Hammer & Blood

A Legacy of Devils novel

Viktor Bloodstone

Alicia,

sometimes you have to be the 1 bear!

FORTRESS PUBLISHING, INC.

WWW.FORTRESSPUBLISHINGINC.COM

Hammer & Blood
© 2020 Fortress Publishing, Inc.
ISBN: 978-0-9887991-6-5

Edited by: Catherine Jordan

This book is available for wholesale through the publisher, Fortress Publishing, Inc.

PUBLISHED BY:
Fortress Publishing, Inc.
1200 Market Street
Unit 17 / Box 137
Lemoyne, PA 17043

WWW.FORTRESSPUBLISHINGINC.COM

August 6th, 1995. 1:07 PM

Papa cut out my tongue. He said it was for my own good.

I coughed up blood and couldn't stop, 'cause it was hard to swallow with only a stub. Then Papa pressed a glowin' white fireplace poker against the stub to keep me from bleedin' out. He said he was fixin' my mistakes.

"Can't have you talkin' to the cops. You'd just get yourself in more trouble than you already are," he said. "Jesus, boy, you turn legal adult age two days ago and you got the cops comin' after you."

I couldn't say nothin' back. I had no tongue, and my mouth still burned from the poker. Before he cut out my tongue, I told him it was her fault, that girl. She shouldn't had did what she did. But Papa said she was a rich bitch, and it didn't matter none if it was her fault—which it was! I was the one who was gonna get in trouble. "Rich bitches are all like that," he said. And now the police were on their way.

We weren't rich. Nope, in fact, we was dirt poor. A house and barn in the middle of the woods was all we could afford. We didn't have much on the first floor of our house: a table to eat at, a few hard chairs, stove to cook at and cabinets to keep the cookin' tools, bunch of animal heads on the walls to re-mind Papa of him bein' stronger than them.

I heard the sirens before I saw the flashin' lights. Papa looked out the window next to the fireplace. "Jesus, Almighty." He turned on me, grabbed a fistful of my shirt. "What'd you did, boy?"

I shook my head; all I could do. He pushed me, kinda punched my chest, and let go. My rump hit hard, but I didn't feel the pain on a count of my mouth hurtin' as much as it did. "Never no mind, I know what you did, boy. Was it just the one girl?"

I looked down at the brown, warped floorboards. None of 'em matched. Some overlapped, most had gaps to the dirt below, ready to catch my toe when I goes barefoot. I picked the splinters on one of the floorboards and shook my head.

"How many? How many, boy?"

I held up three fingers on one hand and four fingers on my other.

"Jesus, Almighty, you done fucked up." He took off his hat and I knew I was in trouble. Big trouble. Bigger trouble than the time I fed that 'possum with the foamy mouth behind the outhouse. Papa never took off his hat. Most days he slept in it. Sometimes I forgot it weren't a part of his God-given head.

Papa was mostly bald. What hair he had grew in stringy clumps at ear level and twirled like worms to his shoulders. He'd tell me at least once a week that Mama made him go white early, but I was what made him go bald. I didn't know how much of that was true, 'cause I never met my Mama. I didn't even know her name. As best I reckon, it was either Shrew or BattleAx. I did know she was a witch. Papa would tell me that at least once a week, too.

"You fucked up good," Papa said again. He repeated himself when he got angry. Last year, when the police came sniffin' 'round about rumors of Papa's moonshine in the barn, he swore over and over. Me and him worked up a good sweat movin' his distillery pieces into the woods, coverin' 'em up with branches and leaves. Today his anger was much worse. "All kinds of fucked up, boy."

I remained sittin' on the floor as Papa rushed around gettin' his shotguns. His hands was shakin' as he loaded 'em all, shells fallin' to the floor. He didn't pick none of 'em up neither, just grabbed more shells from the ammo boxes. All his shotguns leanin' on the wall by the window looked like a fence.

The sirens got louder and louder. I covered my ears, but as the red and blue lights from outside got close enough to change the colors of everythin' inside the house, the sirens stopped. Then came slammin' of car doors and men yellin' warnings, yellin' for me—*me!*—to come out. Papa didn't pay no mind. He clutched the gun's muzzle and punched a hole in the window, then started shootin'.

When the gun was empty, he tossed it aside and grabbed another. "You fucked up, boy, but you're still my boy and this is still my house and my land. A bear fights for its cubs and cave, and I'm gonna do the same. Sometimes ya gotta be the bear."

After Papa went through all the gun's shells, the police finally started shootin' back. The noises made my head feel like it was about to explode. I had to hold it together, hands pressed against my ears. Pretty sure I was screamin', but I couldn't hear myself none. Everthin' was gettin' all shot up.

Papa jerked back and yelped. He got shot in his left arm. It was lookin' bad, just hangin' there, soaked in blood. His face twisted in pain and he groaned. Hope it hurt as much as my tongue.

He tried to aim the gun with his right arm, but it kept fallin'. He swinged it upward and got the muzzle to rest on the window ledge. That was when bullets blasted down our door.

The police shot again, this time the bullets sprayed Papa. He fell with his gun, droppin' onto his back in the blood all over the floor. His eyes didn't shut. He gulped and gulped, repeating his swallow like he was tryin' to call forth some nasty cuss word. I felt bad for wishin' ill-will upon him for cuttin' out my tongue. He was only tryin' to help me, after all. He looked at me, blood bubblin' out of his mouth, and whispered, "Sometimes ya gotta be the bear."

I knew he was in bad sorts. I knew people couldn't take that many bullets, and I knew he was dyin'. But by the way he arched his back I swore he was tryin' to stand back up. Then the police stormed through the front door. More bullets turned his head into a messy pulp, kinda like the time I put a firecracker up a cat's ass.

I cringed as globby parts of Papa's head splashed all over my chest, in my mouth, on my arms.

I was always big for my age. Papa joked that Mama cheated on him with a grizzly. Even though I was younger than all the police here I was more than a head taller than the tallest of them. And wider in the shoulder, too. But there were a lot of police, one was even a woman.

I jumped up and threw the table at them. It hit a couple, but there were too many. They surrounded me quick and closed in just as fast. The woman jumped on me from behind. She wrapped her arm around my neck and pressed her titties against the back of my head. Papa always said titties were the devil's horns. That confused me, 'cause I *liked* the devil's horns! Like on those camper girls. I liked the way they bounced as the camper girls ran, and flopped around as I tied them up, and felt against my skin as I put my face between them. I didn't like it none when the girls screamed and cried as I played the weddin' night game with them. Maybe they just didn't know the rules?

That police woman's titties distracted me. Even though they was in a uniform, they still felt nice against my head. Nice enough to make me think of 'em without the uniform, nice enough to make me wanna see them bounce durin' the weddin' night game, nice enough to make my fuckstick—as Papa always called it—hard. I couldn't move too good with a hard fuckstick.

The other police men hit me. Hit me so fast I couldn't stop 'em. I couldn't feel my burnin' tongue no more, and when I fell to the ground, I coughed. There was a lot of blood and some of my teeth came out. The police kicked me. Again, and again. I was curled in a ball and coverin' my face with both hands. I know it was the police woman who ended it with one big kick to my fuckstick 'cause a man don't kick another man there.

One of them camper girls kicked me there after three days of weddin' night games. As I was rollin' around on the ground, she untied the other two girls and they runned away, cryin'. I was too scared to tell Papa about it until today.

The police rolled me over and practically pulled my shoulders out of their joints to put handcuffs on me. Three pair, in case I got a second wind, they said. I tried to stand but my legs was jelly. They dragged me outside and put me in the back of one of their cars.

"Fuck waiting for an ambulance," one of the police men said. "He doesn't deserve it."

Even though I couldn't see none outta my one swollen eye, I focused on the woman and her devil's horns. I remembered how good they felt against my head. I remembered the camper girls and how good they felt. My fuckstick remembered, too.

July 11th, 2000. 9:52 PM

Ptolemy "The Mathematician" Lindquist watched the people around *The Blaze*, a night club that always attracted a crowd. He was here to kill one of the patrons.

He sat at a small table from the trendy place across the street and enjoyed a cocktail while the nightlife flowed along the city streets. It was a beautiful night—clear and temperate—so he decided to sit outside. His target had been inside *The Blaze* for about half an hour, and Ptolemy had already seen a few variables he didn't like. He almost decided to go home, but while he savored his Maker's Mark, he made and received a few texts that would help him corral those variables. He now had a plan.

Drinks paid. Good tip. Phone number slipped to the waitress. Sure, he was a bit older—late-40s. He had yet to find any white strands in his thick black hair, and while there might be hints at laugh lines, his smile was charming with no facial hair to hinder it. At almost six and a half feet tall and well-muscled, he added credence to the phrase, "Age is just a number." The way the waitress smiled and blushed as she put his number in her pocket told him he'd hear from her later. She smirked when he put on his jacket, black leather with shimmering blue flames rising from the bottom. Garish, but not enough to push her lingering gaze away from him.

Phone to ear, he started down the sidewalk, adjusting his arm to find a comfortable way to position it – the damn jacket was too tight, but he needed it. The person he called picked up. "I found him," Ptolemy said. "He's inside *The Blaze* wearing a leather jacket with blue flames on it. Yeah, kinda lame."

The call ended, and he cracked the flip-phone in two, then tossed it into the nearest trashcan. He withdrew another disposable phone from his jacket pocket. Tapping the numbers, he crossed the street and aimed for *The Blaze*, but in the opposite direction of the burgeoning line filled with dozens of people, all trying to get into the same overpriced location. *Andy Warhol was right*, Ptolemy thought, *marketing unites us all*.

The sidewalk had its pedestrians, some adding to the line, most ignoring the homeless man sitting on the sidewalk, his back against a building. "Yeah, he's at *The Blaze*," Ptolemy said into the new phone. "Tall, wiry, goth-looking guy, including long black hair and long black overcoat."

Ptolemy hung up and dropped the phone into the homeless man's lap along with a few twenties. "God bless you, sir!" the man yelled to Ptolemy's back. He kept walking and pulled out another disposable phone.

"I found him at *The Blaze*. A cowboy of all things. Stetson, boots, vest, the whole nine." Ptolemy closed the cellphone and slipped a few twenties to the bouncer opening the side door.

The club was nothing special. Over the years, Ptolemy had been to plenty all around the world. This one had the same yeasty beer aroma, the lingering whiff of weed, the hint of stale sweat. The lounge was on the first floor, dance floor on the second. The ceiling reduced the music to its basic beat; the rhythmic thumping could be heard anywhere in the lounge, but not oppressive enough to force louder conversations. Alcohol did that.

A drone of voices filled the room. People milled in pockets of two to ten, enjoying a cocktail before heading upstairs to offer themselves to the ritualistic mass of gyrating bodies. He was young once and had enjoyed this type of atmosphere. On occasion, he allowed himself a little fun, even though he was here tonight for a different reason.

He slid out of his jacket and in the same movement tossed his phone in the nearest trashcan. He scanned the room, looking for... Found it. Two blondes in little black dresses standing at a high-top table built for two. Perfect.

Headed toward the women, he passed close to the bar, a bit too close, some might say. In one of the leather high back stools a young man held court with his entourage. Gold and gaudy, the rings, necklaces, bracelets among them cost more than an average worker's yearly salary. When they all tilted their heads back for a shot of a drink that was an unnatural shade of chartreuse, Ptolemy slipped the jacket over the back of the young man's barstool.

The jacket was too loud for Ptolemy's taste, but he hated to see it go to waste. Real leather, quality workmanship.

Leading with his smile, Ptolemy moved onto the pair of blondes. Their gazes wandered around the room until they noticed Ptolemy. Both shifted their stances, becoming more attentive. By the time he reached their table, they were smiling.

"Hi. How are you two tonight?"

That was all it took to start their engines, their mouths revving the conversation around the social racetrack. Ptolemy felt more like a spectator than a participant as they zoomed through their life stories, including the meet-cute way they knew each other. Fine by him—it meant he didn't need to devote much attention to their conversation, and he was happy with his view of the young man noticing the jacket on the back of his bar stool.

Exuding alpha male status, the young man stood from his stool and looked around with a snarl on his lips, as if angry about the jacket. The posturing was short-lived as his friends encouraged him to keep it. He put it on, sat back down, and ordered another round of shots.

One of the blondes took a pit-stop by asking Ptolemy, "So, what do you do for a living?"

"I own my own business," he answered while executing the practiced maneuver of crossing his arms over on the table, so the sleeve of his shirt slid up enough to expose the President Day-date Rolex on his wrist. Diamond dial, 18 kt yellow gold. And the girls were off to the races once more. They slowed down as a commotion started near the bar. The girls finally stopped talking when the screaming started.

"Gun! He's got a gun!"

People cleared away from the man with the gun. He was tall and wiry, his hair long and as black as his overcoat. His gun was small enough to sneak past the bouncer, and he pointed it at the young man at the bar wearing the black leather jacket with blue flames.

Club attendees clamored for the door, others backed against the walls or dropped to the floor. Ptolemy put his arms around the blondes as they screamed and crouched behind the table. "Follow me," he said, and duck-walked them to the nearest couch where they hid. Ptolemy poked his head out from behind the couch to watch.

The young man in the leather jacket had his hands up. The man in the overcoat squeezed the trigger twice. Bullets pulped the young man's eyes—blood and an egg-like goo sprayed the gunman, who didn't flinch. The onlookers screamed.

The gunman in the overcoat turned, then stopped when he saw a pointed gun held by a man wearing a Stetson, steel tipped boots, and a vest—the whole nine. "I gotcha now, Mathematician."

Mr. Overcoat looked confused. He pointed at the dead man with his gun and said, "*That* is The Mathematician. *I* killed him."

"Naah. *You* are The Mathematician."

Mr. Overcoat gestured to himself and said, "Do I look like someone who runs around calling himself 'The Mathematician'?"

The cowboy shrugged. "Just a good disguise, is all."

"I couldn't agree more!" shouted a man who crept out from the nearby shadows. His hair was sculpted into a faux-hawk and he wore all black. He sported sunglasses and aimed a gun at the cowboy. "Because I got a tip that *you* are The Mathematician."

"Me?" the cowboy asked. "It ain't me, partner. It's him."

The show was getting good, going exactly as Ptolemy had calculated. If only he had a bag of popcorn.

Mr. Overcoat pointed with both hands at the lifeless body on the floor. "It's him! He is The Mathematician. I killed him."

The man in sunglasses laughed. "The dead guy? You think he's The Mathematician?"

Mr. Overcoat now aimed his pistol at the cowboy. "Well, *he* thinks I'm The Mathematician!"

"Okay, let's hold on now. Let's—"

Sunglasses laughed again, cutting off the cowboy. "You're pretty fucking stupid to think you were able to kill The Mathematician so easily."

Sirens rang in the distance. Cops respond quickly when a call comes in about gunshots in crowded places. Kudos for them being on high alert in regard to potential massacres, which was where this was headed. "How about we just—?" the cowboy tried but was cut off again.

"Did you just call me stupid?" Mr. Overcoat yelled.

"Ah, hell," the cowboy muttered right before the three-way gunfight erupted, leaving no surviving participants.

More screaming. And the sirens were getting closer. Ptolemy and the girls made a hasty retreat on hands and knees out the building's side door.

Ptolemy made sure the girls were unharmed. They both expressed their gratitude by giving him their phone numbers. He bid them goodnight and took off down the closest alley. Confident he was far enough away from the night club, he pulled out another cellphone—the secured one he used for business. He heard the click of the other line, then sighed as a form of greeting.

"So, you were right about seeing new players hanging around the club?" the electronically modulated voice on the other end asked. The bizarre amalgam of male and female had a calming effect as it spoke. Ptolemy didn't know the person on the other end, so he referred to the androgynous voice as "Broker."

"The cowboy, the goth, and that goofball who wears sunglasses all the time. Thank you for getting their contact information to me, by the way."

"You're welcome. New guys are always easy to contact, more than happy to give out their direct line."

Ptolemy rubbed his chin, thinking. "I just want to know who put a contract out on me."

"I've been digging around, but I can't find any contracts on you. Do you think these new guys have a side bet with themselves? A pool to see who can take out the master?"

"Possible, but it doesn't quite feel like that. Tonight's numbnuts make attempts number three, four, and five."

"I'll keep digging. Speaking of contracts … did you complete yours?"

"Dirk Templeton?" Ptolemy smiled. "Yes. Just as easy as his twin brother, Derrick, from last month. He loved the stupid jacket."

"I'll collect and transfer the money right away."

"Excellent. Thank you. Anything else in the pipeline?"

"I'm negotiating another contract with The Philanthropist. You'll have the details in a couple days."

Ptolemy snorted. "Probably him trying to kill me. I bet he's trying to find someone cheaper."

The voice on the other end laughed, as best a synthesizer could simulate. "He calls himself The Philanthropist because he hires you to take out high-level members in organized crime syndicates. You do so much for him; there's no way he'd trust anyone else."

"True. Very true."

"Mathematician?"

"Yes?"

"If I find out anything, I'll let you know."

"Sounds good. Bye."

Ptolemy was The Mathematician because he was calculating. To be calculating, he needed to have information. *All* the information. Unfortunately, he was missing a serious piece, a rare occurrence for him. Was this a sign he was getting too old for this line of business? The idiots who gunned for him tonight were young, as were idiots number one and two. He figured he was their senior by *at least* two decades. Maybe it was time to disappear. This missing piece bothered him, stuck in his craw. He needed to find out who was hunting him.

His personal phone rang. Only one person had that number. Could be because of what happened tonight, but he flipped open the phone and answered with a little more panic in his voice than he would have liked. "Hey, sweety! Is everything okay? You all right?"

"Yes, Daddy, I'm fine."

July 11th, 2000. 10:47 PM

"Do you always have to sound so dramatic?" Calista Lindquist asked into her cellphone. Sitting on her bed, she simultaneously fended off Tanner's groping hand while attempting to clasp her bra.

It was difficult to hear her father's voice with her flip phone lodged between her shoulder and ear. "You're my only daughter, Cali, and it's a dangerous world."

Two hooks clasped, one to go, until Tanner bumbled his way into completely undoing her progress. Feeling weird about sitting half-naked in bed with her boyfriend while on the phone with her father, she cupped the blue lace bra against her breasts. Lying next to her, Tanner chuckled and mouthed the words, "What are you doing?"

Frowning, she managed to contain her undergarment with one hand, and used her other to point to her phone. "I know, Dad, but holy shit."

"Language," Ptolemy scolded in Dad tone.

Cali sighed. "Dad. Seriously? I'm twenty-two."

"I just don't want you sounding like a hussy."

"A hussy?" Cali laughed the words, surprised she was able to speak them in the first place. "It's the twenty-first century, and no one says 'hussy' anymore. Not even in a feeble attempt at humor."

Tanner shifted closer to Cali. He tried to pry her arm from her chest. She slapped him away, but when she realized it was a losing battle, she hopped off her bed. Free from any challenges, she hooked her bra with ease. Tanner scooted across the bed, arm's length from Cali. His slid an index finger between her lace panties and her skin, and gently pulled downward.

"It's only seven months into the new century, and my humor is always on point, but I'm sure that's not why you called."

"Can I swing by your house and grab the big suitcase?"

"The big suitcase? How long are you going to be at this mystery location?"

"Long enough to need the big suitcase."

"Oh, so a day and a half."

Rolling her eyes, Cali pulled up her panties. "Ha, ha. It's five days."

"Five days? Who are you going with?"

"For once in my life, I want to interact with other human beings you don't vet like you've done with everyone from my kindergarten teacher to my boyfriends. I need some form of privacy."

"I'm a dad. I worry. Will Tanner be there?"

Cali stepped away from Tanner. "Yes, he will be there." Cali hated herself for smiling, but Tanner's perfect body made it okay. A decade from now she'd probably be discussing him with a therapist, dissecting the time in her life when she couldn't stop making bad decisions.

Tanner shifted again, his back against the headboard. As if accused of a crime, he crossed his arms and frowned. He mouthed, "He doesn't like me."

"I don't like him," Ptolemy said. "I am impressed, though, that his parents had the foresight to name him for the one career he'd be good at—sun-tanning."

"Dad!" Cali scolded, turning her back on her boyfriend. "Don't be mean. Now can I borrow the big suitcase?"

Ptolemy sighed. "Sorry. Yes, that's fine. When are you leaving?"

"In two days."

"I'll be home in three. We'll just miss each other."

"We'll catch up after I get back."

"Okay. Love you, only daughter of mine."

"Love you, too. Bye."

Cali flipped her phone closed and tossed it onto her vanity. She crossed her arms and scowled at Tanner. "Seriously? You can't go five minutes without getting all over my tits? I was on the phone with my dad, for fuck sake."

"Oh, come on. You're designed to make me think about sex. Your tits are fantastic. Why else would you have bought them?"

16

"Not to be pawed at like they're cat toys."

Cali knew she was a pretty girl. Her martial arts classes had sculpted her five-foot-nine frame into a statue of lean-muscled fitness. But she never sprouted past an A cup. Her father's money paid for the martial arts and the gym membership and shooting lessons at the gun club, not to mention braces on crooked teeth, so why should boobs be any different? Less than a year ago, she decided to treat herself by using her father's money to boost her confidence. A form of early celebration—she graduated from Bucknell with a marketing degree and a 3.70 GPA two months ago.

Tanner, with resting jerk face, put his hands behind his head, and flexed. The only carbohydrates he ingested came in the form of alcohol, which he burned daily at the gym. There wasn't a single hair on his body to detract from its perfection. He called it genetics, though Cali knew it was a razor, depilatory cream, or laser treatment, not that she cared. Tanner replied, "Seems fair since you've pawed me plenty of times."

Cali grabbed Tanner's boxers from the floor, then threw them at his face. Direct hit. "Give it a rest, Tanner Testosterone. Testannerone. That's what I'll call you from now on, Testannerone."

Tanner moaned and ran his hand through his chestnut hued hair, thick yet always styled, no matter how long the marathon of mutual pawing lasted. One of the benefits of being a dude-bro, he'd say. Cali hated that. He was all too quick to dude-bro with other dude-bros. Cali's least favorite dude-bro conversation would start with one of his kind saying, "Nice ink," in reference to the shoulder tattoo of a dozen intersecting black lines, and ended with Tanner replying, "Thanks. It's something tribal."

It wasn't all vapid topics and forehead crushed beer cans, though. He was a different person when he was alone with Cali. He was nice to her and sometimes able to keep up with the topics she wanted to discuss. She liked those moments together. This wasn't one of them.

Tanner slid out of bed and pulled on his boxers. "Did I tell you Hook was joining us at the lake?"

"What? I thought we were going on a couples getaway."

"We are. He's bringing his girlfriend."

Cali sneered. "The girlfriend of a drug dealer. Can't wait to meet her."

"He doesn't like it when you call him a drug dealer."

Cali put on the tee shirt she wore earlier. She sat at her vanity and grabbed a brush in attempt to bring sanity to the big, blonde mess. "Then he shouldn't call himself Hook and say stupid shit like, 'I'll hook you up with whatever you want,' and 'I'm your hook up, day or night.' Sounds like a drug dealer ad campaign to me."

"He prefers the term 'enlightenment specialist.'"

"He wouldn't know enlightenment if the Dalai Lama shit in his cereal. I can't stand that guy."

"Now you sound like your dad."

"Ha, ha."

"Did you vet Hook the way your old man vetted me?"

"A simple internet search tells the world of all his drug arrests. No vetting necessary."

Tanner grabbed his shirt and jeans from the floor. He stared at them, as if reconsidering, then dropped them and jumped back into bed, returning to his seated position against the headboard. "I wonder what he does."

"Who? My dad?"

"Yeah, I wonder what he does, what he *really* does for a living."

"Umm, I've told you. He's an adjuster for the federal government."

"That sounds like a bullshit job title you tell everyone when you're a super-secret spy for the CIA. Insurance companies have adjusters, the government doesn't. Unless he adjusts people's status from living to dead." Either to prove a point or to live out some repressed fantasy, Tanner made finger-guns with both hands and shot the dozen stuffed animals Cali had lined up on a shelf, some even twice.

Finger guns, Cali thought. *Fucking seriously.* "I doubt that's what 'adjuster' means."

Tanner's eyes widened, a thought striking him like a bolt of lightning. A wry smile crept across his face as he pointed one of his finger-guns at Cali. "I got it. I know what he does. He's an assassin. A hit-man. Right now, he's

18

training his sights on a target, ready to fire one lone bullet for a million-dollar payday." Tanner cocked his thumb and made a popping noise with his mouth.

Cali laughed as she continued to struggle with her hair. "You're an idiot." She wanted to be an enlightened individual but couldn't stop herself from thinking this was cute. She laughed again, this time thinking about her dad, a man who condemned profanity and still used the word "hussy," as an assassin.

"Being a hit-man would be soooo cool."

"We have vastly different definitions of what cool is," Cali replied.

Tanner dropped his gun and moved to the edge of the bed. "What's wrong with you? We spent all night having awesome sex. Why are you being so bitchy?"

Cali reached for an elastic hair tie. As she fought her hair into a pony-tail, she looked Tanner in the eye to make sure he paid attention. "I'm bitchy because you 'forgot' to tell me that an intimate week of six people just turned into a party week with eight people."

"Did I forget to tell you Maxwell can't make it?"

Cali seethed. No Maxwell meant no Melody. Subtract one out of two BFFs, add one druggie skank. Tanner tried an expression of sympathy, but his resting-jerk-face wouldn't allow it. Cali went to her closet. "Un-fucking-believable!"

"I'm sorry! Things got busy and it slipped my mind."

"Busy? You go to the gym and then lounge by the pool all day!"

"Hey! I do other things."

"Save it. I don't want to hear it."

Cali flipped through her clothes, repeatedly slamming hangers against each other. She still needed to pack, but she wasn't seeing her clothes as she processed the new information. Even though she'd have to spend five days with three dude-bros doing dude-bro things and being forced to social-ize with a stranger, Dakota would be there. She loved Dakota as much as she loved Melody, which made the situation at least tolerable. But, God, she real-ly wanted to spend the week with both of her friends, because... A realization hit her as she pulled a red crop-top off the hanger. She turned around as a form of apology acceptance and asked, "Maxwell won't be there?"

"He said something came up."

"But it's his father's house."

Tanner shrugged. "Max gave me a key and the code to the alarm system."

"When?"

"Yesterday."

"Yesterday? When you couldn't meet me for lunch?"

"Oh, for Christ's sake, Cali!"

Cali tossed the top aside and slipped into a pair of leggings. Packing would have to wait. Even though it was late at night, she needed a jog. She was pissed that Tanner had no idea what was at stake with their relationship. This weekend could wind up meaning the end of them.

July 13th, 2000. 7:31 PM

Home. Zebadiah Seeley was home. But it was different.

It had been five years since he had last seen it. Five years since the police dragged him away after they killed his papa. Five years in prison. Then, suddenly, for no reason, they pulled him from his cell, gave him back his overalls and boots, put him in a van, and dropped him off at the end of the dirt road that led from the main road to his house.

The road cut through the forest and was hard to see, nature reclaiming it slowly. Saplings and thorn bushes grew all over, but Zebadiah remembered the path, even after five years. He didn't care that the thorns pulled at his clothes, didn't feel the cuts they left on his skin. He wanted to get home. But his house… his house felt different.

It was still a simple two-story farmhouse, but moss and mildew changed the color of the wood from brown to shades of greens and grays. Graffiti added other colors. Red letters spelled out, "Blood House." Naked women's bodies were drawn with white spray paint. Black symbols he didn't recognize, including an upside-down star inside a circle. He liked the naked bodies but didn't know why words and pictures were on the outside walls. And all the broken windows. The police had shot out a few, but all the windows were broken now. When he walked through the doorway—the front door no longer there—his stomach sank.

The main room was a wasteland, a warzone devastated by invaders. Dust swirled around his feet as he stepped inside. It looked alien. If he hadn't known there used to be a table and chairs, he would have never understood the splintered pieces of wood scattered about. Shards of window glass hid under layers of dust. The left side of the fireplace was nothing more than a pile of broken stone. The animal heads, Papa's trophies, were gone. Piles of crushed beer cans and shattered whisky bottles laid against the far wall. He didn't know who they belonged to, but they didn't belong here.

21

In the fading light, even after half a decade, Zebadiah saw the stain, all that was left of Papa. Each step through the big room hurt. More graffiti on the walls made the pain in his chest worse. Words and pictures like the ones on the outside. All different colors. Different words like, "Die rapist die," and "Satan lives here." Pictures of an angry, ugly face with a small beard and two horns. A hand with only a middle finger sticking up. A long, hairy fuckstick. This made Zebadiah grab his own fuckstick. He hadn't used it for five years other than to piss. Only men lived in the prison. Only men prison guards. Only men cops came and went. That didn't stop the prisoners from playing wedding games.

Zebadiah didn't like men, didn't like what the men did with other men in the showers or behind sheets draped from top bunks. He didn't like what the other prisoners did to him. From his very first day, the guards turned a blind eye when he was held down by three, four, five prisoners who took turns with him. They shoved their fucksticks in his shithole and kept at it even after he started bleeding. The blood made them laugh. Day after day, other prisoners took turns, helped hold him down.

Zebadiah was a couple of inches short of seven feet tall, but hadn't been strong enough to fend off three, four, five other prisoners at once. He devoted as much time as possible with the metal plates in the exercise yard. Day after day, year after year, fuckstick after fuckstick. Finally, after a few years, he had the power to make it stop. He fought off three prisoners, killing one with his bare hands. He spent time in solitary confinement, and afterward he killed two more. The prisoners left him alone after that. But there were still no women.

Standing in the center of the main room of his house, he remembered the police woman from five years ago as clearly as if she were choking him today. How she looked. How her devil's horns felt against the back of his head, how nice they were, how he wanted to squeeze them. Yes. It was time to get the barn ready. He had to fix the house, but later. First, he needed to visit his barn.

The barn was a hundred yards away, on the other side of a field. Like the driveway, nature asserted itself in the form of waist high grasses, thick

22

patches of brush, and tall sporadic trees. His pace quickened, the excitement of his childhood days rushing through him.

The barn was more of a home to him than the house. He and Papa had worked moonshine together, until Papa shut it down after the government men came snooping around. They then used it as a place to butcher cows. Papa stole one now and again from neighboring farms on the other side of the mountain. Papa always said that overcoming the challenge of leading a cow through a forest justified him using Bertha to crush its skull. Bertha was a sledgehammer with a head bigger than two footballs. Zebadiah had no idea why Papa called it Bertha. In between catching, killing, cleaning livestock, Zebadiah used the barn to get away from Papa's ill mood, or to relax, or play wedding games with girls he caught. He liked the smell of left-over slaughter scraps, the sweet tang of rotting meat. It made the back of his jaw tingle with a strange sensation of hunger and comfort. The girls he brought to the barn didn't like the smell, though. It always made them throw up.

Energy and excitement hurried his step as he got closer to his destination. Closer and closer and…

Zebadiah stopped about a few paces from the barn.

Why was light coming from the inside? Why were there noises? Voices? Someone was in his barn. People were in *his* barn!

His first thought was to charge inside and kill everyone. Like in prison; kill whoever made him mad. This wasn't prison, though. In prison, it was just men, sometimes with little handmade weapons. Outside of prison, the world was bigger. The weapons were bigger.

He crept toward the nearest corner of the barn. More graffiti, pictures, symbols, and words. Did the people inside the barn put them there? The wood smelled of mold. Rotted holes formed between some of the boards, some big enough to see inside.

Tubes of florescent lights hung haphazardly from the ceiling and the bottom of the loft. The light was white and dull, washing out everything. Two rows of long metal tables formed an aisle-way in the center of the barn and ran almost the entire length from front to back. Glass cups filled with colorful liquids took up space on the tables. Rubber tubes ran from propane tanks to burners on the tables. A maze of glass led from burner to burner. Small bags of white powder were stacked into big piles. Four men stood in the center of it all.

Zebadiah didn't like this. Didn't like this at all. He could hear Papa say, "Be the bear," as if the old man stood right next to him.

Yes, Papa, he thought. *I will be the bear.*

July 13th, 2000. 4:07 PM

"There's only one lake here, right?" Cali asked.

"Yeah," Tanner grunted from the driver's seat. It was Cali's Mustang, but she wanted to be in charge of the Global Positioning System. The navigational device was the size of a postcard and nothing more than a moving map on a small screen. It had yet to hit the shelves of electronics stores, but her father had been able to get one for her. Cali did well with maps, but considered the device a modern miracle. Tanner never seemed to grasp it. The last time he had used it, they ended up in a different state.

"Why the hell is this house so hard to find?" Cali asked.

"What does GPS say?"

Every time Tanner mentioned the GPS there was a tone in his voice as if he were talking about a person and not computer hardware. The GPS didn't register half of the offshoot roads, and it froze every few minutes. "Feels like we've been missing turns."

For most of the drive, sturdy trees grew up one side of the mountain while thick forest sloped away from the road on the other. Intermittent dirt roads or pull-over areas offered a refuge for the nervous driver. Cali had been to the lake before, but via the cute little town built on the other end, never from this direction. On maps, the body of water resembled a swollen letter "S." The north end of the lake held civilization, the southern end accommodated hunters and fishermen. Cali had no idea that Maxwell's lake house would be so close to wildlife and gun-toting, camo clad sharpshooters, and now concerns about the accommodations bubbled up from the back of her mind. Was this "house" really a log cabin?

Tanner sighed. "I don't know. It's been a few miles since we passed a convenience store. There's gotta be one coming up. We'll stop and ask for directions."

25

"Despite the hilarity of a gender role reversal, we're not stopping and asking for directions."

"What? Why?"

"Do you not know where we are? We're on a desolate road in the middle of a forest looking for a lake house at the base of a mountain. There is no fucking way we're stopping at some ramshackle convenience store run by a toothless crazy old man who will tell us the place we're staying at was once owned by a sociopath seeking bloody revenge and we're going to die."

Tanner laughed. "Seriously?"

"Seriously."

"Wow. Okay. Just so you know, the last convenience store we passed was a FastStop. You know, the same chain as the FastStop two blocks from your apartment? I'm pretty confident that the next one we pass will be bigger than a shack. And we're not totally in the middle of nowhere. I think there's a small town at the other end of the lake."

"There is. I've been to that town. It has a Starbucks and McDonalds. Antique shops. Clothing stores. Cute cafes. And convenience stores without creepy old men."

"So, let's find a place to ask for directions."

"No. I need an address in the GPS, which means I'd have to delete the lake house's address, and I don't know any addresses for anything else in town. Plus, I feel like the road we're looking for should be coming up."

Tanner huffed. "Fine! But if we don't find it soon, we're gonna stop at the next convenience store. I doubt it will be run by a creepy old man, and there are no area sociopaths. Except for Zebadiah Seeley, of course."

Cali's eyes widened. "Who?"

"You never heard of Zebadiah Seeley?"

Cali hated the way he laughed his words, like she was a dumb ass for not knowing what she shouldn't know. "No," she snipped. "Why the fuck would I know about Zebadiah Seeley?"

"Dude. Everyone's heard of him! Five years ago, he held three girls prisoner in his barn and raped them every day for like half a week. They escaped, but there were four girls before them who weren't so lucky."

"Oh my God! How do you know this?"

"I saw it on the news. Figured the topic would make for a good senior paper in high school. The police raided his house and killed his dad in a shootout."

"Why? Why are you even telling me this?"

"You asked."

"I did not ask."

"Sounded like you did."

"I didn't!"

"Guess I made a bad joke that became less funny the more you talked."

"The more I—? Here! Turn here!"

Tanner slammed on the brakes. He managed to control the fishtailing as the car screeched to a halt. Burnt rubber filled the air. "Jesus Christ, Cali!"

"Sorry!" Cali's hands were shaking. "I wasn't paying attention. You freaked me out with all the psycho talk. Back up, I think I see it."

Mumbling profanities under his breath, Tanner did as instructed.

"See it?" Cali asked.

Tanner didn't reply and guided the car down the road. Paved, but barely visible, the road cut into the forest. Overgrown branches scraped against the car as he made the turn. Besides being narrower, the road looked no different from the one they turned off.

Cali vowed she'd only be taking this road one more time—to leave. With or without Tanner, depending on how much of an asshole he was going to be this week. She hated it when he didn't reply to a direct question, so it wasn't looking good for him right now.

"The GPS says it should be at the end of the road."

More silence.

This was frustrating. She just wanted a nice relaxing week of booze, sun, and sex. First, the absence of one of her best friends, then the addition of her least favorite friend of her boyfriend's. That was before the trip even started. Then getting lost in the forest on a dead end road... "Fuck me. Oh, wait. I think I see an opening in the trees. Might be a driveway?"

Tanner slowed and took the slight turn. A wave of relief washed away most of Cali's stress as the forest opened to a lawn, then to a driveway leading to the house.

"Holy shit, Cali, look at this place," Tanner said, gawking out his window while coasting along the driveway.

She understood what he meant. The house he lived in was larger, but *this* one was a vacation home. A spare house, a leisurely place to relax and slum it for a week or so. Cali had no idea what Maxwell's father did for a living, but she was going to ask the next time she saw him.

Civilization hadn't abandoned the world and Cali breathed a sigh of relief. They were still in the wilderness where nature made the rules, but something about a well-manicured lawn, a massive Cape Cod style house, and a white gazebo comforted her. There was even a small motorboat moored to the end of a pier, in case she wanted to work on her tan while gently rocking in the water. The chaise lounges set up by a fire pit mere yards from the lake said that woodland creatures would not be on the menu. She no longer feared having to build traps and capture squirrels and rabbits for food while lost in the mountains. Thanks to her father, she had those skills if she needed to use them. For some reason, he thought learning survivalist techniques was a fun hobby, and taught Cali what he knew.

The driveway looped around the front of the house, then formed a paved pad in the back. Cali couldn't stop smiling as Tanner parked. After he turned the car off, she undid her seatbelt and shifted to face him. He turned to her. She reached out and touched his cheek, gliding her fingers from his ear to his jaw. He cupped her face in his hand. They leaned closer. Tanner's lips parted... then he said, "Let's go inside and fuck in all the rooms before anyone gets here."

Cali hated herself for laughing, not entirely sure if he was joking or not. By the time she got out of the car, he was already inputting the security code after unlocking the back door. Cali liked what she saw so far. An elaborate chandelier hung in the center of the open foyer. A grand staircase led to the second floor. A doorway to a sitting room was to the left of the entry. To the right was a huge dining room with a table for ten. Two ornate cabinets were filled with china that would never be used for anything other than something to busy a housekeeper with dusting.

This was more like the vacation Cali was expecting. All previous exposure to untamed wilderness forgotten, all prior transgressions perpetrated by Tanner forgiven.

"Being the first ones here means first choice of room," he said.

Cali giggled and threw her hands over Tanner's shoulders, her fingers swirling the short hairs on the back of his head. He smiled, and she wanted to take a moment to bask in it, study the way the creases around his mouth softened the angles of his cheeks, the way it made his eyes less intense. He could be a jerk sometimes, but it was his smile that pardoned those moments. She moved in closer for a kiss, but was startled by the clang of metal from another room.

"I thought we were alone?" Cali whispered. Her head swiveled toward the hall, from where the noise drifted. "Thanks to you, now all I can think about it that psycho killer."

"Oh, don't be so dramatic."

"Maybe not the specific one we talked about, but a new one. A more psycho, extra stabby, extra killy one."

"I doubt it's a psycho killer."

"Fine. A burglar. Either way, someone's in the house."

Tanner and Cali tiptoed down the hallway. A closet on the left wall utilized the space under the stairs, and a half-bath was on the right. Cali assumed the hallway led to a kitchen because the clang sounded like a dropped pan.

Tanner stepped in front of Cali. She appreciated the effort, but she would fare better against a burgling psycho killer, thanks to the martial arts training mandated by her father.

Metal against metal emanated from the other room. They both paused. "Utensils?" Cali whispered.

"Rule out a burglar," he whispered. Unless the utensils were made from real silver, there would be no logical reason to burgle a kitchen.

A psycho killer was *definitely* making those noises, probably trying to find the best knife to slash the throats of unsuspecting victims. Cali clenched her fists.

Pressed against the wall, they continued to the end of the hallway. More clanking. Tanner held up three fingers. Cali had no idea what that meant. Then two fingers. A countdown? Then one finger. He couldn't possibly be thinking about jumping into an unknown situation, could he? He could.

Cali reached for his arm to stop him, but he already launched himself from the hallway. Fist reeled back, he jumped into the kitchen.

A woman screamed.

Pots fell to the floor.

"Jesus fuck, dude!" Tanner yelled.

"What the fuck, man!" Hook replied, panting. "You scared the shit out of us."

"Us" being Hook and his non-burglar, non-psycho killer, druggie bitch girlfriend Cali hated on principle alone. Hook had a collection of the most questionable tattoos all over his body. A stick figure on its hands and knees vomiting razor blades forever emblazoned Hook's left set of ribs, a cat's ass with tail lifted to proudly display its rectal orifice on the right set of ribs. An upside-down middle finger hovered over his right kidney. A three-legged horse raced across his left thigh. And those were the tasteful ones. He also had two dozen smaller pieces that made no sense as to why anyone would want to immortalize them. Hook's tattoos made Tanner's "something primal" shoulder piece look like a genius decision.

But the woman? Her shimmering black hair hung past her shoulders and her dark eyes held a level of alertness that Cali didn't expect. The retro cat-glasses—pink frames with black filigree—were adorable on her, so natural she might have been born with them on her button nose. Tiny piercings rimmed her left ear, and her tattoos were beautiful—a full sleeve of birds and butterflies fluttering all around her left arm, and a flower-framed waterfall flowing down her right thigh.

"You all right, babe?" Hook put his arm around his girlfriend's shoulders and squeezed her close. They were the same height and his fervor almost knocked them both off balance.

The woman laughed. "I'm fine. Just startled." Her voice was smooth, confident, and soothing. She patted Hook's chest as she left the confine of his arm. Moving to the new guests, she extended her hand. "Hi. I'm Linda. You must be Tanner and Calista?"

"Please, call me Cali," she said as she accepted Linda's hand.

"Cali. Sorry we scared you guys."

"No worries," Cali said. "A funny story to tell Jordon and Dakota when they arrive. I feel like *we* should apologize for interrupting *you*. Getting started early?"

A hint of pink blushed Linda's cheeks. Her bikini top was flattering on her thin, athletic build, and she wore a simple wrap around her hips, somewhere between a sash and a skirt. "Yeah. Figured we'd catch some sun before everyone got here. Then we got hungry and wanted to see what the kitchen had to offer."

"Beautiful day," Hook said as he opened the refrigerator. He grabbed two beers and tossed one to Tanner as he finished his thought, "to get hooked up!"

The men whooped and laughed. This made Hook's permanently squinting eyes almost nonexistent. His upper body jerked in rhythm with his laughter, his long hair rippling.

"Find anything good?" Cali asked Linda.

"Yeah! The fridge and cabinets are stocked."

"Babe's a good cook," Hook added, punctuating his statement by smacking Linda's ass as he walked by. Eyes widened from surprise, she laughed and playfully smacked his shoulder. Cali wondered why Linda was with him, but figured it might be best to keep judgments at bay. Most people could say the same about her and Tanner. There was just some unexplainable X factor that kept her attracted to him. Clearly, there was a similar X factor for Linda as well. Cali sometimes wished she could find that X factor and stomp it like a bug, especially when the guys gave each other a whooping high-five and then ran outside like children.

"Men," Linda moaned and grabbed two beers from the fridge.

"Amen, sister." Cali accepted the bottle and toasted Linda's statement. Cali's hatred for the woman was waning. "Now that my adrenaline levels returned to normal, I just realized I didn't see any other cars in the driveway. How'd you two get here?"

"Taxi."

Cali chuckled. "I bet that was interesting. Did the driver charge extra for getting lost?"

Linda looked confused. "We had no issues at all. The ride was nice, and the driver dropped us off at the door."

Cali went back to hating Linda.

July 13th, 2000. 8:41 PM

It was all Jenny Fratenelli's fault. She let Paulie feel her up when he was twelve. They were in the seventh grade together. A rumor had spread through school that she was an easy trip to second base with the potential to advance to third for the first guy who got her a concert ticket. Some fad boy-band that Paulie gave zero fucks about. Sure, Paulie ogled all the naked boobs he could handle from his stash of nudie magazines hidden under his bed, but to *touch* them? Paulie was willing to take some risks. He swiped a five from his sister, a ten from his brother. The twenty from his dad's wallet was riskier—he'd get a whooping if caught taking it while the old man snored away a six-pack in his favorite recliner in front of the television. The big score was forty from his mom's purse. It was a busy night at the restaurant, and she was never too good with keeping track of her tips, especially when an out-of-town customer let her know what hotel he was staying at.

He still needed another thirty bucks, so he branched outside his house. The next week at school involved a picked pocket, teaching a group of students how to play craps and then cheating them, and the very cliché moment of shaking down a couple of nerds for their lunch money. That week also involved zero focus in class and flipping a middle finger to all homework.

He got enough money for the tickets.

The venue was walking distance from Jenny's house, and her house was walking distance from his house. His parents didn't care, and hers weren't around—her dad had disappeared, and her mom was always at work. Jenny was so excited to go to the show, she let Paulie touch her boobs *before* they went. Afterward, he walked her home and hoped he could touch them again, wondering about the rumors of third base. The rumors weren't wrong. He even scored a homerun!

33

While making sure his clothes weren't inside out as he put them back on, he let her know how he got the cash. This thrilled her and she declared herself his girlfriend on the spot. Their next few months together were great. Whatever she asked for, he shoplifted from a store or stole from someone in the neighborhood. When she wanted to try pot, he got her pot.

Paulie found a local dealer but had no money. The dealer wanted to get a foothold in a new market, so they worked out an agreement, and Paulie quickly became the guy to see at his school. A few months later Jenny dumped him for a football player. Paulie didn't care. His new lifestyle certainly made it easier for him to get free pussy. He no longer had time for school now that he was making good money selling. Junior year of high school, he flunked out. He left home, but to afford even the shittiest of shitty apartments, he needed to sell more, run more, handle more for faceless bosses whose names alone carried respect and fear.

The last time Paulie saw Jenny was a decade later at a strip club by the airport. She recognized him and offered a blow job for a bump, a hit, a puff, or even just a damn shot of top shelf booze. Paulie took one look at her streaked mascara and lip blisters and decided he didn't need that kind of drama in his life. He tossed her a twenty, squeezed her tits one last time, and never looked back.

He would have been promoted by any one of the people he worked for, if not for his constant gambling. More specifically, his constant losses. He always paid what he owed, so he never lost any fingers or had to deal with broken bones, but he always owed. More jobs, more sales, more shipments to move, but sometimes he'd fuck up a shipment. Like a recent one with Maddox. Last week, some bitch he met at a club took a five-pound brick of pot after he had passed out in the motel room where they partied. He hadn't done a great job hiding it, but the bitch should have respected! Now he was in the passenger seat of a Range Rover while bouncing around a back-road through some nowhere forest with Maddox, one of his faceless bosses whose name alone commanded fear.

Maddox introduced himself last week with a fist to Paulie's gut and a few open-palmed slaps to the face. After one last shove to the floor, they worked out an agreement, a list of chores for Paulie to pay back the pot he had lost. Paulie walked away with his life and only minor bruises, so he thought the agreement was a good one, until he and Maddox pulled up to the barn.

Twilight asserted its dominion over the world and Paulie wondered if there would be bugs. Bugs loved the wilderness. Hell, those fuckers loved any light source at night, and the full moon was coming up over the horizon.

Two men wearing cheap ventilators looked up from packing the white powder when Maddox and Paulie entered. The men were leaning over long metal tables laden with all kinds of chemistry equipment. Paulie didn't know the processing details, but he certainly knew the product.

Florescent lights hummed overhead in the barn, calling out to the bugs. Moths and gnats and beetles swarmed around the fluorescents, dipping lower and closer to Paulie's head. He swatted at them. "I hate bugs," he whispered under his breath.

"Quitin' time, boys," Maddox said with a smile.

The men took off their ventilators and shook Maddox's hand. The one with a shaved head and a black teardrop permanently dripping from his eye glared at Paulie. "Who's this?"

"Johnny and Rock, meet your new friend—Paulie," Maddox said.

Rock, the one with the black teardrop, grunted without even glancing at Paulie. Johnny sneered enough to show he was missing a few teeth. The stubble on his loose skin made his cheeks look like sandpaper curtains. His hair sprouted in different directions and his eyes held countless stories, none good. Paulie wasn't sure why Maddox trusted this guy to handle the product, but hey, he wasn't the boss, and he wasn't going to question.

Paulie, being the shortest of the group, looked up and stuck out his hand. "'Sup."

No one reached out to shake, so Paulie clapped his hands and rubbed them together. He felt like an ass, but he'd show them he wasn't one, that he had initiative, and make himself look good. "All right, guys, what's the plan for tonight? We load up the truck and get the fuck outta here and make some money on this?"

Maddox laughed and put his arm around Paulie's shoulders. Maddox's iron-hard muscles flexed through his tailored suit. With a sweep of his arm, he gestured to a folding chair in the middle of the room. "Johnny, Rock, and me are gonna get the fuck outta here. *You* are gonna sit your ass in that chair and be the night shift crew keepin' watch over my shit."

"By myself?" Paulie didn't like the way his voice cracked.

Maddox chuckled. "Yeah."

"Why do I gotta be night shift by myself?"

"Because I said so." Maddox patted Paulie's cheek, the last tap more like a slap. "You needed a job. This is the job. Keep my shit safe. Ain't no one gonna come here, 'cause no one knows this exists. But if someone *does* knock on the door, answer it with your gun. Got it?"

Double-checking to make sure he could support Maddox's order, Paulie reached behind his back and touched the pistol tucked in his pants. Knowing it was there offered some form of comfort. Couldn't shoot bugs, though, and Paulie eyed a few of the damn critters buzzing around the lights. "Yeah, Maddox. I got it."

"Good." Maddox led the men toward the barn opening. Paulie followed, wishing he'd been armed with a can of Raid. "We'll be back tomorrow. Johnny and Rock will show you how to process the product."

Paulie lingered at the edge of the barn entrance, watching them climb into the Range Rover. Before Maddox closed his door, he called out, "Hey, Paulie?"

"Yeah?"

"No sleeping on the job." Maddox shut his door. The thud resonated through Paulie as he listened to the SUV purr to life and drive away.

He was alone.

"Fuckin' stupid to fall asleep here. Creepy as fuckin' hell." Paulie shuffled around the barn taking stock. One side of the barn housed stalls; nothing of interest in there other than spare propane tanks. Paulie then wandered toward the loft. He stood on his toes hoping to see what might be up there other than darkness, but he was nowhere near tall enough. He gazed at the wooden ladder. "Fuck that nightmare fuel," he muttered. No way was he climbing into that bad dream. He ambled back to his folding chair and flopped down. It shifted and threatened to buckle. *Mental note—don't do that again.* He then made another mental note to stop getting in these situations. He was lucky the punishment wasn't worse, but it still sucked. Stop fucking up, that was all he had to do. Finding his deep introspection successful, he pulled out his phone and decided to text his favorite hookups to see if any of them would be available tomorrow. "No fuckin' signal. Course not."

He slumped in his chair, arms and legs going limp like a doll's. He stared at the ceiling, past the shadows created by the limits of the florescent lights. Past the disgusting, winged, flittering bugs. He wasn't sure if he truly saw it or not, the darkness playing tricks on his eyes and mind, but an image started to form. A red devil face came into view.

He jumped from his chair, hand reaching for his .38. Taking a moment to steady his breathing, he squinted. The lights weren't strong enough to see the details, but the smiling devil face was nothing more than a graffiti image in red spray paint.

"Fuckin' idiot." Paulie laughed at himself, no longer needing his pistol. *Alright, time to make the best of this situation, try to take the edge off.* He was in a room full of a substance meant to get a party started. He didn't know what kinda party, but he knew one way to find out.

He grabbed one of the wrapped bricks and thought about popping it open. Deciding against it, he put it back on the stack. Johnny and Rock didn't seem like they were up for any sort of promotion soon, but they probably knew how many bricks were in the stack. Plus, Johnny and Rock weren't the tidiest people—Paulie didn't need a whole package to get through the night. There was plenty of leftover powder he could scoop together.

Just as he gathered enough to take a snort, the floorboards creaked.

He wasn't alone after all.

July 13ᵗʰ, 2000. 8:57 PM

Zebadiah stood quietly in the barn doorway. This strange man sitting in the chair didn't belong here. These tables and lights and containers and tubes and powder didn't belong here. This was Zebadiah's barn. His Papa was dead, so that meant everything was now his. His house. His land.

The man in the chair pulled something from his pocket. A cellphone. Zebadiah had no experience with them other than what he saw in prison. He and Papa never had a need for any kind of phone for the house let alone a phone for the pocket. He didn't know why, but of all the contraband prisoners put value in, cellphones were the most valuable.

The man on the chair poked at his cellphone and swore the whole time. He raised it in the air like he was offering it up to God. Zebadiah didn't know how cellphones fit into religion, but he knew that making an offer to God was useless. He used to pray and make offerings, beg God to make his Papa stop beating him, to send him a girl who didn't cry during wedding games, and to keep the other prisoners away from him. God never helped. Zebadiah had to help himself, had to become stronger, bigger. He had to take back his life, just as he had to take back his barn.

He stepped inside.

The man looked up. His face angry at first, then confused.

"Holy shit!" the man yelled as he jumped out of his chair so fast that he flipped it over. "Who the fuck are you?"

Zebadiah couldn't answer. No tongue meant he could only speak in vowels and he didn't like how it made him sound. The other prisoners made fun of the way he talked, so he never spoke. He didn't need to talk to this man, anyway. He was going to grab him and break him.

The small man reached behind his back and pulled out a tiny gun. He aimed it at Zebadiah, clutching it tightly in both hands.

Zebadiah stopped. He'd been punched, kicked, choked, slapped, stabbed, but never shot. He heard it hurt more than anything else, and he knew a bullet could kill.

"Christ, you're a big fucker," the small man said, his arms trembling a bit and his eyes widened like a cow's after it got shot in the head. "Okay, look. I've killed before. I don't like it, but I've done it, so let's not go that route, okay? Let's be cool, okay?"

Zebadiah didn't like this man—he was small and twitchy. He looked like the rodents living within the prison walls, eating dropped food or sneaking off into places they shouldn't. They squeaked at night. Always squeaking. Like this man. Zebadiah stepped forward, and a quick blast of thunder erupted as a portion of the ground next to Zebadiah's feet exploded.

"Fuck, that's loud in here!" the small man yelled. "Okay, let's not do that again. Next time, it won't be the ground I shoot. I don't want to kill no one, okay? Let's start over. Let's be friendly. My name is Paulie. Who are you?"

Zebadiah didn't care about names. He didn't stop moving toward the rat.

"Okay, man, now you're making me think you want some of this stash here. I can't let that happen. This place belongs to my boss, and he'd want me to shoot you if you don't leave now."

This place belonged to his boss? No! It belonged to Zebadiah, not this small man's— Paulie's—boss! Zebadiah's fingers curled, ready to grab Paulie.

"Oh, come on, man. I see what you're doin'. You don't want this. I don't want to do this, but I will."

Zebadiah stomped forward, his boots sending up dust.

"I'm serious, okay? I'm aiming right at your chest. Not your arms or legs, your chest."

Zebadiah reached out for Paulie's neck.

Thunder again.

A flash.

Hot pain all through Zebadiah's chest and shoulder. It hurt real bad, most painful thing to ever happen to him, but not as bad as he had imagined.

He rolled his shoulder and raised his arm over his head, hoping it still functioned. It did. Good. He kept walking toward Paulie.

He didn't make it a full step when Paulie shot him again. Again and again. Zebadiah felt each bullet tear through his skin and into his chest, shoulder, belly. He looked down the length of his body and wondered if this was going to be the end. This was how he was going to die.

The bullets felt like hot pokers digging deep into him, but nothing that made him feel like he was dying. He ran a hand over his chest, his fingers poking through the holes in his overalls, the holes in his body. A dark red ooze coated his fingers. Any time he had been stabbed, there was blood. *A lot* of blood.

There should be more blood.

"What the literal shit is happening?" Paulie mumbled.

Paulie. Zebadiah almost forgot about Paulie. Almost.

Zebadiah charged the smaller man. Paulie tried to run but tripped over the fallen chair and dropped his gun. Zebadiah was on him, but Paulie wasn't easy. He punched. He kicked. Mostly to Zebadiah's head. He even managed to break free of Zebadiah's grip.

He reached for Paulie, this time grabbing the sweaty, slippery man by both ankles. Paulie's head hit the ground. He wasn't squirming, but he still clawed at the ground to pull himself away.

There was no escape for Paulie.

Zebadiah didn't want Paulie here. He didn't want the metal tables with glass and liquids and powders here either. He planted his feet and set his hips. With less effort than expected, he lifted Paulie and allowed him to dangle like a rat, then swung Paulie like an ax onto the metal table.

The crash was thunderous, and Paulie landed face-first into glass cups and tubes. He lay there grunting and bleeding. He bled like Zebadiah expected, liquidy and spilling fast from his face. Why wasn't Zebadiah bleeding the same way? He had holes in his body, but his blood oozed like tree sap, not the way Papa bled when the cops shot him. Zebadiah looked down and fingered the hole in his sore belly.

Paulie slid from the table and thumped to the ground, leaving a wide trail of blood through the broken glass. His face was pulverized, broken and open like a ripe watermelon. Blood poured from Paulie's flattened nose into his swollen eye. Glass shards stuck out of his right cheek. His lips were blooms of ground meat, but they were moving. The man was saying something. Zebadiah leaned close. Paulie whispered and gurgled through the blood bubbling out between broken teeth. "Bith... Jenny Fanelli... Her faul..."

Zebadiah didn't know what that meant. Maybe Jenny was someone Paulie played wedding games with. He didn't care, he squeezed Paulie's neck until it popped.

Zebadiah grabbed Paulie by the back of the shirt and lifted him off the ground. He wasn't going to leave him here, and thought he'd chop him up and bury him. The dead man's arms and legs dangled, making him look like an animal.

And Zebadiah was hungry.

July 14th, 2000. 1:08 PM

Completely reclined in her chaise lounge, Cali basked in the afternoon sun's rays. Exactly what she wanted for this week. Yesterday had its rough patches, but meeting Linda helped smooth things out. Tanner and Hook had abandoned them in the kitchen to run down to the end of the pier and jump in the water. The jerks even started the boat and motored around the lake. Cali didn't care because Linda was intoxicating. About an hour later when Tanner and Hook crashed their conversation, Cali couldn't help feeling irritated. The guys were wet and loud and they wanted to party. Luckily, Jordon and Dakota arrived. Cali's enthusiasm for the day rose when her lifelong friend walked through the door.

The six of them had a mellow evening—pot, booze, food, smiles. Hook did a bump of coke even though no one else wanted any. Linda made kabobs that hissed and sizzled in the fire pit. The meat's spice combination sent Cali straight to Nirvana. Dakota was proud of herself for remembering marshmallows for dessert, though there was a ton in the overflowing pantry.

Dakota got drunk before midnight. That usually happened when she felt ignored. Cali didn't think she had ignored her during dinner and banter around the fire, but maybe she had? The night ended with three minutes of below-average sex—Tanner softly snored in her ear, the smell of his alcohol-infused sweat perfuming the air. Cali eventually drifted to sleep while thinking about all of Linda's stories she couldn't wait to hear.

Today had started with a traditional breakfast of pancakes, bacon, and eggs. Of course, Linda found creative ways to use vanilla and cinnamon in the pancakes to send Cali's tongue to Heaven. But what followed breakfast was confusing.

The men had to go on a pot run. Somehow Hook, the king of all hemp, ran out of weed. Cali had known him for a few years now, almost as long as she'd known Tanner. Most of her stories and memories of Hook started with, "One time, at this party…" and ended with him passed out. He wasn't intelligent. He wasn't funny. He wasn't interesting. He wasn't even that entertaining. Yet, on her way to the bathroom, Cali overheard an argument between him and Linda regarding her desire to join him on the pot-run.

"You don't need to come along," Hook said.

"I know, but I want to," Linda replied.

"It's just me and the boys."

"Come on. It's always just you and the boys."

"You don't like the girls?"

"Cali's cool. Dakota hasn't said much."

"There you go. Hangout with the cool one and talk to the quiet one."

"But I'd rather go with you."

"When you whine like this, it makes you sound like a bitch."

"Yeah? When you talk like that, it makes you sound like a fucking douche."

Cali tiptoed to the bathroom and closed the door right before Linda stormed away.

What the literal fuck did she see in that guy? Sure, he could be attractive in that messy-haired bad-boy, squinting and snarling sort of way. Even though he had no fat to hide his toned muscles, he was on the thinner side. Too thin for Cali's tastes, but that was hardly enough to make her question the sanity level of her new friend. He had nothing to offer Linda, so why would she want to make a pot-run with three dudes? Why couldn't she go a few hours without being around Hook? If Linda was clinging on to a borderline loser so fervently that she didn't want to be without him for the length of time to run an errand, why was Cali so quick to get rid of a potential winner like Tanner? Was she being too demanding? Too shortsighted? Too entitled?

As Cali exited the bathroom, Tanner was aiming for their bedroom. With the exchange between Linda and Hook fresh in her mind, she wanted to try an experiment to see how Tanner would react. "Why do you have to make a pot run?"

He never did well in these situations, ones where she ambushed him for seemingly no reason, so his level of deception was at a minimum. He shrugged and kept his answer short. "'Cause."

"That's not an answer, Tanner."

"You should have gone to school to be a lawyer."

"I know. You've mentioned it before, and often. Still doesn't explain why you have to go on a pot run with Hook."

"What's the big deal?"

"The big deal is that it's supposed to be a nice, relaxing couples getaway with our friends. We've done no couples things. You and I haven't done anything together since we got here."

"Jesus, Cali, we just got here yesterday. The six of us had a real nice time hanging out last night."

"Yeah, around the fire pit drinking and smoking the last of the pot, apparently. I still can't believe Hook ran out. I thought he walked on a path of hemp leaves everywhere he went. Anyway, we did the same things we could do anywhere. We're by the lake. We should do lake things."

She strayed from topic just enough to allow Tanner an out. He softened his facial expression and put his hands on her hips. Gently, he pulled her to him, and looked deeply into her eyes. "We will. Promise. Just a little male bonding on the way to get some party supplies, and then the rest of the week will be couples lake stuff."

"Okay." She kissed him, and then left the hallway, but not before saying, "If Hook is buying locally sourced, make sure you inspect it first. We don't know what kind of backwoods nonsense happens around here."

Even though she wanted to see his reaction regarding the pot run, her words were sincere. She wanted more time with him. She was determined to make the best of the situation and went outside to join Linda and Dakota for a little sun.

Cali reclined in her chaise lounge, soaked up the rays, booze, and Linda's latest story about the time she saw a lion in the wild while helping build houses in an African village.

"Amazing. You make traveling around the world seem easy," Cali said.

Linda smiled. "I wouldn't say it was easy, exactly, but certain areas of Africa are in dire need of help. Everything got fast tracked. After some paperwork and modern medicine, I was in Africa helping build houses for impoverished tribes."

Cali chuckled. "I mail off a check or two whenever the commercials of starving children make me feel guilty, and you go over there to help rebuild whole villages."

"It's not like I have a burning desire to right all the wrongs of the world. I had an opportunity to help a few people. Plus, it was a free two months in Africa! Hell of an experience, especially the safaris."

"I just don't think animals should be caged up like that," Dakota snipped as she stretched out on her chaise. Bright afternoon sun bounced off Dakota's sunglasses. The reflection off her long, platinum blonde hair was just as vibrant. Cali and Linda both turned on their sides and propped themselves on an elbow to observe the young woman between them. They each lifted their sunglasses and exchanged a confused look.

Cali started to feel bad—she had been enjoying conversations with Linda that Dakota didn't participate in. Lounging on either side of Dakota and talking over top of her didn't help matters. But did she actually think safaris were the same as zoos?

"Well, these safaris were a little different," Linda started, no hint of sarcasm or condescension in her tone. "All of the animals were allowed to roam free as a way to raise awareness."

Dakota sat up. "Really?"

Linda nodded. "Really."

Dakota pondered the words for a bit. Even though her sunglasses took up half her face, they did little to hide her baby doll features, a button nose between chubby cheeks. Pursing her heart-shaped lips while deep in thought, she looked like a little girl trying to be an adult. She nodded as if her approval meant something. "Yeah, that's cool. I like it."

45

Before laying back down, Dakota drained half the caipirinha from her glass. Cali and Linda exchanged another look, one ending in a knowing smirk, a shared secret that helped strengthen the bonds between new friends. What the hell is wrong with Linda?

Cali couldn't figure her out. There was something wrong with her. There had to be, despite Cali's best efforts to ferret it out. She liked Linda. Intelligent. Articulate. Witty. Kind. Cali knew very well she had a girl-crush on her and wanted to change her own life to be more like Linda.

Cali took a pull from her caipirinha, a Brazilian drink made with cachaça, a fancy liquor made from fermented sugarcane. It was delicious. Linda made it and it was just like her experiences—much richer than what Cali expected. They had both been to Brazil, but traveled it in different ways. Cali used her father's money to stay at the best beachside resorts and fussed to management when the swim-up bar's drinks weren't to her taste. Linda experienced the country, sharing soul-changing adventures with people she'd met in the hostels where she stayed. Cali paid top dollar for a caipirinha that she never knew was made with watered down cachaça, while Linda made her own with the locals. The cocktail made Cali think of Tanner. He was a watered down caipirinha found at any resort, not an authentic one found at select locations.

Cali had been mulling over the upcoming changes in her life, and the reason why she wanted this trip to be perfect. This would be her last couples week. She hadn't told anyone yet, but she accepted a job offer with Harkins & Powell, an advertising firm in California. She intended to share the good news, but she wanted one last week with Melody and Dakota, one last week with Tanner.

It was the age of internet and travel, so it wasn't like she'd never see her friends again or needed to say goodbye to Tanner. But things were going to change, and she wanted to assess her relationship. This career path might be transient, and she wasn't sure what kind of baggage she wanted to bring. Sure, Tanner had plenty of money and could travel to wherever her future might take her. But did she want that? The idea of breaking up with him in a few weeks had been growing stronger every day. Until Linda. Specifically, why she was with Hook.

"All right, ladies, we're heading out," Hook said as he and the other two men encroached on their lounge time. "Be back in a few hours."

All three men wore camp shirts, khaki shorts, and man sandals. Tanner and Jordon looked like models in their attire. In contrast, Hook looked like an extra from any movie set on a modern island beach—red Hawaiian shirt completely unbuttoned, strands of puka shells wrapped around his neck, frayed ends all along his shorts, and sandals held together by wishes and prayers.

Cali lifted her sunglasses and looked from Jordon to Tanner. "Did you intentionally wear matching shorts?"

Dakota laughed. "Your shirts are only one shade of blue different from each other. And… Are those the same Ray-Bans?"

Tanner nodded. "Yup."

"Why?"

"'Cause we're bros, that's why."

Cali rolled her eyes so hard it felt like they did a three-sixty.

The only immediate difference between the men was their size. Jordon was tall and had rounded roid-muscles, his percentage of body fat the only thing lower than his single-digit IQ. Tanner had three inches of height and thirty pounds over Jordon, despite the lack of steroids. Hook was average in every sense of the meaning. Maybe below average.

Cali smirked as Dakota and Jordon gave each other a parting kiss. Their platinum hair glimmered the same way in the sunshine. Most people called them Ken and Barbie, but Cali and Tanner secretly referred to them as the Chris and Cathy from *Flowers in the Attic*.

"Be back soon," Tanner said, and kissed Cali's cheek.

"Okay," she replied, more interested in the deep kiss shared between Linda and Hook.

Gliding their fingertips over each other's cheeks, they finally parted. Hook said, "Later, babe."

"Be safe," Linda replied.

The guys headed toward the car. Cali watched Tanner, wondering if she should have shown him more affection. Maybe if she stopped treating him like something she saw every day, then maybe she would see something new? Calling out a parting, "I love you," didn't seem right, but when she called out his name, she hoped the right words would come to her.

"Tanner?"

"Yes?"

"Could you grab some more cachaça on your way back?"

July 14th, 2000. 7:48 AM

A barn in the middle of nowhere. That was the location of Ptolemy's next assignment. Broker had been right about The Philanthropist setting up another contract. On the surface, the assignment seemed easy enough, an up-and-coming drug lord. Ptolemy had been doing this long enough to know two things: there was never an easy assignment, and the most important meal of the day was breakfast.

"House. Play Enigma," Ptolemy commanded as he entered the kitchen. He loved his kitchen, from the butcher block island in the center to the Viking stove interrupting the counter's flow. But his favorite part was the 60 jar, AllSpice Wooden Rack that sat adjacent to the stove. Non-slip rubber pads and waterproof labels were a cook's dream.

His house wasn't what many considered "homey." Monochrome colors of black and white with varying shades of gray and a splash or two of silver covered every inch of the 5,000 square feet. Minimalist art in the form of abstract paintings. No plants. No knickknacks. Though a black vase sat on an end table with a single red orchid—Cymbidium Fuss Fantasy.

Many people would find his house beautiful, but few would find it comfortable. That didn't matter to him. This was his home, and he could relax here. The couch was inviting, the wine was chilled, his music beautified every room, the bed offered a night of perfect sleep. "House. Pull up details for today's assignment."

A light gray screen on the side of his refrigerator glowed softly as black lettering appeared. He read over the details again while cracking open three eggs into a small bowl for an omelet. Next, he cut a half-inch thick slice of ham into perfect cubes. Before he could move onto the green pepper, his perimeter breach warning sounded off. A simple red light flashed, one of many tucked in the corner where two walls met the ceiling. His open concept floor plan meant no walls to hinder his sight-line—one could never be too careful in his line of work.

He grabbed a dishtowel and wiped his hands as he hurried from the kitchen to the living room. Laptop open on the coffee table; he tapped a few keys to pull up an aerial representation of his house. Southwest corner, something moved away from the house, toward the forest.

Ptolemy assumed it was an animal that got too curious. The exterior floodlight probably popped on and scared it away. He checked through the feed, just to be sure. Ptolemy was correct in his assumption. The hindquarters of a white-tailed deer leapt into the forest. Second one this week, but this one seemed a little odd. Distorted, as if the deer ran through rain. He moved to the closest window and looked out. Not a single raindrop fell from the sky.

Ptolemy appreciated nature, which was why he lived deep in the forest and why his house had floor-to-ceiling windows. But he liked to keep nature outside. Squinting, he looked toward the forest where the deer had disappeared. No rustling, no signs of life. Was there a deer? Was he seeing things?

Ptolemy sighed. He had hoped for more time, as every human being did when they contemplated unpleasant change. No expert on physiology, he knew enough to accept that as people got older, their bodies changed. As did their minds. He wasn't one of those people whose identity was tied so closely with what he did that he wished to die while doing it. Retirement was his goal, a real retirement, and he had promised himself he would do so when his body said it was ready. Paranoia proved itself a valid concern in his line of work, but the feeling was leading to constant anxiety. A message from his body, telling him he might be ready. He had already moved on from one life-threatening career before. After all, that was the whole point of tomorrow night's annual dinner with Kamu, Meg, and Mako. To celebrate moving on. To remember their missions. And who they lost.

Hawke.

Athena.

Draping the dishtowel over his shoulder, Ptolemy sighed again and went back to the kitchen.

Absently whisking his eggs, he contemplated what retirement might look like. It'd be as luxurious as his current lifestyle without needing to roll dice with Death. His daughter had up and coming life goals. Career. Adventure. Family. These would be exciting periods for her, and he wanted to live long enough to see them. Yes, it might be time to retire.

He thought about today's job. How many more before making the big change? Two more? Three? First, he needed to finish his breakfast. Back to his omelet. Chop the green pepper and … His knife wasn't where he'd left it.

Survival instinct was automatic—he dodged the knife swipe and caught it in his whisk. Deflecting the strike, he released the whisk and grabbed his dishtowel. He twirled then snapped it locker-room style at his attacker's face—a wannabe ninja, judging by the skintight, full-body outfit. No room for hidden weapons, no pouches, pockets, or belts. The ninja jerked backward, then lunged with arm extended as if wielding a fencing foil and not his Wusthof 8-inch Chef knife.

Ptolemy grabbed the towel by its ends, bringing it down on the knife-wielder's arm. In one fluid motion, he wrapped it around the ninja's wrist and pivoted, slamming his back into his attacker's chest. A hard yank of the arm and whipping his body forward, Ptolemy flipped his assailant onto the island, satisfied with the meaty slap and grunt of pain. But the intruder wasn't injured enough—the ninja used momentum to deftly roll off the other end of the island. Ptolemy wanted answers, and one of his other kitchen knives could ask the right questions. Unfortunately, the knife block was empty. He ducked just as the paring knife thwacked into the cabinet door directly behind his head.

Ticked that someone was using his favorite cutlery set against him, Ptolemy grabbed two frying pans from the stove. One close to his body like a shield, one extended outward, he was ready for another knife attack from his assailant. No, not one assailant. Three! They were fools, too, with ridiculous patterns on their outfits. All three wore head to toe black, but each bodysuit was accented by dark gray patterns in the material, barely perceptible. One moron had tiger stripes wrapping him from back to front, a slash over each eye. The other fool wore horizontal stripes. No… On second glance, not stripes. A single stripe crossed over his eyes and then spiraled around his body down to his ankles. The last idiot had starbursts over his eyes, shoulders, elbows, chest, hips, and knees.

Starbursts had been the first attacker. He now faced Ptolemy and stood on the other side of the island. Tiger-stripe gripped the boning knife and the bread knife. Spiral held his fists up and bounced from leg to leg like a video game character.

Ptolemy started with Spiral out of principle. It was one thing to have style, even if it was flashy, but this moron took idiocy to a whole new level, so Ptolemy threw a frying pan at him. Like a titanium reinforced missile coming in hot, it clanged Spiral right in the forehead and knocked him to the ground.

The other two approached from either side to the island.

Ptolemy swung the second, larger pan to fend off Tiger-stripe's slashes. In a coordinated effort, Tiger-stripe stepped back, allowing Starbursts to swoop in. The pan was the perfect size for his head. The hit, and resulting clang, wasn't hard enough to knock him out, but it disoriented him enough to allow Ptolemy to kick him in the chest as he deflected another knife slash from Tiger-stripe.

Ptolemy hurried to gain advantage over Tiger-stripe before his companions could right themselves, but he was the fastest of the three. Pan in hand, Ptolemy swung to block the stab of the boning knife. He then spun and smashed his elbow into Tiger-stripe's head. Apparently, Tiger-stripe had the thickest skull of the trio, because he took the hit and spun as well, delivering a slash to Ptolemy's waist.

The pain was mild. Ptolemy had been cut plenty in his lifetime—this one wasn't going to be his undoing. Tiger-stripe slashed with the bread knife and stabbed with the boning knife, keeping Ptolemy on the defensive. He swung the pan once to deflect a stab, then back again to alter the arc on a slice. Tiger-stripe moved his head just enough to show that he was focusing on the pan. In the moment he readied the boning knife for another attack, Ptolemy flipped the pan out, landing a jab into Tiger-stripe's face, knocking him for a loop. Ptolemy needed to get out of this enclosed space.

Spiral had gotten back to his feet. He rolled his shoulders, stretched his neck, and then cracked his knuckles. Seriously? Ptolemy planted his hands on the butcher's block countertop. Like a farmer scything wheat, he swung his feet around. If the resulting kick to the chest didn't break ribs, he'd be amazed and disappointed.

Ptolemy sprinted to the living room and assessed the situation. Tiger -stripe held both knives and was ready for more. Starbursts seemed no worse for wear, either. Spiral was on his feet but held his ribs. At least he had quit the superfluous movements. Then he did something confusing. Hunched over from the obvious rib injury, Spiral rolled up his left sleeve to expose what looked like a tiny computer screen. Leaning against the island for support, he tapped at the screen strapped to his forearm. Tiger-stripe and Starbursts skulked into the living room, sizing up Ptolemy.

Ptolemy backed away toward the fireplace. With no lamps or knick-knacks, his only ersatz weapons were the poker and shovel. Tiger-stripe and Starbursts matched his pace, step for step, and started to spread out. Tiger-stripe was the immediate threat, but Ptolemy didn't discount Starbursts. His plan was simple; grab the poker and shovel and beat the shit out of Tiger-stripe before Starbursts could get to him.

Until a faint buzzing sound… It came from the north-eastern area of his house, the hallway between the living room and the bedrooms. A mechanical buzz.

Two flying machines zipped into the living room. Ptolemy ducked to keep his head from getting taken off by the things. They arced away from the wall and zipped upward, ready for another attack.

Drones? Are these things drones? Ptolemy wondered as they hovered close to the ceiling. He had no personal experience with the square drones, each side over two feet long with propellers at the corners. They moved like radio-controlled helicopters without bodies. But these were no toys. Spiral was controlling them via the wrist computer.

With three hostiles still on their feet, one of them armed with knives, and two flying machines capable of God knows what, Ptolemy decided to utilize his last resort. He hated to do it and really didn't want to, but he had no other choice.

He dropped his hands to his sides. The three intruders pulled up, undoubtedly confused by his change in posture from defensive to casual. This was going to make a mess, but Ptolemy would have to deal with that later. Keeping perfectly still, he said, "House. Play *Rhythm is a Dancer.*"

Eight laser-sighted guns dropped from the ceiling, tasked to target and shoot anything that moved. When Tiger-stripe and Starbursts turned to run, dozens of bullets dropped them before they took a step. Spiral tried to duck and cover—enough movement to create rows of holes along his body and destroy the keyboard attached to his forearm. The flying machines crashed to the hardwood floor, their propellers no longer spinning.

"House. Stop."

Ptolemy waited for the guns to retreat into the ceiling before he dared to move. The security system worked well. He counted only six holes in the walls from stray bullets, and more importantly, none in himself. A minor cut and sore muscles, but he'd live. It was bad enough that someone was trying to take him out, but now they were trying to do so in his home. This assault went beyond a bunch of new assassins attempting to make a name for themselves. Someone had put a legitimate hit on him, and Broker didn't know anything about it. Or did he?

Ptolemy trusted Broker. Too much of a history. He'd call Broker to get a crew in here to clean and gather clues about who these three idiots were.

Ptolemy picked up one of the flying machines. Heavy, but lighter than it looked. He'd take them to The Empress, a tech guru he contacted any time he needed weapon upgrades. But that would have to wait. Even though his morning was ruined, he still needed breakfast.

July 14th, 2000. 1:37 PM

Cali's Mustang dipped and bounced, Hook speeding along the path. The terrain was rough, and even though the speedometer read ten it felt like a hundred. Tanner didn't like that Hook was driving, but only Hook knew where they were going. It was easier to let Hook drive than try to take directions. The last time Tanner took the wheel, he and Cali got into an argument. They had been doing that a lot lately. Hell, they had gotten into one an hour ago over the pot run. Christ, she had come out of the bathroom and asked him why he had to go. Seriously? What the hell was that about?

Why did she waste her time getting a marketing degree? She grilled him like a lawyer, which was what he thought her true calling should be. Sure, there was money in marketing, but there was power in being a lawyer. Power led to politics. He had daydreamed about being the husband of a political leader more than once. That position would be a middle finger to his old man who never missed an opportunity to tell Tanner he was a spoiled, lazy, entitled brat. It almost made Cali's insufferable mood swings worth dealing with.

The Mustang's undercarriage was being tossed by nature. A bounce, a drop, a slam of his shoulder against the door. She was going to be *pissed* when she saw all the little scratches and dings, the dirt caked tire rims. More fighting. More yelling. Who knew what kind of mood she'd be in when they got back to the house, especially after a few hours under the influence of the other girls. Dakota was harmless, never having a thought any deeper than a mud puddle. But Hook's weird girlfriend? Tanner didn't like the way Cali had become attached to her. And what the fuck was cachaça anyway?

Tanner's head smacked off the passenger side window. "Ow! Fuck! Slow down!"

"Dude." Hook chuckled. "This road is a jungle path. I told you to hold tight."

"Yeah, I'm just really distracted."

"About what?"

"Cali. She's been acting weird lately. She didn't want me to come along."

"Ha! I had the opposite argument with Linda this morning. She wanted to come along."

A branch slapped against the window and Tanner jerked back. "Really? Why?"

"Don't know. Crazy bitch, I guess."

"I guess. Where'd you meet her?"

"Same place I meet all my girls—a party."

"Classy as always."

"All right, chill. We're almost there, so take off your shirt."

"Do I really need to do that?"

"Course you do," Jordon said. He leaned in from the backseat and blew kisses into Tanner's ear. "You're the muscle man."

"Ha fucking ha," Tanner grumbled and swatted at Jordon the way he would a fly.

"No, seriously," Hook said. "You're the muscle of the operation. Take off your shirt and muscle up."

Tanner unbuttoned his shirt. "You do know I'm more than just the muscle, right?"

"Jesus Christ, princess, yes, I know you're more than the fucking muscle. You're a partner. I'm a partner. Jordon's a partner. Maxwell's a partner even though he ain't here at this moment in time. We're all fucking partners. I get it. These guys we're meeting don't give a flying rat's fuckhole about our share percentages. We all got a part to play in this little dance. Jordon is playing the part of the college-educated, smart money guy. I'm the weaselly guy with the mouth who set this whole thing up. You? You are the fucking muscle, and we want those muscles on display."

"Fine." Tanner balled up his shirt and tossed it in the back seat. He was hot, and he'd been sweating. The white tank top clung to every striation of his muscles. He thought about flexing his biceps and kissing them as a subtle "fuck you" but decided this wasn't the right situation. Things were stressful enough and being a dick wouldn't help. He fondled the shark-tooth dangling around his neck. "Should I keep the necklace?"

Hook curled his lips and sucked his teeth. "Seriously, man? Who under the age of fifty still wears a shark tooth necklace?"

Jordon kicked Hook's seat. "Says the guy with puka shells around his neck."

Hook looked down as if he forgot he was wearing them, then looked back to the road. "Keep the necklace, Tanner. It's retro. Might give us a west coast vibe. A 'we don't play by your set of rules' vibe."

"I think they'll figure that out pretty quickly anyway," Tanner said, one hand on the ceiling, one on the door to brace against all the jostling. "How much longer of this shit?"

"Should be coming up."

"How do you know?"

Hook sighed. "The dude said a mile from the main road."

"It's been a fucking mile! I'm not sold on the idea that either of you even know how long a mile is."

"Then open your eyes and look for a path leading to... I think this is it."

Small trees faded into tall grasses, and Hook guided the car along a recently made path. They had come to a barn.

"Remember, Hook," Jordon said as he leaned forward again. "You're the one squealing like a pig if things go south."

"Yeah, yeah, yeah. Oink fucking oink," Hook mumbled.

"You sure this is right?" Tanner asked.

"You wanna knock on the barn door and ask if we have the right drug lab, or if it's the other barn down the street?"

"No need for knocking. The barn door is wide open," Tanner said. Three men could be seen inside, and they seemed agitated, pacing in tight paths, arms and hands swinging through the air in angry gestures. "Are we sure we want to do this?"

Hook parked beside a black Range Rover. "I'm fucking sure that you and Maxwell and Jordon once came to me saying you wanted to get in the party game, make some money, be your own businessmen. I was perfectly fine peddling pot and pills, but you guys talked to me about a future and growing my business and becoming equal partners and how you have all these buyers lined up at your girlfriends' college and all that happy horseshit. Well, guess what? If you wanna sell serious fucking drugs, then you first need to buy some serious fucking drugs. And I ain't going in there by myself, so come on Muscles and Money."

Like many things in life, being a nouveau drug lord seemed better on paper. Tanner tried thinking of a few reasons to scrap the whole idea and turn around, but Jordon killed all hope of that by climbing out of the backseat after Hook. Tanner took a deep breath and realigned his expectations, then got out of the car.

There would be guns. He expected it. As long as he and Jordon kept their mouths shut and Hook did what he needed to do, then the guns would stay holstered and hidden. Tanner didn't trust Hook with much, but he trusted him with this. Everyone had an arena where they were the champion gladiator, right? Drug dealing was Hook's arena. Even if the guys in the barn pulled their guns, even if this was a setup and they were about to get robbed, then it was only a few thousand dollars. Hand them the money and leave, that simple.

Tanner took a deep breath. His hands were sweating, his heart pounding. He smelled fear. He prepared himself for the guns, the drugs, even for getting robbed.

But it turns out it wasn't fear he had smelled. It was death, and he wasn't prepared for the large pool of blood the three men stood around.

July 13th, 2000. 9:18 PM

Zebadiah carried Paulie through the field to his house, dead body slung over his shoulder like a sack of corn feed. He fiddled with one of the bullet holes in his chest as he made his way through the field. It was hard to see in the waning twilight, no matter how bright the moon.

He couldn't quite fit his finger in the wound, but that didn't stop him from poking at it. It didn't hurt, but felt more like a memory of pain. It didn't bleed either. Well, not in the way the blood had flowed from Paulie. Zebadiah's blood now oozed thick, like spilled jelly. At first this scared him, but he was still walking and moving. He was still breathing. He was still hungry, still salivating as he thought about food. He'd have to go hunting, maybe catch a nighttime critter like a fox. First, he wanted to dispose of Paulie's body.

The house was quiet and empty like it was supposed to be. He flopped the dead man down in the center of the main room. The kitchen didn't seem as big as when he was a child. He wanted to burn the body, but there was no way the wood burning stove could handle the lump lying in the main room. There was nothing here for him to cut with. He looked around for answers and found potential when he glanced out the window. Trash.

Papa had always been a hoarder. A "collector" he would say with a phlegmy laugh. They couldn't afford to throw anything out, let alone get anything new, so they kept what they had in disorganized piles outside. Zebadiah strolled among the six, seven, eight mounds, examining them. Papa had made small piles with his stuff. From the looks of things, other people had added to the piles over the years. Maybe the same people who broke out his house's windows and put graffiti all over the walls?

The trash piles contained interesting things. All kinds of furniture in different stages of rot and disrepair. One heap was made from broken electronic equipment like gutted radios and busted televisions. There was even a

59

half-rusted car beside the house, situated like a welcome gate to the rubbish. He didn't know one car from another since Papa had no need for them. If Papa needed to get to town, he'd find a way. And on the rare occasions Zebadiah attended school, a bus would pick him up along the main road. There were no tires on this car, and it was windowless, decorated with bullet holes and another crudely painted fuckstick on the side. He'd have to come back to get a better look at it later. After he cleared out and reclaimed his barn. And got rid of Paulie's body.

Zebadiah didn't have to search the piles too long to find something useful—fifty-five-gallon drums, four of them. He chose the least rusted barrel, sturdy enough to hold wood, and dragged it closer to his house. He filled it with paper, twigs, and larger branches. Luckily for Zebadiah, the dead man had a lighter in his pocket. He got the fire going easy enough, then fetched the dead man from his house and dropped him next to the barrel.

Thoughts about trying to rip his arms and legs off danced through his head. Didn't seem like it would work, though. He glanced to the junk piles and hoped to find something useful in there. Before he tried that, one more thought made itself known. More like a reminder—the underground shed.

Ten paces west of the house, Zebadiah swept away years of growth and dead leaves, the natural camouflage that kept it hidden. The pad lock was secure, but rusted. It took only four kicks from his boot heel to break it from the doors.

The shed was small, and he needed to turn and duck to fit inside. Steep stairs with three walls of shelves, and a lantern hanging from the ceiling that he didn't know how to use. Zebadiah didn't know how to work Paulie's cellphone, but when he flipped it open, it lit up. The light wasn't bright, but it was enough to find the double-sided axe.

Zebadiah stripped the man and fed the clothing to the fire. The flames danced green and blue for a time, but quickly faded to orange and yellow, then burped up ashes. After two swings of the ax, Zebadiah had the arms in the burn barrel. A quick whiff of burning hair, a sizzle, a pop from the skin cracking, and soon enough he'd be able to throw in more. Strangely enough, he wasn't sickened by the smell. His stomach still rumbled.

The full moon light made its way through the trees, but not where Zebadiah needed it. He pulled the torso closer to the barrel, the firelight helping. He tried to use the ax blade as a knife to cut into Paulie's belly to empty out his guts, but it was far too dull. As the fire burned strong, he wished he had a better cutting tool and wondered what else Papa had in the shed. A memory of a specific tool struck him. It wouldn't help with his situation, but his curiosity took over. Was it still there?

He wandered back to the shed, and before setting foot on the stairs, a dirty, musty, foulness hit his nose. Something from within the forest? He looked around, deeper into the woods. Movement. A rustle of leaves? Too impatient to waste time thinking about it, Zebadiah chalked it up to the sounds of nature.

Down the stairs he went, the faint light from the cellphone led the way. Papa's prized tool was here… It was still here!

The sledgehammer. Bertha.

Papa loved this thing, possibly one of his proudest possessions. Said he made it himself. Zebadiah recognized he was a slow learner, but he was quick enough to know that Papa had no such tools or skills to create something like this hammer. The thing was metal, long handle and all, with an enormous head. One of the few times Zebadiah went to school, he learned about mythical gods and one who lived underground toward Earth's hot center. The god made great weapons, like this hammer. During those moments of his childhood when he'd look at his father as a good provider, he'd fantasize that maybe he traveled into the Earth and stole Bertha from that weapon-making god. In reality, Zebadiah knew his papa had stolen it from one of the hillbillies on the other side of the mountain, probably the one with only ten teeth and burn marks up and down his arms.

Papa used it to kill cows. One blow and the cow stopped mooing. Truth knew no home in Papa's mouth, so he'd say he used Bertha to put the cow out of its misery quickly as possible. Zebadiah knew its purpose was to quiet the stolen animal before its calls for help were heard.

Zebadiah marveled at its weight. Papa had to use both hands to lift it and his whole body to swing it. Zebadiah lifted it with one hand. He felt why

Papa liked this hammer. It was all the power in the world in one tool. All the power in the world in Zebadiah's hand.

He doubted he'd ever use it to kill cows. Maybe he'd use it to pulverize the dead body, or on the stuff in his barn and the men who put it there. But as he climbed the shed's stairs, he discovered he had a much more immediate use for it.

A bear. A big brown one had the dead body by a foot and was dragging it away. The bear must have been hungry if it was looking for food right before nightfall. Zebadiah cursed himself for not taking the time to examine the smells and noises before going into the shed. He could have scared it away before it got ahold of the man. No. He was thinking wrong. No need to hunt when an animal got this close.

He ran toward the body and grabbed Paulie by the neck. The bear didn't seem to care until Zebadiah pulled, stopping the bear in its tracks. It tugged and jerked Zebadiah forward. He should have been afraid, but he was impressed with his ability to stop the animal. Zebadiah was not about to let the bear walk away so easily. Digging his feet into the ground, he bent his knees a bit, and yanked with all his might. The bear's head snapped, and the beast released the foot.

Slobber sprayed from the bear's mouth as it shook its head and growled. Zebadiah stood firm and knew deep within his heart he could kill this animal without the need of a gun. The bear reared up on its hind legs, its front claws in the air. It roared, a pastor of strength, preaching a prophecy of death. Zebadiah was unmoved by the sermon and answered in kind, yelling with his arms in the air, gripping good ol' Bertha in his hand.

The animal dropped to all fours and gave one final snort before charging. Zebadiah crouched and braced for impact. Right before their collision, the bear stopped and raised up on its hind legs again. It came down with purpose, knocking Zebadiah to the ground. Jaws clamped on Zebadiah's left shoulder, teeth piercing his skin. The bear tried to shake its head, but it didn't seem to have a good hold and its face was too close to the ground.

The bite hurt, but much like the bullet wounds, it was more of a memory of pain, his body feeling what it thought it should feel. Pinned, Zebadiah had no leverage, his kicks meaningless against the thick fur. He still had his Bertha, though. Zebadiah was unable to swing her, so he used her to punch the bear in the head. The first couple hits yielded nothing except louder growls, but the third hurt the bear enough to make it let go, and the fourth encouraged it to get off Zebadiah.

The bear shook its head and circled Zebadiah as he got to his feet. The bear must have been hungry because it didn't take the opportunity to run. Instead, it attacked. Zebadiah was ready.

It lumbered forward and reared up again. This time Zebadiah swung Bertha, connecting with the bear's ribs. Zebadiah wasn't ready for it to twist the way it did. A claw swiped his torso. Blood oozed from the three slices, but the injury didn't slow him down. He swung again, driving the hammer into the bear's chest. The bear's eyes widened as it stumbled backward. Zebadiah didn't miss his opportunity, nor his next four swings: shoulder, back, back, neck.

Panting, Zebadiah raised Bertha in the air. He felt like a mythological god ready to smite a creature refusing to do his will, ready to crush its head. At that moment, he heard his father's voice:

"Sometimes you have to be the bear."

Papa was right. Zebadiah lowered Bertha and walked over to where he had left the ax.

July 14th, 2000. 1:22 PM

Idiots. Fucking idiots, each one of them.

Maddox made a mental note to find a higher caliber of help. He wanted to get a jump on the day, get back to the barn to see how Paulie did last night. He treated Paulie like a chump, but he was beginning to think it might be Rock and Johnny who were the chumps.

Late. Both morons had been late when he arrived to pick them up. It was bad enough that they had lost their driver's licenses. Who ever heard of a crime lord driving his help around? Idiots were late and idiots weren't trusted to drive. The last thing he needed was the demise of his drug lab because of a ticket, so now he was driving his Range Rover to the barn with Johnny and Rock in the back.

Paulie seemed like he might be a good candidate for a promotion. He was eager and certainly knew the business. He had been around awhile and seemed smart enough not to be too smart. Maybe Paulie just needed the opportunity? Back when Maddox played football in high school, some guys were terrible during practice, but beasts during game time. Was there a beast lurking in Paulie's short frame?

Maddox chuckled to himself at that thought as he turned off the main road and started down the uneven path winding through the woods. He sensed both Rock and Johnny giving him side-eye, probably wondering what he was laughing about, but too afraid to ask. So angry by their tardiness Maddox threatened to shoot the first person to talk. Fuck them. Let them wonder. They're out, Paulie was in. Maddox decided to invest the time to groom the little guy to be his second in command. Not to mention, Paulie wasn't young. He had been around long enough to make connections. Maddox needed all the connections he could get, now that he offed the Templeton brothers. It took a shit-ton of time and money to find "The Mathematician," but it was worth it. A void had been created by removing the Templetons and Maddox was going to fill it. But he needed help, a second in command he could trust. No one else on his payroll was any more qualified, certainly not the two idiots in the car with him now. Paulie wasn't perfect, but he might be the answer.

He'd drop Rock and Johnny off at the barn, then take Paulie back to the city. He had a couple deliveries to make. Sure, the dumbass lost a delivery, but it was only a few pounds of pot and it was because some hooker screwed him over, both literally and figuratively. Maddox was in a forgiving mood about that transgression. He, too, had fallen victim to the enticing deceptiveness of a woman. Paulie would get another chance to prove himself with the scheduled deliveries for today while Rock and Johnny had some penance to do for their tardiness. Double the daily production. There was always demand for his product, especially with new buyers paying a visit today.

A few rich frat boys trying to break into the market. Morons. Saw too many television shows making this business look easy. It wasn't, and they were extra stupid for thinking they would grow big enough to be players in the same game Maddox was trying to win while buying and selling his product. Morons were starting with five kilos, too. Stupid to believe they were going to move it easily. They'd probably get busted before they got halfway through the stash. But, hey, they were coming to the barn with cash up front, so Maddox was more than willing to make the deal. Even if they somehow moved it, then Maddox would simply double the price, because they'd be stupid enough to double their order.

Maddox pulled up to the barn. No other cars yet. Frat boys better not be late. Maddox had enough of tardiness today and emphasized his point by slamming the door shut as he got out of his SUV. Johnny and Rock followed in awkward silence, still not tempting a bullet to the face. Even if they had been allowed to engage in conversation, it would have stopped once they saw the scene in the barn.

Maddox drew his gun and moved to the closest support post for cover. Johnny and Rock did the same thing until Maddox waved them on to secure the place. Johnny took the right side while Rock took the left, leading with their guns as if they were hound dog noses. Moving quickly, they checked behind every post, poked around in every stall, and then climbed the ladder to the loft. Nothing but mud, rodent remains, and long rotted hay.

While Johnny and Rock were making their way off his shit-list, Maddox examined the scene. Blood. Not a slaughterhouse, but plenty of still damp pools around one of the tables. Broken glass and spilled chemicals were contained to a small area. Maddox assumed someone had been thrown against this table, and he assumed that someone was Paulie. But whoever threw him was huge. Really fucking huge, judging by the size of the footprints leading from the scene to the other end of the barn and out the back door.

Clasping his gun with both hands, Maddox followed the dried blood splatter and footprints to the field behind the barn. They disappeared within the thick brush and tall weeds. Heat radiated up his neck as his speeding heart added fuel to the furnace. He didn't like this feeling, an apex predator suddenly falling from the top of the food chain. *Jesus, look at the size of these prints! Are those size eighteens?*

Maddox rolled his tight shoulders, then he walked back to the area of blood and broken glass. Johnny and Rock joined him in silence. He certainly appreciated that they were smart enough to be afraid of him. Now, to figure out who, or what, had incited his fear. "Anything?"

"No, boss," Johnny answered. "No evidence of nothin'."

Rock walked around the table and then pointed to the ground. "Hey. There's a gun here."

Maddox crouched next to it, grateful for any form of evidence. He set his Glock on the ground and picked up the one in question. A simple .38 Smith and Wesson Special, six empty shells in the chamber.

"What the hell happened here?" from the barn doorway.

Out of reflex Maddox flicked his wrist, snapped the chamber shut, snatched his gun from the ground, and aimed both at the interloper. Johnny and Rock pointed theirs as well.

"Whoa! What the fuck, Johnny?"

A few inches shorter than six-foot, red Hawaiian shirt, mussed hair, puka shells, and man-sandals. His hands were in the air, eyes wide as saucers. A quick assessment and Maddox deemed this guy harmless. Maddox debated about shooting him anyway. The douchebag knew Johnny, though, so Maddox glanced over for an explanation.

"It's cool, Maddox. That's our man, Hook," Johnny said, then lowered his gun as an attestation to his statement. "He's the one buying the five kilos."

So caught up trying to figure out what had happened, Maddox forgot about the meeting with these guys. A mouthy little guy, a pretty boy, and some jackass with tribal ink on his gym muscles. *Yeah, these idiots will one day challenge me for top dog. Sure.* For now, he'd sell them the five kilos and tell them to fuck off.

"What happened here?" the kid with the tribal ink asked.

Maddox didn't like the way the kid's eyes were wandering, checking out his setup, the broken glass, the scattered powder, the blood stains. At first Maddox thought the kid might have been trying to get a good look so he could learn how to make the product, but he didn't seem inquisitive, more like he was going to shit himself. He was staring at the mess, not the setup.

"Who the fuck are you guys?" Maddox demanded.

Unable to pull his eyes from the blood, the tribal-inked kid, who was no doubt the muscle of the trio, pointed to the pretty boy. "I'm Tanner. That's Jordon."

Hook moved closer to the carnage. "Was this an accident?"

"No," Johnny replied. "We got robbed."

"Not robbed," Rock answered. He pointed his pistol at the packaged bricks at the end of the other line of tables. "Not a single one of them is missing."

"Someone sending us a message?" Johnny asked.

"About what? There's blood, but no body. Nothing stolen. Unless you count Paulie." Maddox flipped open his cellphone. It barely had a signal. He punched in Paulie's number, not really expecting an answer. Either he got whacked and couldn't answer or ran away and shouldn't. As soon as it went to voicemail, Maddox hung up and returned the phone to his pocket. "If I were leaving a message to a rival," Maddox said, glancing at all the damage, "I would have broken *everything* and then burned the barn down. There was a fight, that's for sure. Someone lost, but... where'd Paulie go? A fraction of equipment is broken, and some product is ruined. It's enough to piss me off, but what's the message?"

"Then it has something to do with Paulie?" Johnny asked.

"No shit." Maddox stroked his goatee while mulling over the Sasquatch-sized footprints in the dirt outside. "Paulie's not a tall guy, and he doesn't have feet this size. And there's no drag marks. The man with the big shoes probably carried Paulie out of here by himself. Probably slung him over a shoulder, then went..." Maddox considered the print's trail. "Not to a vehicle. Because those footprints trail into the field. Yeah. Paulie must have been the target, but I don't know why. He loses a shit ton of bets, but always pays his debts. Owed me for a lost shipment of pot. That's why he 'volunteered' for the overnight shift. Maybe he owed something to someone else, and they weren't as charitable as me."

Arms crossed over his muscled chest, Rock looked at the mess and shook his head. "Shame. And now we got this to clean up."

Maddox sighed. "Fuck. I needed Paulie to make a couple of deliveries today."

"He'll do it," Johnny said, eyeing Hook with a smirk.

Maddox couldn't get a read on Hook; the squinty-eyed shmuck had a good poker face. But the other two? Maddox could almost hear their ass cheeks clench to keep from shitting themselves. This was going to be the only bit of fun he'd have today, so why not?

Maddox towered over Hook by a half foot. The little shit didn't seem intimidated, probably used to being the short one all his life. "Ya know, I thought about telling you to fuck off, that the whole deal was no longer going to happen. But Johnny says you're willing to do me a favor. Is that right?"

"You said two deliveries?"

The looks on the pretty boy's faces? Priceless. They went from scared to furious. God damn, Maddox about pissed himself with laughter. He had

Johnny and Rock to clean this place, but he didn't want to leave until he had a better idea of what happened. The deliveries were to two of his street level pushers, so he would lose a full day of business if he postponed. Maddox snorted as he swallowed his laughter and put on a straight face. "Yeah. Local. Both in town."

Maddox was enjoying this. The longer Hook took to ponder the offer, the angrier his friends got. If this were a poker game, he'd mop the table with them. Just for shits and giggles, he added, "Do the deliveries and bring back my cash, and then I'll sell you six kilos for the price of five."

Johnny knew this asshole, so Maddox felt confident that he'd find them if they fucked up the deliveries. A slight chuckle escaped from Maddox when Hook said, "You know what? We got a deal."

July 13th, 2000. 9:46 PM

Zebadiah was panting. At least he thought he was, thought he needed to. He breathed in and out, inhale, exhale, like he always had, and now after killing a bear, he breathed faster. Did he need to?

Well, he was still hungry, so his belly was working. Maybe that meant his lungs needed to work, too? But he didn't feel pain the way he used to and now he bled in a way he never bled before. Maybe he didn't need to breathe no more? There was something different about him, for sure. He'd gotten strong, very strong in prison, but now he felt even stronger than that. Maybe because he was home. Papa always told him this land was special. After Papa would tell him that, he'd immediately start to insult Mama, calling her a witch and a bitch and a whore and a cunt. In any case, Zebadiah decided to keep breathing as he always remembered, whether he needed to or not. And he drooled as he used the ax to chop off the bear's head and legs. Now to find a good way to cook it. Back to the trash piles where he found a small length of chain link fence with minimal rust. Perfect fit on top of the burn barrel to turn it into a grill.

The fire in the drum was going nicely, hissing out words Zebadiah thought he knew, as if the flames begged him to put meat on the fencing-grate. He obliged, placing both of the bear's front legs on it. Hungry. So hungry.

While his food sizzled, he thought more about the bear. He had lopped its head and legs off with the ax, but there was a lot left. Obviously more food, but this was going to take prep work. He didn't want to try to cook the whole animal with all that fur. The smells from the cooking leg fur were awful and he imagined that the whole body would be worse. After a few minutes, though, the fur had burned away leaving the smell of cooking meat to make his guts roll with anticipation. It didn't smell any different than the cuts of cows Papa cooked. Was he smelling the meat because he was looking at it? He knew he was changing. That knowledge made him feel like he was standing inside a dark cave with no flashlight, alone and cold. He was turning into something but didn't know how or why or what. All this thinking hurt his head. So what if he was changing? Pain didn't feel like pain no more and he was stronger than ever! Maybe that's why he was so hungry.

His bear meat... The ax was too clumsy for skinning, so he turned back to the junk piles with hopes of finding something better. They were so tall he couldn't see over the tops. Most of the junk items were metal, though every pile had some form of furniture in it, too. Couches, dressers, tables, chairs. A few sinks, a rusted refrigerator, more than one toilet, plumbing tubes. Zebadiah wondered if there had been enough here for Papa to install indoor plumbing. He looked to the outhouse, then shivered at the chilly memory of mornings where he'd hop out from under his blankets and run to the cold wooden seat.

Why would people throw away so much good stuff? He hated that people had been on his land and in his house, but he understood why they'd been here. No one had been around for the past five years to protect his property. But to throw away things that still had use? He couldn't comprehend.

There were all kinds of devices like televisions and radios and even a few things he didn't recognize. He and Papa had no electricity, so no need for those electronics, but even if they didn't work as intended, they could still serve a purpose. Glass never went bad, the bits of metal could be reshaped, and all the cords would be good for tying wrists and ankles together.

A lawn mower. Someone had gotten rid of a lawn mower. Their loss was his gain. He had no lawn, but that didn't matter; there was value in this mower. He flipped it over and was excited to see the blade. Rust touched all parts of the machine, and yanking the blade free was easy. Yes! It was sharp enough to cut into the bear's belly.

Using both hands, he scooped out the guts and tossed them to the closest pile of junk, the one with the most broken metal. Should any animal want to investigate the smell, then they'd be rewarded with a jagged edge. That meant more meat for Zebadiah. A simple trap. He liked traps.

Zebadiah wanted to skin the bear, but the blade barely made it through the belly. He'd sharpen the blade and skin the bear tomorrow. He needed to store the carcass until then, and had seen plenty of chains and hooks in the junk piles.

His house was small and simple. A lone hallway led from the backdoor to the main room with a room on each side. Three bedrooms were upstairs, connected to each other by doorways. They were mostly empty now, except for beer cans and broken bottles.

He entered from the backdoor and went into the room on the left, the one missing parts of the ceiling. Ignoring the mess, he tossed a half dozen chains over the exposed rafters. He'd use the hooks to hold the bear's carcass. Satisfied with a job well done, he could deny his hunger no longer. Time to eat.

The bear's leg was sizzling when he tore a bite out of it. The sensation was of warmth, but without burning pain. Zebadiah couldn't reach the roof of his mouth with his shortened tongue, but the base of it remained and enough muscle to help with swallowing. Prison doctors told Zebadiah he would still be able to taste, mostly due to smell and taste buds on the roof of his mouth. He was able to taste the bear meat. It wasn't to his liking.

Zebadiah devoured the meat anyway, tearing away chunk after chunk, though disappointed with each swallow. Gnawing on the bone, he wasn't satisfied. He had a craving, and wondered if the other leg would taste better. He grabbed it from the grill. After a few bites, he stopped. It didn't taste right. It wasn't much different than cooked cow, from what he remembered, but he didn't want it.

Frustrated, he tossed the remaining piece aside. He rocked on his heels, thinking. The fire popped. A vivid childhood memory of a similar sounding pop—his father cuffing him across the head for not eating all the chuck steak on his dinner plate—the gristle had been too hard for him to chew seeing how the cut was too close to a joint. Zebadiah's jaw had popped, and a tooth got knocked loose. According to Papa, meat was nutrition. Meat was valuable, and it should *never* go to waste.

He couldn't explain why, but he went back to Paulie's remains. Two swings of the ax and Zebadiah was ready to toss an upper thigh into the barrel. Or … onto the grill?

Zebadiah paused at that thought and he stared at Paulie's thigh. A thick line of blood ran along the meat. Zebadiah traced the crimson liquid with his finger. His blood used to look like this, but not anymore. He pressed his finger knuckle-deep into the meat. It didn't seem right to eat this guy, especially raw. He'd eaten raw cow before. Got sicker than a dog after eating its own shit, but this time … this time he thought different.

Curious, he tore off a small raw hunk, and popped it into his mouth. Chewy, yet rich. Yes! This was how it was meant to be enjoyed. He tore off another piece and another. Grunting, he peeled away the skin and ripped the meat from the bone with his teeth. Blood-soaked globs slid down his throat. It was heavenly, as if his whole body tasted the food.

Once he finished the leg, he tossed the clean bone aside. There was still a whole other leg to enjoy. His teeth tore through skin, and he consumed the rest of his meal.

Belly full, or his new perception of full, Zebadiah tossed the bones in the barrel, the fire dimming to embers. He was no longer hungry, but itchy and tired. The bullet wounds. The itching came from the bullet holes. They were smaller and no longer oozed reddish slime. So tired.

Struggling to put one foot in front of the other, Zebadiah grabbed Bertha and the bear's head before entering the house through the backdoor. He stumbled into the room on the right and collapsed on the floor, excited to sleep. He wanted to be well rested for tomorrow, for the men in the barn who didn't belong there.

July 14th, 2000. 2:04 PM

Linda's ass caught Cali's attention. She didn't expect to see Linda's rounded booty sticking in the air as she passed by the bedroom. Cali just happened to look in and see Linda on the ground, halfway under the bed. She thought about surprising Linda, maybe jumping into the room, and then yelling, or sneaking up behind to goose her. Cali knew the owner of that ass for about twenty-four hours, but she was confident Linda would find it funny.

Cali crept into the room on the balls of her feet. About halfway to her goal, she stopped as Linda shimmied backward and stood. Different scenarios ran through Cali's head, confident that she still wanted to startle Linda, but unsure which direction to go. Linda then surprised her by grabbing Hook's bag and tossing it onto the bed. She unzipped the top flap and started rooting through it.

Cali must have made a noise or subtle movement, enough to signal Linda that she wasn't alone. As fast as a viper strike, Linda twisted and threw a right hook. Electricity shot through Cali's left hand to deflect Linda's fist from her face. Cali spun behind Linda, rolled back-to-back along Linda's body, dropped to one knee, and punched. She missed—Linda slapped her hand away and leapt backward.

Linda's fists were clenched, her eyes made of ice. Suddenly her jaw dropped, and she brought both of her hands to her mouth. "Cali? Oh my God! I'm so sorry! Are you okay? Did I hit you?"

Controlling her breathing, in through her nose, out through barely parted lips, Cali stood and unclenched her fingers. "I'm okay. But what the hell was *that* about?"

"I'm so sorry! When I decided to travel the world, I needed to learn self-defense. A single woman in the jungles of South America—swing first, ask questions later is the key to survival."

Cali exhaled. She brought her hand to her fast-beating heart. "Oh my God, I should have thought of that before trying to sneak up and pounce on you."

Linda laughed. That rich and full music seeped into Cali, making her tingle. "That's hysterical. Your moves are quite impressive by the way."

Cali's cheeks warmed, the surest sign of a blush forming. Tucking a lock of hair behind her ear, she looked down at her bare feet. "Ugh, thanks. My dad made me take like a bazillion lessons in all kinds of martial arts. He thinks the entire world is the jungles of South America."

"Well, I certainly believe more women should be encouraged to take lessons." Linda extended her arms for a hug. "Still friends?"

"Yes, please."

Linda's hug was everything Cali expected and hoped for. Warm. Strong. Inviting. Her girl-crush on Linda had returned, especially since she caught Linda snooping through Hook's stuff. It made her happy to know that her new friend wasn't simply a bimbo satisfied with her druggie boyfriend's behavior. But what was she looking for?

After the forgiving embrace ended, Cali pointedly looked at Hook's open bag and then back to Linda. A slight smirk tugged at her lips. "So... find what you're looking for?"

Linda quickly zipped the bag and returned it to the floor. As she turned back to Cali, she unbuttoned and unzipped her cutoffs. A tickle formed within Cali's chest, wondering if Linda wanted something more from their burgeoning relationship. Linda didn't remove her shorts, though, instead lowering the left side to expose her hip. A life-size skull with an ambient glow emanated from its empty eyes, and a beautifully rendered black rose grew from its open jaw. "No. I had this done last week and I wanted to put some cream on it. Thought I brought some, but can't find it, so I thought maybe it somehow got into Hook's bag."

"Under the bed?"

Linda buttoned and zipped her shorts. She took off her glasses. "You never know. I once lost these and found them in the refrigerator. Stupid, right?"

75

Glasses in the refrigerator. If Dakota would have done that, then yes, that would be textbook stupid. But not Linda. Cheeks flirting with the formation of dimples, and the spark of intelligence behind her eyes made the notion endearing, like she was almost human, not quite a true goddess. A demigoddess, maybe, sired from a reasonably intelligent man and the goddess of awesomeness.

"No, definitely not stupid." Cali turned to the sounds of footsteps coming up the stairs. Even though there were no creaks, and the carpeting was thick, a person could be heard walking if they weren't tiptoeing. Dakota stopped at the door and poked her head into the room. "Hey, lesbians, the guys are back."

"Finally," Cali said.

"I know, right? It's been, like, hours. Hope they got some good shit." Dakota turned and went back down the stairs. Within a few seconds, guitar riffs and the beat of AC/DC's *Back in Black* thumped through the floorboards.

"I'm so sorry," Linda said.

"For what?"

"I feel like I'm coming between the two of you."

"Me and Dakota? Don't worry about that. We've known each other since first grade when I helped her get her fingers untangled from her shoelaces. I've been helping her tie her shoes ever since. And believe it or not, I mean that metaphorically. She'll be fine."

"Are you sure?"

"Yeah. It just takes her a little longer to catch on to things. Let's see what the boys came back with."

Cali and Linda joined the others in the kitchen. Dakota and Hook had already opened the gallon-sized freezer bag of marijuana resting on the center island and were busy rolling a pinch in papers. Tanner held two bottles of beer. He handed one to Cali as soon as she stepped into the kitchen. He kissed the top of her head. "Hey, babe."

After taking a long pull from her bottle, Cali replied. "Hey. Got some good stuff?"

"Locally sourced, no additives, preservatives, or GMOs."

"Ahh, excellent. We can get high knowing we've dealt exclusively in fair trade practices. Where's Jordon?"

"Hitting the head. He refused to piss in the forest."

"Forest? You guys went in the forest?"

"Yeah. Hook's guy was actually in a barn and—"

The electricity went out. The music stopped and the microwave clock disappeared. Hook looked up. "The fuck?"

After a few seconds of confused glances, Jordon entered the kitchen. "Hey, I was in the bathroom and the lights went out."

"It's the whole house?" Dakota asked.

"Looks like it," Hook answered. "I'm gonna check the breaker box."

"A black out?" Tanner asked.

Cali went to the patio doors and looked at the other houses sitting along the lake's perimeter. She saw only two and they were far enough away that if there had been any people there, they'd only be an inch high or smaller. Late afternoon, there was no reason for any lights to be on had anyone been home. However, one house did have a lit porch light. "If it is, it's localized. Someone forgot to turn off their porch lights."

Tanner came up behind her and wrapped an arm around her waist. He kissed her head again and then took a swig of beer. "Without the electricity, it's almost like we're camping."

"Yeah, we're really roughing it. Living off the land like the pioneer settlers."

Tanner remained silent, other than a gulp of his beer. Cali knew he was trying to process her last statement, wondering if her sarcasm was playful or pointed. She wasn't sure of either. They stood on the deck in uncomfortable silence. An eternity passed by disguised as a minute, then the lights finally came back on. She and Tanner went back inside as Hook came up the basement stairs. He held out a small, glass globe circle. "Fuse blew."

Tanner took the fuse from Hook. "This house uses fuses?"

Jordon shrugged. "Maxwell said it's a really old house. There have been a lot of renovations and updates, but I guess they never got around to converting to a circuit breaker box."

"Way to drop the ball, Maxwell," Tanner said to the fuse in his hand. He turned to Hook and asked, "So, you put in a new fuse?"

"No, this is the generator. There are no more fuses. Just an empty box on the closest shelf. We'll have to go get more."

"Are you serious?" Linda snapped.

"For fuck sake!" Cali blurted.

Rolling another joint, Dakota asked, "Can't we just use the generator for the rest of the week?"

"Not enough gas," Hook answered. "I'll be amazed if it lasted until tomorrow."

Tanner hurried back to Cali for damage control. Stroking her arm in an attempt to sweep away her anger, his words sweeter than if he had dipped them in honey. "Hey, I know the vacation is off to a rough start. The pot run took longer than expected, and I'm sorry for that. It ruined any fun plans for the morning. But when we were driving back, we talked about plans for the next few days. On the other side of the lake there's a place that rents jet skis, and another where we could do some parasailing. Jordon said there's a place that will teach us kitesurfing. I promise starting tomorrow, it will be a paradise vacation. Promise."

Cali barely heard his words and put no stock into his promise. She watched his lips move over his perfectly straight and gleaming white teeth, but instead of listening to him, she focused on the conversation between Linda and Hook.

Linda wanted to go along on the errand, ride along with them to a hardware store in town. Hook went on and on with excuses. "You three aren't dressed to go into town. It'd take half an hour for you to get ready while the three of us are good to go." Cali also heard, "You three have been drinking all day, there's no point in pausing your buzz. We'll be right back, and we'll catch up." His words came out of his mouth as smoothly as Tanner's, as smoothly as someone who'd practiced their excuses beforehand.

The frustration on Linda's face was more obvious than if her emotions were tattooed across her forehead. Turning her back to Hook, she crossed her arms and faced Cali. The two women exchanged a look, an unspoken solidarity.

Rifling through her closet of smiles, Cali found the perfect response to Tanner's bullshit—big and bright, an off the rack fake being sold as designer, daring Tanner to recognize the difference. She rubbed his arm in the same patronizing way he had stroked hers, though she doubted he caught the subtext. "Sure, sweety. Hurry back, okay?"

"Yeah. Totally."

She accented her fake smile with a counterfeit kiss.

Dakota and Jordon shared a kiss, the same way Cali used to make her Barbie and Ken kiss when she was seven. Short, cute, lips only, the only exposition being a brief "I love you."

Linda gave no further argument. "Don't fuck around."

Hook rolled his eyes, gave a salute, and left. Jordon and Tanner followed. On his way out, Tanner gestured toward them and contorted his face to imply, *What can I do? I have no choice.*

As soon as they left, Dakota walked toward the patio door waving the joints over her head as if they were prizes won from a hard fight in a gladiatorial arena. "Gonna enjoy some fresh air. You bitches joining me?"

"Yes," Linda replied.

"Be there in a minute," Cali said.

"Everything okay?" Linda asked.

Cali started up the stairs, and said, "Yep. Just going to look for some tattoo cream in Tanner's bags."

July 14th, 2000. 2:21 PM

Tanner fumed. Never being one to keep his emotions in check, he blurted, "What the fuck are we doing?"

Hook watched the road through squinted eyes, as if his narrowed vision would put things into focus. "What the hell does it look like, Tanner? We're driving."

"Yeah. To one of the two drug meets you set up without consulting me or Jordon."

"This again? We talked about this already, every painstaking inch from the barn to the house."

"And bullshit poured from your mouth every painstaking inch."

"What the hell, man? Jordon didn't like it either, but you don't hear him bitching about how scratchy his panties are."

Jordon sat directly in the center of the backseat, arms stretched along the top, gazing whimsically out the passenger side window. "I've learned it's best to keep my mouth shut when Mommy and Daddy fight, because whoever wins usually buys me ice cream."

"See?" Hook slapped the steering wheel with both hands for emphasis. "Despite that dumbass lump of flesh assuredly thinking of me as the mommy in that metaphor, he's not complaining."

Tanner punched the dash. "This isn't a joke, Hook!"

"Yeah, no shit! For the millionth time, Johnny put us in this situation. There's no fucking way we could have said, 'no,' to Maddox. That's the whole fucking reason why we're doing this. And do not friggin' start in on me again about not holding a business meeting with you two. Do not. It was, and still is, a wise business decision to do what a crime lord tells you to do, because you really don't have much of a choice."

"The missing henchman doesn't bother you in the least? And, you know, the blood, all the blood?"

80

"Dude. Seriously. Does Cali, literally, really, truly have your balls in a jar? Did you think we were going to be the first bloodless drug lords? This shit happens all the time. They didn't seem that surprised. Right, Jordon?"

"Right," from the back seat.

"See? If our organization's accountant picked up on it, then why can't you?"

Tanner shook his head and stared out the window. He didn't see the tree density dissipate as they got closer to town. He only saw the barn. Broken equipment. Blood. Maddox's eyes. "Maddox didn't seem surprised, but ... *concerned*."

"Concerned? What are you talking about? The dude's face is made outta fucking stone. He's got two settings—'angry,' and 'Columbian neck-tie pissed-off.' Don't even try to tell me you think you can get a read on that guy."

"I'm not *trying* to tell you. I'm *telling* you. He looked concerned. Right, Jordon?"

"Yep," from the back seat again.

Hook glanced in the rearview mirror. "Yeah? Well, no fucking ice cream for you!"

"Don't be a dick," Tanner snapped. "All I'm trying to say is we should have been better prepared for these things."

"No one could have been prepared for walking into that crime scene."

"We were walking into a drug lab, the very definition of a crime scene."

"You know what I mean!" Hook slapped the steering wheel again. "It's impossible to prepare for this shit. We have to make the best decisions available and alter our plans accordingly."

"Well, it looks suspicious with the girls."

"Does Cali let you visit your balls at least once in a while? Maybe once a month when she can't use them?"

"Dude, I'm serious. She has no clue, and I wanted to keep it that way until our business gets more established."

"You don't have to tell her shit. Tell her what's what and then that's that."

"You're just jealous that she and I have something real."

Hook laughed so hard he snorted, and the car swerved. "You're fucking stupid. If I'm jealous of anyone's relationship, it'd be Jordon's."

"God damn right," Jordon said.

"See?" Hook looked in the rear-view mirror again. "Tell us your secret, and I'll change my mind about not getting you ice cream."

"Communication."

Hook whooped and did a rat-a-tat-tat on the steering wheel with both hands. "Amen, brother! Lack of communication! He tells Dakota what he's doing, and he don't listen to her shit. He's got his balls and they're right where they should be, not in his girlfriend's purse."

"It's got nothing to do with my balls and their perceived location," Tanner said. "It has to do with getting busted for doing something highly illegal."

"We ain't gonna get caught."

"If you keep coming up with these lame excuses, we will."

"Lame? Dude, my plan is fucking genius!"

"We could have waited a couple of hours before Jordon popped the fuse. How did you even know the house had a fuse box anyway?"

"'Cause if we waited, we'd get all caught up in some unimportant bullshit and then we'd be getting back after midnight. *That* would have been even more suspicious than this. And Maxwell told me about the fuses. It was at the last party. You know how he gets when he's drunk. Just goes on about stupid shit. Hell, I have no idea why *he* knows that the house still has an old-time fuse box."

"For fuck sake."

"Hey, you should be thanking me. We showed the girls the fuse and it buys us a lot more time and credibility than that bullshit idea of yours about forgetting your phone at the barn."

Tanner hated to admit it, even within the privacy of his own mind, but Hook was right. Going out to replace a blown fuse was a much better idea than forgetting his phone at the barn. Too many loose threads for Cali to pick at and pull. She would have unraveled that tapestry of lies for sure. But showing her the blown fuse? Even she couldn't argue against physical evidence.

Finally noticing that they were among sidewalks and storefronts, Tanner moaned, "Yeah, yeah, yeah. So, what's the plan now? We're in town already and we don't have a solid plan."

"Pretty easy plan, dude. We make the deliveries, then collect and count the money. Back to the barn to deliver the cash and collect our product. Back to the house before 7:00."

"All right, according to Maddox's directions, the first delivery is about three miles away. Make a left at the next intersection."

At the next intersection, Hook made a right.

"Are you fucking serious?"

Hook laughed as he pulled into the parking lot of a convenience store, nothing more than a fifty-by-fifty box advertising lottery tickets, alcohol, and cigarettes. "Calm your tits, dude. I gotta hit the head and I know the guy workin' right now."

Hook jumped out of the car and ran inside the store. Tanner mumbled, "This doesn't seem right, does it?"

"Nope." Jordon's perfectly symmetrical face rarely carried the burden of any expression other than the dull look of boredom, but now fresh creases formed along his forehead while he watched the store as if it might get up and run away when he blinked.

"What are you thinking?" Tanner asked.

"I'm thinking he went in for more than a quick piss."

"Me too. Should we go—damn that was fast. Here he comes."

Hook hurried from the store with a paper bag in his hand. Back in the car. Door closed.

Hook distributed the bag's contents, starting with a small pouch of beef jerky to Tanner. "Here. This is to keep your muscles all muscled up." To Jordon, he tossed a small cup of vanilla ice cream with the kindergartener's wooden stick attached to the lid. "That's for being a good boy."

Jordon laughed as he said, "You're such a fucking asshole." It didn't stop him from taking off the lid and digging in.

Tanner huffed as he opened the pouch. "What'd you get?"

"Me? I told you I knew a guy, so he gave me a treat that has a little more iron in it."

Hook opened the bag.

Inside was a gun.

July 14th, 2000. 4:31 PM

Maddox paced the barn floor, steering clear of the bloody scene and the broken glass. He'd been edgy all day, and not irrationally so. This was one hell of a puzzle, and he never liked puzzles. As a child, his grandmother made him sit next to her for hours while she worked on her jigsaw puzzles, trapping him within her miasma of stale cigarettes, coffee breath, muscle cream, and hint of body odor. Hours at a time, especially when she'd watch him during the long days of summer. The newspaper puzzles she spent time on didn't interest him either, a wasted page every day. Once he learned how to read sports spreads and horseracing lines, he was set. Nothing to solve. He never understood the concept of puzzles. Answers were information used to come up with plans, not prizes for wasting time ferreting them out. Paulie's disappearance was an unsolved puzzle.

The theory about Paulie pissing off the wrong people was easy to believe. He had plenty of annoying tendencies. But Maddox had his ear to the ground and developed a decent network over the years. He spent three hours on the phone—three-quarters of it wasted with a piss-poor signal. He had to call everyone back multiple times, but he was able to get enough of an intermittent signal to gather pieces of the puzzle. None of them fit together, and that pissed him off. No one knew anything. No one had seen Paulie, and everyone thought Maddox was the only one Paulie was currently indebted to.

Maddox heard shuffling from outside the barn door. It was Rock, traipsing through the field. Why the hell was he jogging?

"What'd you find?" Maddox asked.

"Across the field is that creepy as fuck house in the forest we drove past to get here. Piles of trash all over the place."

"Did you go in?"

"Fuck no!"

Maddox scowled and put his hands on his hips, a maneuver to pull his jacket back and expose his gun. Rock continued, "Sorry, boss. I'll take a bullet before going in that place. I've done some bad shit, seen worse shit, but nothing like that house. It's all run down and gone to hell, with no sign of life, but something ain't right with it. If the devil had in-laws, he'd put 'em in that house."

Maddox processed his words. Rock was more afraid of that house than a gun. "How close did you get? Look inside?"

Rock shook his head. "Not that close. I swear to you, I smelled cooked meat. It wasn't fresh, but I'm telling you, someone cooked somethin' there recently."

Maddox ran his fingers through his hair and stared out the barn door at the field of grass. Late afternoon flirted with early evening, and with the bad reception in this forsaken armpit of the world, it was probably too late to call more of his employees. "Okay. Tomorrow I'll call a crew and we'll all go knock on the door together."

Rock exhaled slowly. "Okay, but I'd feel better with half a dozen or more. Are we so sure that it wasn't someone Paulie owed money to?"

"I ain't sure of anything." His words were half true. Maddox wasn't sure it was someone associated with Paulie. Who could it be? Who would even know about this place? If it were a simple hit, then there'd be a body. If someone wanted to make an example out of him, then Maddox would have heard about it by now. Nothing added up. Someone had killed Paulie and took him away. Maddox was sure about that.

After those three frat boy morons left, Maddox helped Johnny and Rock clean the mess. After they took inventory of the damage, Maddox made calls while Rock and Johnny looked around outside for a couple hours. The effort reminded him why he hated nature with its remoteness and lack of cell service.

"What now, boss?" Rock asked.

"When Johnny gets back, we'll—"

The loft floor creaked above Maddox's head. He pulled out his gun and pointed at the board directly over him. The barn was old, and it certainly could have been an "old barn" noise, but it seemed pointed. Trying to see between the gaps in the boards, he looked for anything. A figure. A shape. Movement. He needed eyes up there and gestured to Rock to climb the ladder.

Rock moved slowly, ascending the ladder with a gun in his one hand while grasping a rung with his free hand. Left foot up one rung, then right foot. Maddox slid from one support post to another, gun up, eyes wide, heart running in circles like a caged rat. He undid a button on his shirt to release pent-up body heat. Beads of sweat rolled from his brow to his jaw. He wrapped the fingers of his left hand around his right wrist for support. A couple more rungs and Rock would be eye level into the loft, see what caused the creak hopefully without getting his head taken off.

Barn entrance! Something at the main entrance! Maddox aimed at the doorway, finger on the trigger. Johnny. And the fool was oblivious to how close he came to dying. Shaking his head, he sauntered through the doorway and said, "It's gettin' dark in the forest."

Rock brought his gun to his lips like a surrogate index finger. "Shhh," he mouthed, then pointed at the loft.

Johnny stopped mid step. He mouthed, "Fuck. What happened?"

Rock rolled his eyes and gestured to the loft again with his gun.

Maddox debated about shooting them both. It would make this situation a whole lot easier. They had added little value to anything today.

As if something bit his ass, Johnny drew his gun and poked his head out the barn door. He yelled, "There's something out there!"

"What is it?" Maddox asked, coming out from under the loft.

"Don't know. I'm gonna check it out." Johnny ran back outside.

Maddox ran closer to the barn door and Rock jumped off the ladder to join him. They slid to a halt when Johnny's scream came from outside. Maddox had heard many screams before, of grown men crying and begging, gurgling noises of pain bubbling up from the depths of fear. This went beyond all of them, an accumulation of every pain and anguish all at once. He winced when he heard the scream a second time. It was followed by sickening noises Maddox couldn't quite reconcile, and then a thump. Something heavy had dropped to the ground? Maddox and Rock looked to each other, neither brave enough to face what they were hearing from outside the barn. Another heavy thump. Then a wet crunch. The noise repeated, again and again. Each hit sounded like dishes breaking while wrapped in soggy cardboard. Or bones cracking within a dead body.

The noises stopped.

"The fuck?" Rock whispered.

Maddox tightened his grip on the gun, ready to shoot. He didn't know what was going on outside, but it was pissing him off. He needed to get this situation under control.

Johnny entered the barn through the air. He landed with a slap on the ground, his clothes wet and red. There was still a body in those clothes, but it was a pulped mess on the floor. Arms and legs were bent at unnatural angles; bones poked through jagged, bloodied holes. Johnny no longer had a head — ragged strips of ripped flesh hung from his neck.

Rock burped, then puked. Maddox fought with his guts to keep from doing the same thing, but the quivering jelly in his bones set like concrete when a hulk of a man loomed in the doorway. The man's size unnerved Maddox, but what terrified him most was the bear's head worn over his own. Tongue lolling out and over its bared teeth, the bear's head looked like more than a mask. It was a real bear head.

Was this what happened to Paulie? Taken by this freak show? Over seven feet tall, this guy's arms were bigger than most people's legs. His meaty hand was armed with a huge sledgehammer. His filthy overalls clung against his hairy chest. None of that mattered. This bastard killed one of his men, maybe two of his men. Maddox needed to dish out retribution.

"Rock!" Maddox yelled, slapping his employee's back to gather his senses. "Get your shit together, man."

Rock straightened and wiped vomit from his chin. Skin pale and eyes wide, he aimed his gun at the man with the bear's head. "Fuck! Fuck you!"

His aim true, Rock squeezed the trigger a few times. No effect. Seemed to just piss the man off, and he advanced toward them. Rock fired away, as did Maddox. They sure as shit weren't shooting blanks, but their bullets weren't stopping the man. By the time Maddox emptied his gun, Rock was screaming and running toward the bear head wearing freak.

Rock was not a small man, probably the largest in Maddox's employ if he had to guess, but watching Rock punch the hillbilly in overalls was like watching a kindergartener attack an adult. The beast backhanded Rock, knocking him away. Rock slid across the floor, scrabbled to his feet, and charged again. This time, the monster of a man swung his sledgehammer like a bat, and with a solid crack he sent Rock flying into a nearby lab table. Glass and liquids sprayed everywhere. The creature's speed belied his bulk. Rock hit the floor, and the beast was there, swinging his sledgehammer.

Maddox deduced that Johnny had met his demise in that same way, at the end of the sledgehammer. But to see it happen? To hear the noises of a human being getting pulped? Maddox knew how his nightmares were going to go for the next few years.

He needed to kill this man, to stop him from ruining his product. To stop the awful noises of him smashing Rock with a sledgehammer. The thump and splash of each swing. But how? This dude absorbed almost twenty bullets and they were less effective than mosquito bites. Was he wearing a vest under his overalls? Maybe, but he got hit in the shoulders and the exposed parts of his chest as well. Was he so hopped up on something that he couldn't feel pain? Maddox reconciled that this man-beast had inhaled enough of his product to think he was Superman. Why the hell else would he be wearing the head of a bear?

The folding chair! Maddox ran to the chair. He stepped on one leg and pulled the other. It popped easily from the fastener. Another good pull by adrenaline fueled muscles and he ripped the leg off. The metal at the breaking point was jagged, sharp enough to puncture skin with the right amount of force. The way Maddox felt right now, he knew he could deliver that kind of force.

Maddox ran across the barn at the bear-man, the whole way reminding himself not to look at Rock. No matter how bad he imagined Rock looked, he knew deep in his heart the reality was worse, and if he saw it, even for a glimpse, it would be enough to throw off his attack. *Just focus on the target*, he thought. *Just focus on that big fucker.*

The jagged metal punctured an exposed part of the freak's skin, right below the shoulder blade. Maddox drove it in about half a foot deep, hoping it hit his kidney. Momentum slammed him into the bear-man with enough force to knock the guy off his feet. He planned to kick the bear-man's head while he was down, repeatedly, and then use his own hammer against him. Too caught up in the action, Maddox forgot not to look down.

Rock was in worse shape than Johnny. His torso was mash, flattened past the point of having any discernible form. His arms and legs weren't touched. Neither was his head. Eyes wide and staring, mouth open, there was no pain on his face, just surprise, as if he were alive and watched his body turn into a large pool of red gelatin. If he *were* still alive, he could have warned Maddox about the bear-man getting to his feet.

The punch hurt. It was awkward, catching Maddox right under his armpit, but hard enough to lift him off his feet. He twisted to roll when he hit the ground. Fire burned through both shoulders and his chest, and each inhale was a knife stab. But his legs still worked, and it was time to use them. The bear-man might be taller, but he was a lot heavier. Maddox could outrun him.

On his feet, the pain behind his chest eased, replaced by fear. Maddox became instantly religious and thanked the first god that came to mind, the one that his grandmother yapped on and on about those long summer days, because he'd come out of this with just some bruises. No broken bones, no punctured organs. The bear-man walked toward him, the metal chair leg sticking from his back. No matter how high this guy was, he should be bleeding. But he wasn't. Time for Maddox to go. He'd be back with a crew.

He had to run the distance of the barn to get out the back door. His first few steps were painful and slow, but he picked up the pace, easily fast enough to outrun the bear-man. Before he made it to the door, a man in head-to-toe black dropped from the loft and blocked his way.

July 14th, 2000. 4:13 PM

Ptolemy hated the forest. A city offered ways to disappear, to stay invisible. A city allowed ghosts to walk among the living. Not the forest. It was determined to remind Ptolemy of his every move. Footprints if the ground was too soft. Branches and twigs and thorns to snag clothing and flesh. No one would notice a strip of clothing and some blood on the city streets, but a snagged piece of clothing in the forest? There would be enough DNA for authorities to write a memoir about their target.

His tactical outfit was tight and snag proof from head to toe, minimalist for this mission. He had a gun strapped to each thigh, a lighter in one small pocket, a Swiss army knife in another, and specialized goggles from the Empress that not only protected his eyes and reduced the sun's glare, but allowed him night-vision should the need arise. All he had to do was take out a wannabe drug lord. Simple enough. He just wished it wasn't in the fucking woods.

His clients paid well, but there was always a special request that came with an assignment. Make it messy to leave a message. Make it quiet so no one would ever know what happened. Make it look like an accident. Make it look like someone else did it. This one, though... The client—a regular known as "The Philanthrapist"—wanted the mark taken out in a barn.

The directions to the barn were impeccable; Broker always gave him the best information. The barn itself was another story. Dilapidated. Peeling paint. Wall boards separating. No doors on either the front or back entrance. He didn't want to mess around with either entry. Too conspicuous. Scaling the wall—mildew colored and covered in graffiti—to get to a window that led to a loft was more his style.

Ptolemy wanted more time to plan, to get a better understanding of the environment, the situation. With the same bite at the back of the throat that came with drinking a chardonnay when expecting a moscato, he had started to creep across the loft until he heard voices. His mark was already in the barn, standing below the loft. And he wasn't alone.

Ptolemy was a consummate professional and distasted collateral damage. Maddox was the only mark on his list. There was one other man with him, a large bald guy, and they were pissed off about someone named "Paulie."

From his vantage point, Ptolemy saw a line of tables with all kinds of chemicals on them, an assembly line of drugs. One part of the assembly line was smashed up. Maddox and crew were obviously squatting. This was not their barn, not their property by the way the bald guy was talking about the house across the field. Clearly there had been an accident or a fight. Things had gotten sloppy. Maybe that was how Maddox wound up on Ptolemy's assignment sheet.

Ptolemy couldn't get a clean shot at Maddox as he moved under the loft. Option one: jump from the loft and shoot everyone in the room like some psycho. Option two: shift position to see if there was a big enough gap in between a couple planks of wood to get a better shot. Option three: patiently wait for the target to move out from under the loft to get a better shot. Under normal circumstances, he would choose to wait. But these weren't normal circumstances. He still wasn't a psycho—he could accept creating collateral damage as long as he was one hundred percent sure they deserved it. The bald guy could be a blue-collar worker hard on his luck just trying to support a family. Even if he did deserve it, there might be more of Maddox's men around. Too noisy, and they'd come running. And that's not including this "Paulie" who they were looking for. Odds were he either got whacked by last night's intruder or he ran, but until there was one hundred percent confirmation of either, he was an unknown variable.

The only option that remained was to find a gap in the floor boards large enough to plug Maddox and slip out of the barn before anyone knew what happened. There was the risk of Maddox having other men, but if Ptolemy were fast enough, that wouldn't matter. But as soon as Ptolemy shifted his weight to reposition himself, the plank under his foot creaked.

Fuck!

Ptolemy held his breath.

Maddox looked up in his direction.

Fucking old barns!

Ptolemy hated to be inelegant, hated finishing a job by shooting up the place, but Maddox had ordered the bald guy up the ladder.

Knees bent, core tight, Ptolemy repositioned his aim toward the top of the ladder. As soon as the bald man's cranium appeared, Ptolemy would shoot and jump over the loft railing. Maddox would undoubtedly shoot from below, but he'd be aiming where Ptolemy was, not where he'd be going. The bald man took another step up the ladder.

Shoot and jump. Shoot and jump. Ptolemy readied himself for anything. Or so he thought. A thin guy ran into the barn. *Great, now I have to be a random psycho and kill everyone.* But the thin guy started squawking about something outside and then left to investigate. Luckily, Maddox and the bald guy decided that whatever was happening outside took precedent.

Perfect! Pop Maddox while he was distracted and head out the way he came in.

Until he heard the scream. The second scream was just as horrific and terrifying.

The body of the unfortunate lackey flew into the barn as if the day got tired of chewing on him and spat him out. And then the outside came in.

A bear. A bear did this, mauled the guy, and tossed him back inside the barn. No. Not a bear. Bears didn't wear overalls. A man. A beast of a man over seven feet tall wearing the head of a bear over his own.

Ptolemy knew what it took to set up situations to make something impossible happen. A brand-new car on a dry road skidding at the right moment to strike and kill a man. A windowpane falling ten stories to hit a person on the sidewalk below while harming no one else. The safety features of a home furnace failing in a single house in a suburban neighborhood, taking the life of only one person. Ptolemy worked in the world of impossible, and he knew there was truly no such thing. But the way that giant in overalls wielded his sledgehammer made Ptolemy doubt everything he knew about physics. The bear-headed man swung it with the ease of using a movie prop made of foam on a stick. Then Ptolemy witnessed something even more impossible.

The bald guy shot the man wearing the bear's head. Bullets struck the center of his chest. More bullets followed. All to no avail. The giant finally attacked; the sledgehammer proved devastating.

Maddox fought back, and on a certain level Ptolemy respected that. His actions were as useless as the bald man's, now pulped into pink globs. It turned his stomach, but all Ptolemy had to do was stay quiet and let this bear head wearing psycho take care of his hit for him.

The rational part of Ptolemy's brain suggested that the man must have been wearing some form of body armor under his overalls. He desperately wanted to believe that because it was the only sensible explanation. But the psycho's overalls left plenty of exposed skin, and Maddox had just plunged a broken chair leg into the monster's back.

Ptolemy wanted nothing more than to run away, as his mark was attempting to do. But he had a job to finish, and an opportunity to do so without using a single bullet. He leapt from the loft and landed in front of his target.

July 14th, 2000. 7:49 PM

Cali felt bad. Not just because the room was spinning, but because of her thoughts regarding Tanner. Why did she want to break up with him again? On paper, he was amazing. Tall. Handsome. Great bod. Even though he had no major career aspirations at the moment, she knew he'd be successful at whatever finally became his focus. And he had plenty of money to keep them both comfortable until he figured it out. *Why did I think that?* she asked herself. *I have money, so why do I feel like I should wait around for him to decide what he wants from life?*

Okay, so her money was her father's money, but she had nearly unlimited access. No—that was another bad thought. She wanted to make *her own* money. To pave her own way. She was tired of needing her father to support her, and she hated the idea of jumping right into the wallet of her boyfriend. Did that give her the right to be so mean to Tanner?

In retrospect, she felt like a bitch for snapping at him during the drive to this house. She should have told him she loved him before he went out for weed—the very stuff contributing to the fuzziness in her spinning head. She could have been nicer before he went out to get a fuse for the fuse box. Guilt added yet another brick to her burden after finding nothing more than clothes and condoms when she had snooped through his stuff.

But you know what? He's a dick, the tequila said as it took the room for another spin. *You're right,* she replied. He was lazy. Not just with his life, but in this relationship. There was no evidence of respect or admiration. There was no discussion about going out with Hook and Jordon; he just went. *Oh, tequila, how can you be so right, yet sometimes soooo wrong.*

After the guys had left, the girls threw a mini party. A form of feminist protest showing they didn't need the men to have fun. Strong margaritas flowed like waterfalls while a pot cloud hovered at the ceiling. Dakota passed out on the couch. Linda and Cali poured another glass and shared some giggles, over what, Cali couldn't remember. Linda excused herself to use the bathroom, and Cali felt a sudden urge to lay down. She trudged up the stairs to her designated bedroom and slid into the comfy, comfy bed. Right in the center, on her back with her arms outstretched was the perfect place to argue with tequila about breaking up with Tanner. She was no closer to one decision or another. Dakota had made passing out seem like such an attractive alternative, and the thought of doing so crossed Cali's mind. Until Linda appeared in the doorway.

Linda shuffled to the bed and crawled in with Cali. Head on her shoulder, Linda draped her arm across Cali, just under her breasts. Cali tensed. More confusing emotions joined the alcohol swirling inside her. It had been four years since she had been with a woman, the obligatory college freshman experiment. At the time, she wasn't sure if she liked it or not. She certainly liked Linda, but wanted to be her, not necessarily be with her. Maybe this time would be different? Maybe she had been too drunk to appreciate it during college? *Of course*, she just remembered, *I'm pretty drunk right now.* What about Tanner? Sure, thoughts about breaking up with him had been dancing through her head these past few weeks, but to cheat on him during their vacation together? That would be hardcore-level bitch.

"I'm not gay," Linda mumbled. "My tummy doesn't feel good, and I need to cuddle. You're my ersatz teddy bear."

Cali relaxed and brought her arm in to embrace her newest friend. She smiled as they shifted to get more comfortable. Linda smelled like vanilla. "You're so drunk you think I'm a stuffed animal?"

"Yep. Well, your tits at least. Which look amazing, by the way."

Cali laughed. "They're fairly new. Don't puke on them or you'll void the warranty."

Linda chuckled, then sighed. "I so wanna be you when I grow up."

"Me?" She was surprised. Linda had been a new standard Cali wanted to achieve. How could such a strong, confident woman wish to be someone who viewed herself as a rich, boring brat? "Why would you want to be me?"

"You know where you're going. You know what career you want; you have a great boyfriend. You're smart *and* pretty. And tits. And you got a rock hard, slamming bod. I changed my mind. I'm going gay for you."

Cali tensed again.

Linda shifted and said, "Kidding, you homophobe."

Cali remained tense. "Ha, ha. I'm not phobic, just trying to work some stuff out. I'm not as together as you make me out to be. I know how my future is starting, but I'm… I'm not sure if Tanner is in it."

"Whoa." Linda released Cali and moved up the bed to sit, her back against the headboard. After Cali did the same, Linda grabbed her hand. "That sounds pretty serious."

Cali squeezed Linda's hand. This woman's support and undivided attention made Cali feel like the only person in the world. "Yeah. I guess?"

"You implied that you're thinking about breaking up with your boyfriend of what…three years?"

"Yeah."

"That's serious, sweety. What's going on?"

Cali shrugged. "I don't know. I'm probably being a spoiled rich girl complaining about spoiled rich girl issues."

Linda gave Cali's hand another squeeze. "A bank account balance isn't inversely proportionate to emotional justification. What you feel is what you feel."

"Wow. I think I'm more in love with you than I am with Tanner."

"Yeah, I get that a lot. It's what I do. I pretend I'm not gay around straight women to lure them into my web of gayness. I'm a lesbian sex spider."

Cali laughed. "See? I think that's what I'm missing with Tanner. You gave me validation, whether I needed it or not, or deserved it or not."

"I was just being nice to you. Is Tanner not nice?"

"Yeah… no… I mean, he never treated me meanly, and he does have moments of niceness, when we're alone."

"When he lets his guard down?"

Cali sighed. "It started like that, but lately it's an expected comfort. A permission to fart in front of each other, a lack of manners, an opportunity for him to point to his dick any time I say I need to talk."

Linda chuckled, a pitiful one of solidarity through experience. "Yeah, that's also Hook's way of letting his guard down."

Cali bit her bottom lip, so the question she shouldn't ask wouldn't come out. Tequila said, *If you never ask, you'll never know.* "So…?"

"Why is such an awesome girl like me with Hook?"

"Umm… yeah?"

"Kinda the same reasons, but different. The whole sensitive bad boy thing. Except, lately, he's been less sensitive."

"I'm sorry. Has he… ever…?"

"Hit me? Oh, God no. I'd tear his balls off and wear them as earrings. He's just been less attentive, more focused on drugs."

Cali snorted. "*More* focused?"

"Yeah, I know, right? But I think he might be getting into serious shit. Moving past party stuff and into much harder stuff. I'm worried about him. I'm worried that he and Tanner and Jordon are sneaking around doing drug stuff right now. You know, more than just getting pot."

It was Cali's turn to squeeze Linda's hand. "Tanner hasn't mentioned anything to me about Hook doing anything more stupid than usual. Not like he's an open book either, but I haven't noticed any changes."

Would I have noticed, though? Cali wondered. *I've been caught up in my own head, my thoughts and dreams and future. Maybe I haven't been paying enough attention?*

Linda rested her head on Cali's shoulder. "Thanks. My tummy feels better, and I could use some snacks. Maybe another drink to take the edge off."

"I like this idea." The room had stopped spinning. Thankfully, it didn't restart when she got off the bed. Walking down the stairs proved to be no challenge. This was a good plan.

The throaty snores of Dakota greeted Cali and Linda as they walked over to the couch. No vomit anywhere, so that was good. Her feet were propped on the couch's arm while her arms lay soldier straight by her sides. One side of her hair stood inches above her head, and a boob had escaped her bikini top.

Linda brought her hands to her heart. "Daaaw. She looks so peaceful when she sleeps."

Cali mimicked the action. "She does. She really does. I wanna draw a dick-n-balls on her cheek."

Linda covered her mouth to stifle a laugh. "No."

"I do. I really, really do. Dick-n-balls. Right on her cheek. I bet the guys wouldn't tell her and she'd go the rest of the week never knowing until she looked in a mirror. She'll ask where the dick-n-balls came from and I'll say I don't know how the dick-n-balls got on your face. You better not tell her, or I'll cut you."

Linda took Cali's hand and pulled her from the living room into the kitchen. "You're not drawing on your sleeping friend, you're not going to cut me, and for the love of all things holy, please stop saying dick-n-balls."

Cali pouted. "Dick-n-balls."

"I'm going to ignore that. Now, we have a big bag of chips to munch on until the guys get back. What should we wash it down with?"

"How long have the guys been gone? An hour? Hour and a half?"

"Try five hours."

Tanner's been gone for five hours, probably doing drug stuff, the tequila said. *Drink me.*

Oh, tequila, you're soooo right sometimes....

July 14th, 2000. 4:43 PM

Ptolemy dropped from the barn's loft and landed in front of Maddox.

"The fuck?" Maddox yelled as he skidded to a stop. He swung, but Ptolemy dodged with ease and grabbed Maddox's arm. One twist was all it took to face Maddox toward the lumbering bear-headed man and one push was all it took to end his assignment. Of all the ways he thought about killing Maddox, what he witnessed wasn't one of them.

Palm covering Maddox's entire face, the bear-headed man squeezed. Maddox punched and kicked, pushed against him while trying to escape his grasp. The only time the monster let go was to position both hands around Maddox's neck. With the meaty snap of pulling a large drumstick from a plump turkey, the creature yanked Maddox's head off his body. A crimson wave splashed the bear's face.

Job done. Time to extricate. This was not the moment for Ptolemy to process what he had just witnessed, so he jumped and grabbed the loft's ledge. The beast dropped Maddox's headless body, picked up his sledgehammer and threw it. A thunderous crack of splitting wood; the hammer destroyed the support post under Ptolemy. The old wood gave way, dropping out from under him with the cacophony of trees falling in a forest. The landing hurt his knees, and he narrowly avoided the jagged edges and exposed nails. He turned to sprint out the back door. And stopped.

About a third of the loft had collapsed, blocking his escape. Ptolemy contemplated his options. Running through his adversary didn't seem likely. He had two handguns holstered to his thighs, but after watching two other men waste a couple dozen bullets on this monster, Ptolemy doubted his guns would make any difference. To his right were the stalls. There were a couple of propane tanks in each stall, but nothing of immediate use. Tables ran the length of the barn in front of an open area under what remained of the loft. That was the best potential for escape.

Ptolemy extended his arms, palms out in front of him, showing he meant no harm. "I don't know who you are or why you don't like these guys, but I'm not with them. That's obvious, right?"

No answer. The man wearing the bear head just stood there, panting, fists clenched. Ptolemy took a measured step forward. All he needed to do was clear the debris and slip into the open area under the loft. From there he could sprint to the front of the barn and out the door. He continued, "I mean, that guy was trying to run, and I stopped him, right? You didn't like him, and I didn't like him either. So, I stopped him for you. I'm going to leave now, and you can do whatever you need to do."

A few more tentative steps. The man didn't move, didn't react. Ptolemy was close enough to hear him breathe. Close enough to see that the fur of the bear's head was real, matted by Maddox's blood. The sockets were hollow, no eyes. Ptolemy couldn't help but think of Nietzsche's line, "If you stare into the abyss, the abyss stares back at you." One must be a monster to find monsters. To fight monsters. Whoever this man was, he was no longer human. He was a monster. One primed to kill.

As Ptolemy took another sideways step toward the open area, the bear-headed man lunged. Fast, but clumsy. Ptolemy ducked under the massive hands reaching for him. Judging by the way he had thrown the sledgehammer, he was right-handed. Ptolemy grabbed the bear-headed man's right wrist and extended his arm straight up, exposing the armpit. Middle knuckle out, Ptolemy punched furiously, hoping this creature's nerves were capable of being rendered numb. The creature swung his left fist across his body and connected with Ptolemy's shoulder.

The tight angle caused the hit to be more of a push, but it was enough to send Ptolemy tumbling into the open area under the loft. As fast as Ptolemy got to his feet, the bear-headed man blocked his egress. But his right arm was moving slower. Ptolemy wasn't sure if this creature felt pain, but his punch had done *some*thing.

Knees. Ptolemy went low and delivered a lightning-fast kick to the man's knees. The man dropped to the ground and Ptolemy delivered kicks to the chest and punches to the bear's face. He knew the bear's head was real, but didn't know the dimensions of the man's face underneath, so he kept his punches low, connecting with his neck and jaw. Ptolemy didn't need to kill the man—and that seemed impossible considering what he had available—he needed to confound him enough to run. All he needed was to see the bear-headed man wobble.

It still wasn't enough.

When Ptolemy turned to run, the man lunged with enough reach to grab Ptolemy's ankle, and the strength to throw him toward the fallen portion of the loft.

Luck guided Ptolemy through the air. The bear-headed man hadn't mustered enough force to cause any harm from the throw, and Ptolemy used the shoulder he landed on as the pivot point, jumping to his feet, thankful that he had avoided jagged debris. He couldn't let that creature get ahold of him again.

Ptolemy's instinct took over, logic and strategy no longer useful. Ptolemy grabbed a nail tipped wood plank and swung it like a bat. Nails tore through the beast's shoulder, gobs of skin flying away to reveal oily meat underneath. He swung again, striking the monster's arm as he brought it up to protect himself. The board cracked in half and the creature lunged at Ptolemy again. Missed!

Ptolemy rolled under one of the tables, jumped to his feet, and shoved the table and all its contents at the creature. None of the chemicals did anything other than get the man wet. He swatted the table away with ease. Ptolemy needed enough time to position himself in the stable behind him.

The monster charged and Ptolemy jumped to grab the crossbeam, then kicked as hard as he could. Feet squarely against chest, he sent the man crashing into the debris of the loft's collapsed section. Ptolemy accepted that he couldn't keep his opponent down, and scaled the wall between this stable and the next. He squeezed through the gap between the wall and the ceiling when the man came charging. Soon as Ptolemy hit the ground, the wall crashed down. Jump! He made it out of the stable to the barn's center before getting crushed, but the bear-headed man was on him in no time.

Barreling into him, the monster wrapped his arms around Ptolemy. Chest to chest, he lifted Ptolemy off his feet and squeezed. Ptolemy cried out. Both arms free, he pressed against the bear-headed man's neck and pushed, which resulted in getting squeezed harder. Fighting was useless, mere flesh and bone against an unstoppable engine of death. This was an enemy he couldn't defeat. No longer able to inhale, Ptolemy fumbled for his guns. They were his last resort.

Ptolemy pressed both barrels against the monster's neck and unloaded two full clips. The bullets tore through with ease, spattering flesh and tissue in loud bursts of black ichor. The heat and gases seared the skin on the man's neck, a smell of cooking rot Ptolemy wouldn't soon forget. How the hell the creature's head was still attached didn't matter. Ptolemy was free.

As he scrambled to the barn door, Ptolemy procured his lighter. He knew little about the drug making process, but was confident the chemicals were flammable. The creature absorbed bullets and kept moving—he was an abomination. And he needed to burn. Ptolemy took a few seconds to ignite a small pool of liquid on the ground. He didn't need to say anything pithy nor stick around to watch the barn burn. He ran from the place happy to never see it again.

July 14th, 2000. 4:54 PM

Pain. Zebadiah lay in his barn, writhing in pain. He had no idea how many times he had been shot. The men who had invaded his barn shot him. He didn't feel much until the man in black. Two guns, over and over and over again in the same spots. It hurt so badly that he wanted to close his eyes, take a nap. His lids fluttered shut, but he forced them not to close. He saw color. Flickering oranges and yellows. Fire!

Zebadiah struggled to his feet. His head didn't move right. It didn't move the way he wanted it to move. He saw where he wanted to go, but his world was at an angle. He frantically ran his fingers over his face, the bear's face. Everything seemed right with that. Lower. His neck. Half of it wasn't there! Flaps and strips and gouges and bones. And blood. Over his hands, his blood flowed from his neck. A new kind of blood, though, black and oily.

Zebadiah stumbled, disoriented by how his head was hanging and confused at how he could put his finger through his throat. The fire was small. He'd stomp it out if he could get to it in time, but he had to move. One foot in front of the other became harder. Were his feet getting heavier? His legs felt like they were made of mud, but he had to keep moving before the fire got any bigger. He raised his foot to stomp it out, but collapsed and fell into the flame.

He rolled around, arms flailing as he combated the fire, his black blood flying around in stringy globs. It hurt, but losing the barn would hurt more. Hands slicked with his own blood, he slapped at the flames. It worked! His wet hands, his blood, had extinguished the fire, and he was still alive. Barely. He had almost forgotten what pain felt like, but he was full of it now. And he was hungry.

His head flopped to the side since he was unable to muster the strength to hold it upright any longer. Meat! In the fury of fighting the man in black and stopping the fire, he lost track of where he was. Blessed be, as Papa might say, he found himself next to the skinny man he stopped outside. He had pulped that man and then threw him into the barn, hoping to shoo away the other two. That didn't work, and there was the man in black who had been hiding in the loft. Despite all that, Zebadiah had successfully defended his barn, and now he was hungry.

Moving felt like razors scraped his insides, his arms hard to command, his head bobbling about as he dragged himself to the meat. One last pull and he collapsed again, his face splashing in a pool of blood. Red blood. Unsure if he could feel or smell or taste, he closed his eyes and sensed life. A bone had poked through the skinny man's skin and on it was a chunk of meat. Zebadiah pulled the meat off the bone, slid it into the bear's mouth, his mouth, and chewed. But he couldn't swallow.

Fingers wriggling like discontented worms through the pulped flesh of the skinny man, Zebadiah sought out smaller chunks. Squishing through his fingers, he scooped up the pulverized meat and brought it to his neck. He didn't know if this would work, but he figured why not try. He had no other choice.

He slid the slop past his neck's shredded skin flaps, and pushed the chunks into his throat. But his arm could only go so far. More. More meat. With both hands, he grabbed whatever bits of meat he could find and shoveled them in. Not enough. Mashing the intruder created only a few globs here and there. He tried to tear apart the skin, but it was too tough, and the blood made it slippery. A murky thought of looking around the barn for a knife passed through his mind, becoming murkier by the second. Maybe one of the other intruders had one? Didn't matter. He was still too weak to move that far.

He shoved his right hand in his throat again, this time using his left to push it farther. The effort helped, but only minimally, his knuckles rubbing against his chest bones. He needed something else to push the meat the rest of the way into his stomach. Stomach. He looked at the pulped intruder's stomach area. There was enough of a rip in the intruder's belly for Zebadiah to get his hand through and pull out the guts that look like sausage.

This was slippery work, but he was able to pull out more than an arm's length and work it into his neck-hole. Parts of the tube squished between his fingers, but he kept pushing, shoving the slimy mess into his neck. It was working. The mass of meat fell into his stomach. He felt it.

His body tingled. The bullet holes itched. So did the gaping wound in his neck, but it was more intense. The hole was getting smaller and his strength was coming back. He crammed more belly sausage down his throat until he felt strong enough to tear through the rubbery rope with his teeth.

The hunger hadn't stopped. He craved more meat. Much of his body still itched and ached, but he did his best to ignore it as he stood. With his head back where it should be, though he was still a bit wobbly, he looked around his barn. Anger burned within him as he viewed the damage, as did the urge to protect, to kill. To be the bear. To use Papa's hammer.

Zebadiah had a hell of a chore ahead of him to fix up his barn. There were more pressing matters, though. He had three slabs of meat to take back to the house. Two were mashed up, but he could get more meat from the broken bones. The third slab was in great shape, just missing its head. He grabbed that one first, hoisting it over his shoulder.

There was the man in black to think about. Would he come back? Were there others looking for these men or the tables full of colorful liquids and white powder? No one came to his house yet, but that don't mean no one would. He needed to be ready in case there were more unwanted visitors. Papa had taught him all kinds of traps. He liked traps.

He found Bertha and trudged toward his house. He'd need one more trip for the other two slabs. A stray thought hit him hard enough to make him pause. He hadn't taken a breath for a long while, not while he was fighting, not while he was feasting. Zebadiah no longer needed to breathe.

July 14th, 2000. 9:02 PM

Tanner checked his phone again. No new texts. He wasn't sure if that was a good thing or a bad thing. He had assumed Cali would be blowing up his phone with voice mails and texts bugging him to tell her where he was. Instead, he only received one stating, **you forgot the cachaca** and that was hours ago. Was she giving him the silent treatment? Was she *that* angry with him? He flipped his phone closed and slid it into his pocket.

The barn was coming into view and the dirt road was getting rougher. If Cali weren't "silent treatment" pissed at Tanner yet, she would be if she found out he let Hook drive her car through the backwoods.

The drug deals were successful, went off without a hitch. Hook didn't need to flash his gun even though he desperately wanted to. Now all they had to do was give Maddox his money, grab the six kilos of product, and get back to the lake house to make amends with the girls. Before shit got too serious, Tanner turned to Jordon in the backseat and asked, "Any word from Dakota?"

"No. Nothing," he replied, bracing himself to keep from slamming his head against the ceiling.

"Pussies," Hook laughed as he pulled up to the muddied parking area in front of the barn, next to the black Range Rover. "I haven't checked my fucking phone all night."

"Yeah, yeah, yeah. You wear the pants. We get it," Jordon mumbled.

Tanner considered defending himself against Hook, but fuck it—he'd rather hand over the cash they got for delivering the drugs to Maddox's street level dealers and be done for the night. He wasn't looking forward to whatever argument there was going to be with Cali, but it was much more appealing than going back into this creepy ass barn, now dark and deserted. But... it should be neither dark nor deserted.

107

"Wait. Something's wrong," Tanner said as Hook turned off the car, extinguishing the only source of light.

Hook tilted his head back and dropped his shoulders, a kindergarten-er readying himself to battle against broccoli. "Oh, for fuck sake. Are you gonna whine about this again?"

"I'm serious, Hook! Why are there no lights? Where are they? Are they even in there?"

"It's an old barn in the middle of nowhere."

"Yeah, but there are a few hoods of florescent lights. I saw them last time we were here."

"Maybe they don't want to turn them on to draw attention? Maybe Maddox is a fucking hippie tree-hugger and wants to save the environment through energy conservation? Who the fuck knows?"

Tanner looked through the windshield and squinted. Hook was half right—there could be several reasons why the lights weren't on. No need for him to panic. Yet. "Turn on the headlights. If they're in there, we give them the money, get what we bought, and get the hell out of here."

Hook sighed, then turned the key. "There. Headlights on. Happy?"

"No. I still can't see what's going on in there. Something's blocking the back doorway."

"Probably the door, genius."

"This barn doesn't have doors, *genius*. We need to turn around."

"I agree with Tanner," Jordon said.

"Of course, you agree with your gym buddy, male model looking, rich twin. Hey, I'm the one who has to work for a living and I'm the one who deals with these people on a daily basis, but does anyone ask what I think? Course not. Guess what? We're not going anywhere until we give Maddox his money." Hook got out of the car.

Tanner grabbed the flashlight from the glove compartment and slammed his door. "Don't start that shit, Hook! This has been your game the whole trip, so don't fucking whine how Jordon and I aren't letting you play."

"Can you be any fucking louder?" Hook whispered, the anger in his voice obvious, as he led the way to the entrance. "Of course, it's been my game, because you, Jordon, and Maxwell have no clue how to play it. You don't even know what game you're trying to play."

"Guys?" Jordon said as he came to a complete halt before the barn's threshold. "What the fuck?"

The barn looked like a war zone. The car's headlights exposed part of the interior while Tanner shined his flashlight farther inside. A patch of dried liquid a few feet inside the entrance, part of a smear of black, like used motor oil, but a large portion was reddish-brown. "This still part of your game, Hook?"

"Fuck you, Tanner," Hook whispered as he pulled his gun from his pocket. He held it with one hand, keeping it by his side and pointing it downward. A precaution as he stepped into the barn.

"What are you doing?" Tanner whispered. "We have no idea what happened here."

"Yeah, no shit. That's why we're going in to investigate."

"Not a good idea."

"Then what is? Calling the cops? Or leaving with a drug lord's cash? This is a drug lab, and these things blow up all the time. If that happened, then Maddox or his guys could be hurt." Hook peered into the barn. Quieter than before, he whispered, "If Maddox is hurt, do you know how big a favor he'd owe us if we rescued him?"

This didn't look like a lab explosion, especially since the fire-hazard of a barn was still standing, but that didn't stop Hook from going in farther. Also didn't stop Tanner from following. Jordon tagged along as well, pulling the top of his shirt up to cover his nose and mouth. "Jesus, it stinks."

Tanner shined his flashlight anywhere the headlights couldn't reach. Under the loft. In each stable. Around the tables. The massive patch of blood among the broken glass in between two tables.

"Hello!" Hook called out.

Tanner jumped as if he stepped on nails with bare feet. "What the fuck, Hook? What happened to stealth?"

"That was before we knew what happened."

"Dude, we have no fucking clue what happened here."

Hook pulled out his phone and flipped it open. As he punched numbers, he continued, "Uh, yeah, we do. It's fucking obvious—there was an accident of some kind. That part of the loft gave out, and it fucked someone up right around here. Looks like he got cut up real bad. Whoever else was with him got him out of the barn. Last time we were here, I heard them talking about a house across the field. Might have gone there."

"Are. You. Fucking. Serious? That makes no God damn sense. There's more blood here. More at the door. And some over there."

"Coincidence?" Jordon asked.

"Possibly," said Hook. "It was a big accident with a lot of fucking glass." Hook closed his phone and mumbled, "No fucking signal."

"What about the tables. Why the hell are some bent to shit?" Tanner pointed his flashlight from table to table for verification. "Look, a few are over there."

"Jesus Christ, Nancy Drew! I don't know the details! Half a fucking loft fell on them! Criminals or not, there's gonna be some level of panic. Shit got thrown around."

"If that's true, if they needed to help someone who's all cut up, why drag him through a field to a house instead of taking the SUV?"

"Do you know where the hospital is around here? Because I sure don't, and they probably didn't either. And before you go on about 911, you just heard me bitch about no signal as I tried to call Johnny. If someone lives in that house, then maybe they have a landline. We should head up there to see if Maddox is around."

"Oh, God," Jordon moaned. He paced in small circles. "Oh, God. Oh, God."

"Soooooooo not a good idea, Hook," Tanner said. "How do we know this wasn't some rival who fucked up all this?"

"Because Maddox is the big dog. Rumor has it that he went hardcore and hired an assassin to knock off a couple of his rivals. He fucks rivals, rivals don't fuck him."

"When we saw him last, he was talking about one of his men, a guy named Paulie—"

"I don't know Paulie, and I don't give a fuck about him. What I *do* give a fuck about is the giant stack of Maddox's cash we have in the car. Now let's take a little hike across the field of grass and check out the creepy-ass house on the other side."

"No," Tanner said.

A cold front passed over Hook's face, freezing away emotion, even the usual spark behind his eyes. He pointed his gun at Tanner.

"What the *fuck*, Hook?" Jordon yelled, both hands on his head. The game of madness had just taken an unexpected turn.

What-the-fuck was right on the money. Tanner had used guns before, nothing more than expensive toys he played with at the local shooting ranges and gun clubs. He never had one pointed at him—until now. He'd known Hook a long time and hoped this was just desperation-induced posturing. But as Tanner raised his tremoring hands over his head, Hook's face looked all too serious. "Dude," Tanner whispered, fear preventing him from talking any louder. "That is unnecessary."

The car's headlights created ominous shadows, deep and black throughout the barn. The darkness circled Hook and embraced him in a menacing hug. His eyes were nothing more than abysmal holes in his skull. After a few heart-crushing seconds, Hook lowered the gun. "You fucking think so? You gonna say the same thing to Maddox or one of his goons when they hold a gun to your face for running off with their money? I got no way of contacting Maddox and I can't get ahold of Johnny. If we leave, then all *they* know is we took their money, and they *will* get it back. So, we gonna stand around and give reasons for a drug lord to kill us, or are we gonna put on our big girl panties and search the creepy fucking house at the other side of this field?"

Tanner looked over to Jordon who was still wide-eyed and shaking. "Hope you wore your slutty ones, 'cause I think we're about to get fucked."

July 14th, 2000. 9:17 PM

Against Tanner's better judgment, they followed the bloodied trail from the barn into the field. The grasses and weeds reached beyond his shoulders, almost to his head in some spots, but there was a definitive path. Wider than one person, but not quite wide enough for two. Every few steps the flashlight revealed hints of a blood streak, or a small splash of black ink.

Tanner's phone still had no signal.

Hook growled. "If you check your phone one more fucking time, I'm gonna shove it so far up your ass you're gonna need to tap your teeth to dial."

"Settle down," Tanner said. "I was just checking to see if we have a signal in case things went sideways. We don't."

"Bullshit. You were being a pussy and checking to see if Cali texted or called. Every time you check, you shake the damn flashlight. You're gonna make me fall and break my damn neck."

This side trip was a shit-show. Running late because it was difficult to find a fuse was one thing but running late because he was looking for a drug lord was another. The best excuse he had for Cali was a flat tire. Yeah, they got a flat tire, and they were too close to the edge of the road, by a ravine, and the tire rolled away and down the hill. *Okay,* Tanner thought, *that idea is the floor.* But he'd consider any other idea besides this lame one.

"Jesus, look at this place," Jordon whispered. They'd finally made their way out of the field and faced a simple two-story farmhouse.

The moon was bright, so Tanner turned off the flashlight. The color of the wood siding could only be described as "fester." It was as ramshackle as the barn and he doubted anyone lived here. The only thing keeping the walls from crumbling was the graffiti, ranging from obscene words to pornographic drawings. "Satan lives here," caught his eye, the moon light making the words look like they'd been painted in blood.

Tanner and Jordon followed Hook around the back of the house. "Holy fuck, look at this. These trash piles must be like, eight, ten feet high? It's all junk. Old junk."

Tanner felt like a visitor on an alien world. Old barns, run down houses, and mountains of trash didn't make up the landscape of his life. He didn't belong here, wasn't welcome here. He couldn't help but focus on the sharp objects protruding from the piles like palisades, overt warnings to keep away. "Where the fuck are we?"

"America, asshole," Hook moaned.

"This is pretty insane."

"Maybe to you rich bitches, but this is how the rest of us live. Abandoned property like this becomes the party house and dumping grounds for the locals. Nothing to be afraid of."

"How about this?" Tanner asked, pointing to a metal barrel with fencing on top. Lying on the ground next to it was an ax, the blade stained brown.

Hook sneered. "So? It's a burn barrel."

"It's a makeshift grill that's been recently used. You smell that? Burned wood and cooked meat."

Hook rolled his eyes. "Here we go again. Missy is getting scared by the creepy house and wants to go home and lose herself in a pint of ice cream."

Tanner clicked on the flashlight. The beam illuminated a pile of bones. Jordon clenched his fists and jumped backward. "Fuck! Are they fresh? Are those are maggots wiggling on them?"

"Christ, Jordon," Hook said. "Just because Tanner put a skirt on doesn't mean you have to."

"Are those human? I mean, they look like human bones, right?" Tanner asked.

That look of coldness swept over Hook's face again, the darkness giving him shark's eyes. "I really fucking doubt that. Now let's check in the house."

"Hook, you can't—"

"I can and I am. Don't make me point the gun at you again. Maddox could be bleeding out in there, we don't know. We'll do a quick search. If no one's there, we'll aim for the road."

"What good is—?" Jordon started, but Tanner grabbed his arm. Tanner shook his head trying to convey that it might be best to keep mouths shut and eyes open. There was something not right with this property, and the faster Hook poked his nose inside, the faster they could leave.

Jordon yanked his arm from Tanner's grip. If he received the message, then he didn't appreciate it. He stormed away and caught up with Hook as he walked toward the front of the house, between the outside wall and row of trash piles. Tanner made a sweeping pass with the flashlight over the ground, the trash piles, the outhouse, the burn barrel. About twenty feet from the house was a collection of leaves piled on either side of a small clearing. Possibly a door to a cellar? Or shelter? Or natural refrigerator? Or Satan's torture dungeon? Tanner had no desire to find out.

They turned the corner to the front of the house, past a car with no wheels slowly being claimed by rust. Tanner jogged to catch up, half afraid that Hook was going to use his gun. Jordon didn't know Hook as well as Tanner did, so whatever kept him from pulling the trigger before might not be there now.

Hook stepped toward the patio, a ground-level row of half-rotted boards mostly covered with leaves and dirt. No front door. Broken windows on either side, and three darkened windows on the second floor. A lone vine clung to the front of the house, snaking its way up the window above the door. Tanner and Jordon lingered back.

"What the fuck is wrong with you two?" Hook asked. "The only things in this house are ghost stories, empty booze containers, and possibly a raccoon or homeless person. And that scares you? You should be scared of a drug lord who knows how to find us to collect his cash."

"Exactly," Jordon said. "All he wants is his cash. We give it to him."

"If he has to hunt us down for his cash," Hook said with a sigh, "then he's gonna want something in return. Something extra."

"Then we give him a few hundred bucks. Another thousand or two. Whatever, I don't care about the money. When we return to the girls, there's a good chance they're going to leave us."

"God damn it, Jordon, if you're too scared to go into the house—"

"We'll go in, we'll look around really quick, but if Maddox isn't there, then we leave. No searching the second floor, no looking around the woods, no following any roads or paths. We go back to the girls and you keep trying to get ahold of Johnny."

Hook ran a hand through his hair, as if scrubbing away the potential consequences of this predicament. He then gestured to the house. "Fine. Jordon, lead the way."

Tanner shined the flashlight on the front door opening. Jordon took one step on the patio—the board broke. The moment it snapped, the vine went taught, and something fell from the second-floor window.

It happened fast, and took Tanner a few breaths to realize that Jordon wasn't standing anymore. Unnatural moans and gurgles added to the sick feelings within Tanner as his friend spastically twitched.

Tanner and Hook rushed to Jordon. A large metal plate had fallen from the window and landed directly on Jordon. Tanner lifted the plate, taking care to avoid the jagged metal strips protruding from it. Removing the strips of metal imbedded in Jordon rewarded Tanner with a gush of blood painting him in red.

Tanner couldn't blink, couldn't breathe. Jordon's blood was in his hair, on his face, in his mouth. Jordon lay twisted and sliced, pierced so deep that blood ran freely from ravines in his flesh. Neck at a terrible angle; his head flatter. His left eyeball draped over his nose. Helplessness tore through Tanner, something he had never felt before. He didn't know what to do as blood continued to flow along the valleys of torn skin and muscle.

"What the fuck?" Hook shrieked, his voice a fever pitch of panic.

Tanner looked at the gory metal plate for answers. If not for the snap of a twig behind him, Tanner would have stared forever.

"What the fuck?" Hook screamed, aiming his gun not at the window or the doorway, but behind them.

A bear.

The bear walked like a man on its hind legs as it exited the forest, which didn't seem right. And... "The fuck?" Tanner whispered. "Is that a sledgehammer?"

"Stop!" Hook yelled, his voice higher than usual. "I'll shoot! I fucking mean it!"

Tanner couldn't wrap his mind around the man. The behemoth was so large the sledgehammer looked like a mallet. Tanner had worked out with large men on the football field and at the gym, but he'd never seen nothing like this. Why was he wearing a bear's head? He was coming straight for them, weapon raised and ready to swing.

Hook squeezed the trigger. Again, and again until he unloaded all six bullets.

The man in the bear's head kept coming.

Hook squeezed the trigger, the empty gun snapping in his hands, and having as much effect as when it was loaded.

Tanner grabbed Hook's arm and pulled him into the house, the freak too close for them to escape any other way.

Wielding the flashlight like a weapon, Tanner scanned the room as he ran. Big, open, littered with bottles and cans, a small kitchen to the left, a broken fireplace to the right, a set of stairs at the back of the room, a hallway straight ahead. The stairs? No. That would limit their options of escape. The hallway. There had to be a back door.

Tanner started down the hall, Hook behind him, and got to the back door. Locked! The door had no windows, and the lock was an old style that needed a key. There were two rooms off the hallway. Pick one and out the window.

Hook stood in the doorway of one of the rooms, mesmerized by whatever was inside. Tanner ran to him, grabbed his arm.

"We gotta go! We..." Tanner's words fell away. He saw the carnage in the room, saw what had happened to Maddox and his crew.

116

July 14ᵗʰ, 2000. 6:06 PM

Home. Ptolemy was happy to be home. The cleanup crew did an amazing job. Fast, efficient. Everything back to its original place. No sign of wreckage or blood anywhere. Broker was a miracle worker.

"House, shower on, standard temperature," he said, dropping his clothes onto the bathroom floor, in no mood to think about their future, which would be the incinerator.

The water was a perfect temperature, warm enough to soothe his aching muscles. A turn, a stretch, water hitting the right spots and alleviating pains he hadn't felt in years. A few he swore he'd never felt before. It had been a long time since he had to defend himself like that. But *never* against an opponent like that bear-headed behemoth.

What was that thing? A crazy man in a mask. Not a simple, store bought mask, though, having been close enough to see and smell the matted fur. The mask was a real bear's head. The man wearing it … was he human? His size was staggering, but plausible. His speed and strength? No way a human his size could move that quickly, even if there were medicinal enhancements. And no drug existed that would give someone the strength to rip another man's head from his body. At least none he knew of.

Ptolemy never asked about assignments. Broker knew his rules: no women, no children, no innocents. Ptolemy had a general idea who his targets were and why they were marked for death. Usually organized crime. The only information he had was the essentials Broker shared with him. If Broker gave him nothing, then it was nothing, like with this Maddox fellow. He knew the Templeton brothers were drug dealers, because Broker had told him, but Ptolemy deduced that Maddox was a drug supplier, judging from the set up in the barn. Were the Templetons and Maddox connected? And what was the drug?

White powder could be anything. Heroin. Coke. Crazy designer nonsense. What if the designer wanted something more than a high? There were countless stories surrounding angel dust and this new drug dubbed "bath salts" where the users challenged the laws of biology. What if the powder in Maddox's barn lab went beyond those drugs? Clearly, bear-headed man owned the barn, and maybe he got a face full of the powder and went crazy? Killed a bear, wore its head, killed the intruders in horrible ways, felt no pain, and acquired super strength because of the drugs?

What about his blood being black ooze?

Ptolemy had a headache—he was overthinking this. The job was over, he got paid, end of story. Shower off. Time for dinner.

The cleaning crew had provided new cookware and cutlery. He appreciated that, having no desire to ingest the blood of his enemies. Ptolemy used dinner prep as a way to take his mind off his worries. He started to cube a chicken breast, and his cuts were uneven. He couldn't focus. He had too many questions. Like, who were his enemies?

"House, call Broker."

The sounds of a phone ringing filled the kitchen while Ptolemy fussed with his new pots and pans. A small pan for quinoa, a larger pan for chicken, a small pot for a little bit of pasta.

Broker picked up, answering in the distorted fifty percent male, fifty percent female voice. "How did the Maddox assignment go?"

"A little crazy, actually. Not sure what kind of drugs he was supplying and concocting, but I'm guessing it was something new or experimental. Question—do you know of any connection between Maddox and the Templeton brothers?"

Broker's chuckle sounded alien-like due to the voice modulator. "Well, as a matter of fact… While digging around to find out who's hunting you, I uncovered a piece of information—Maddox was the one who hired you to take out the Templetons."

Ptolemy paused from his dinner prep to absorb what Broker had shared. After a moment he went back to cubing the chicken breast. "Interesting. Sounds like Maddox wanted to show the underworld how big his clackers are. I'm guessing the hit on Maddox was revenge motivated. Do we think it's personal or professional?"

"Could be either."

"Or both. Anything on the three guys who managed to sneak into my home?"

"Nothing yet, but I just started."

"Okay. Let me know when you find something."

"I will. So, how's Cali? Does she know about the home invasion?"

Ptolemy smiled. Broker was a woman. This wasn't the first time she had expressed concern for Cali's wellbeing. "No. She's spending the week with her boyfriend and some other friends."

"Good. I trust the cleaning crew did a good job?"

"Amazing job. Using the new cookware as we speak for a chicken recipe I found online."

"Sounds delicious."

"How about you join me for dinner? You know where I live. Hell, I'm beginning to think everyone knows where I live."

The voice chuckled. When Broker replied, there was a hint more emphasis on the male aspect of the voice. "I didn't know you played for the other team."

Ah. Trying to recover. Broker was overcompensating. "Maybe I play for both teams?"

The voice laughed, a bolder, deeper tone than before. "I've seen no evidence to support that statement."

Ptolemy had always been a mercenary. No action was worth doing unless there was some form of payment. Studying in school yielded good grades, which led to scholarships. It also yielded the attention of the government. The army gave him combat skills and more education, fast tracking him to black ops missions. After the army he met Meg, Mako, Kamu, Athena, and Hawke. He made quite a living with them, until the final mission that resulted in the loss of his wife and one of his best friends. He then altered his career path. Top level assassins got paid *very* well, this being his tenth year in the business. The first couple of years hadn't gone smoothly. Mostly low-level hits set up in back alleys and basement bars, often ones where his life was in peril. Then Broker contacted him. Ptolemy had assumed Broker was a man. After all, sexism was alive and well in the world of paid killing.

Over the years, evidence suggested that Broker was a woman. Subtle things like Broker's sympathy. Again, the sexism, but a man rarely offered concern to another man, unless they were family. Ptolemy was an only child of only children, and his father passed away before he graduated high school. Broker was a woman. And Ptolemy had suspicions as to who she was.

Naaah, impossible, he told himself, like he always did when his mind started to knock on doors best left closed and locked. But he had been thinking about it more lately. Maybe because he was close to retirement? There was only one option other than retirement in this line of work, and it was an option he didn't like.

Ptolemy shrugged. "Maybe I'm lonely."

"Again, evidence dictates that you can get a woman, or multiple women, to be there within the hour."

"That's what I'm talking about. Right now, I'm making myself dinner. Some fad grain called quinoa and chicken with a side of whole-grain pasta topped with roasted red peppers and mushrooms. Sure, a trip to a fast-food restaurant would satisfy my taste buds for a few minutes. But this meal I'm cooking will satisfy my body, my mind, my soul."

"That's very mature of you, although I doubt all the women in your contact list would appreciate you comparing them to greasy burgers."

Ptolemy smiled. "No, probably not, but you get the point."

"I do. Unfortunately, you're barking up the wrong tree, buddy."

"Woof, woof."

There was a long pause, almost silence. Ptolemy had always kept their relationship professional with minimal personal facts, and he *never* flirted. Why not? He had maybe one or two more assignments left in him, so if she rebuffed his advances, then so what? The faintest noise of Broker breathing, faster as if she were fighting with herself, the battle of head versus heart. Ptolemy had given her something to ponder, something he assumed she never thought about before. Finally, Broker came back with, "Is there anything else?"

"Not unless you have something to say."

"I do not."

"Okay. Good night, then."

"Good night."

The soft click of the call ending filled the kitchen and Ptolemy smiled again. Broker was a woman. No man said good night to another man.

July 14th, 2000. 9:32 PM

Slivers of moonlight cut through the trees outside and into the house's window, highlighting the body parts—what Tanner assumed were human body parts—dangling from chains. Some pieces were skinned, and a few looked as if they had been mashed. The meat glistened with moisture and the room smelled of rot. July heat spoiled the meat quickly in this makeshift butcher's room. A stark awareness stabbed at Tanner's mind, reminding him to move now, before this room became his final occupancy.

The options were to try the other room, or attempt to break down the back door. Tanner had no desire to see what was in any other room of this house. The back door seemed sturdy, but between him and Hook, they should be able to shoulder through it.

"Hook! We gotta move!" Tanner yelled as he started to the back door, hoping Hook would follow.

Hook didn't move until the sledgehammer hit him.

The hammer's head slammed into Hook's arm, snapping bone upon impact, and knocking him to the ground. This was another thing to add to the list of impossibilities Tanner had seen tonight—the man who threw it was still standing in the front door on the other side of the house.

"Fuuuuuuuuuck!" Hook cried out as he writhed on the ground, clutching at his broken arm.

The freak stepped into the house.

Tanner grabbed the sledgehammer and tried to lift it. His effort almost pulled his arms from their sockets. The handle was metal and the whole thing weighed more than one of the big plates at the gym. Hope for using it as a weapon against the freak disappeared, but he could use it on the back door. He needed every muscle he had to swing it, and it crashed through the backdoor with ease.

The freak was halfway across the main room.

122

Tanner dropped the sledgehammer and yanked Hook to his feet by the back of his shirt.

Hook coughed and moaned. "Can... barely... breathe..."

"Your legs still work? We gotta move!" Tanner pushed Hook through the back door. Tanner kicked it shut. It didn't latch, but he only needed to blind the freak for a few seconds.

Hook was in no shape to run. If Tanner tried to help him, then they'd both get caught. As much as he hated to do it, they needed to split up. He helped Hook to the closest scrap pile and whispered, "I'll lead him away, you find a place to hide."

Tears streamed down Hook's face. "I can't, man. I'm all fucked up. Not just my arm. It's my back. I think that hammer knocked my spine out of whack."

Tanner released Hook and pointed to the piles. "You can. Get behind one of these piles. I'll lead him away. I promise."

Wheezing, Hook did as instructed. Tanner ran from the back door in a straight line. The sound of the door frame crashing seemed to come from within his chest. He stopped and turned to face the man wearing the bear's head.

The man started toward him.

Every blood vessel thumped to the rhythm of his heart, his nerves singing to the symphony of fear. He moved backward, keeping an eye on that sledgehammer, while making quick head turns to gauge where he was. The last scrap heap was on his left, field to the right, outhouse behind him. *Keep watching that fucking sledgehammer*, he reminded himself.

The man in the bear's head was closing the gap.

Tanner turned and sprinted along the scrap heaps and dashed behind the one farthest from the house. He thought about rounding back toward Hook, but it would have been too easy for the bear-headed freak to cut him off. Instead, he ran to the adjacent scrap heap, and then stopped to catch his breath. Listening for the monster, Tanner slipped to a junk pile closer to the house and glanced down the gap between the piles. Nothing.

Tanner concentrated on his breathing. No matter how bad the fire in his lungs blazed, he needed to keep his mouth shut. In through his nose as slowly as possible, out over his barely parted lips. If only he could control his heart, pounding hard enough to rattle his vision.

As if walking through a minefield, Tanner navigated the junk pile. He knew where the monster should be, but wanted visual confirmation before he moved on. Any surprises would be potentially deadly. One step at a time. A little bit farther. Just around the curve to the gap in between the piles... and nothing.

Tanner froze. Maybe the freak was rounding the pile farthest away? *Control your breathing, control your breathing,* he repeated, waiting to see if his pursuer was going to come around the trash heap. Ten seconds. Twenty seconds. Nothing.

He had to be there! Tanner needed to know the freak's location. An athlete all his life, Tanner was confident he could outrun the lumbering hulk. It was the sledgehammer he worried about. Crouching with the command to duck primed in the front of his mind, he waddled down the aisle between the two rows of scrap piles. With every few steps, he looked to the piles for potential weapons. No luck.

There was a lot of old furniture, but nothing useful. Sure, a sturdy piece of wood could make a decent weapon, especially if he were able to create jagged edges by ripping off a chair leg or part of a bedpost, but it would take time to wrestle it free. It would make too much noise. And since he didn't want to risk giving away his position by using his flashlight, he couldn't see well enough to search through the piles for anything sharp or pointed.

Tanner crept back to the farthest pile. The freak had to be nearby. Still low. One foot in front of the other. Easy. Steady. A chunk of metal shifted, and Tanner dropped to his knees. He lurched sideways and rolled on his shoulder. Jumping to his feet, he punched twice, swinging at air.

A chubby raccoon scampered away from the junk pile.

False alarm. This time. Tanner crouched and snuck back over to the scrap heap where he had an unobstructed view of the house. No sign of the freak. Where the hell was he?

Hook answered that question with a shrieking, "Fuck!"

Weapon. Tanner needed a weapon.

The burn barrel! Tanner remembered the ax by the burn barrel. Caution be damned as he ran from his hiding spot. He needed to help Hook. A quick run from the piles and he grabbed the ax.

Hook's screams were coming from the front of the house and Tanner sprinted, ax ready. By the time he got there, a shockwave of metal crashing into metal reverberated through the air. He first thought one of the scrap heaps had collapsed, then realized it was an isolated sound. It came from where Hook was situated. A car. The man in the bear's head stood next to the old rusted out car with the sledgehammer over his head. And swung.

The sledgehammer crashed down on the hood with enough force to lift the back of the car, the noise blasting through Tanner's entire body. What was he doing? Why was he demolishing the car? "Fuck!" came from the car. Hook! Hook was in it!

Tanner charged toward the commotion, a knight rushing forth to slay a dragon. He wasn't sure about the sharpness of the blade, but he wagered it could do some damage. With one swing he drove it deep into the monster's side. The giant showed not even an iota of discomfort. Tanner yanked on it when the freak turned. The ax slid out, and Tanner quickly backpedaled. Holding it with both hands, he swung the ax like a baseball bat.

The freak slapped the ax out of Tanner's hands and punched him in the chest. Tanner bounced off the ground and rolled backward. No stranger to fighting and he'd taken plenty of hits on the football field, but the fights were in high school against much smaller kids and in football he had plenty of padding. This blow was devastating. Struggling to get to his knees, he clutched his chest. It hurt to breathe; his vision tilted. He begged his body to stand, to run, but it ignored his every plea. The freak strode to Tanner and raised his sledgehammer over his head.

A scream, a warrior's whoop, came from behind the freak. Hook! With one hand, Hook drove the ax into the man's back. He dropped the sledgehammer! A taste of hope was all Tanner needed to get back to his feet. But hope was a delicacy susceptible to spoilage.

"Fuck you, you fuck!" Hook yelled. "Take that, bitch!"

The bear-headed freak turned around.

"Shit! No!" Hook tried to run back to the car. The monster was faster.

Tanner had made assumptions about the creature. There was a correlation between size and speed. Shorter, lighter running backs were faster than the taller, heavier ones built for punishment. Always. But even with an ax jammed between his shoulder blades, the beast caught up to Hook and snatched him by the ankles, plucking him from the ground like a weed. And swung.

The junk pile next to them was filled with scrap metal, jagged pieces in all directions, durable enough to push through Hook's back and pin his torso while his legs ripped away. His spine separated with a pop and his entrails flopped out with a splash. Pinned to the pile like a trophy on a wall, Hook stared at his innards as they drooped over the trash, guts getting caught up before hitting the ground. His shaking hand reached for the length of intestine looped over a long piece of pipe.

Fear. Anger. Madness. A unique mixture of burning emotions injected into Tanner's heart, inspiring him to speed into action.

The sledgehammer.

It was heavy, but Tanner was ready for the immense weight this time. The man was too tall for a clean head shot, but Tanner was certain he could connect with his shoulder. The impact should break it, maybe even drive the fucker to his knees. Feet planted, muscles tensed, Tanner made a perfect arc with his swing.

Again, he underestimated the man's speed.

On the down arc, the beast twisted and caught the handle. He pushed back and smacked Tanner's head with the neck of the sledgehammer.

Stars exploded throughout Tanner's vision, each one bringing new pain. He staggered backward and dropped to his knees. Bursts of color mixed with the moonlight and made the man before him look like a god. An angry, spiteful one, a superior being who could bend humanity to its will. No, not a god. A legend, a story, a myth.

The freak reached behind his back and plucked the ax from it like a thorn. Tanner had one last flash of clarity. It dawned on him who this was standing before him. After all, he did an entire research paper on him.

As the tip of the ax whistled toward his skull, Tanner whispered, "Zebadiah Seeley."

July 14th, 2000. 9:44 PM

No! Zebadiah tried to stop his swing but couldn't. The ax dug into the head of the intruder. Never in a million billion years did he expect meat to say something he wanted to know more about. This person knew his name, *said* his name. Why? How?

Zebadiah took a moment and looked around, suddenly paranoid. Exposed. Threatened. He felt... he felt... confused. This intruder knew his name and the man in black had escaped. He would need more traps.

Over the past two days, he had been shot and stabbed more times than he could count, not that he could ever count that high to begin with. Papa always said numbers was for city-folk. Zebadiah had survived it all, killed most of the threats. He didn't bleed red blood no more, didn't need to breathe no more neither. All he needed to do was eat what he killed, and then he was good as new. He had power.

Papa said most people thought the only power was money, but he knew there was all kinds of power. So did Zebadiah. There was guns and muscle and this land and his mama. Zebadiah even saw other kinds of power in prison. Words. Trade. Fear. He had learned enough about the world to know power didn't last. When would his run out? Would the shooting and the stabbing eventually hurt? Because he was confident there would be more shooting and stabbing.

Zebadiah tossed the ax aside. He wasn't going to learn how this intruder knew his name, but at least he had more food.

Bertha in one hand, fresh meat in the other, Zebadiah stomped back into his house through the back door. He had found enough chain and metal cable to set up a dozen hanging hooks. Five were already in use. One supported the bear's torso. Three held the bodies of the men from the barn. The one man's head got its own hook 'cause Zebadiah thought it was funny. The intruder who knew his name got the hook closest to the door.

Zebadiah went out back to the junk pile, sat and snacked on the smaller man's innards while thinking about how smart he'd been to set his traps. Sitting and eating, tired from the fighting, he wanted to rest. But there were a few things he had to do before he could sleep. He grabbed the body by the arm and wrenched it free from the pile. He picked up the legs, too, and took both parts to his meat room. Next to get a place on a hook was the intruder who got smushed and cut up by his front door trap. Then he thought again about the man in black, the one who got away.

What if the man in black came back? What if he knew who Zebadiah was like the meat with the split skull? This worried him. The man in black hurt him, hurt him real bad. Papa told him to be the bear, and the bear protected its lair. The bear didn't hibernate unless it was safe. Traps. He needed more traps. He went to the front of the house to reset that trap. As he gathered the rope, he decided there was a better use for it. A different trap he had thought about. Not only did he need more around his house, but in the woods as well so intruders didn't get so close to his house. He moved the metal plate to the side and would worry about that later.

The newer meat called to him, fresh and still warm. As he ate, he knew he'd be right as rain by tomorrow.

Belly now full and eyelids getting heavy, he wondered about his last kill. How did the intruder know his name? And why did that bother him?

July 15ᵗʰ, 2000. 2:10 PM

Cali awoke to the explosions of World War 3. The sunny day and bird song told her that the outside world was perfectly fine—it was her brain that was exploding. With great effort, she turned her head to survey her surroundings. Bed. Alone. She had mixed feelings about that. If Linda had been next to her, then that would've made for an awkward morning—she had no immediate memory of whatever curiosities were explored. Dakota next to her would have been worse, making the rest of their lives awkward. They had known each other for too long to open Pandora's box, the metaphor and the euphemism. But there was no Tanner, either.

She remembered following Linda downstairs. She also recalled a deep desire to draw dick-n-balls on Dakota's face, but Linda had talked her out of it by distracting her with tequila and weed and snacks. Now was not a good time to flip through last night's mental photo album; the riot in her head and the volcano in her belly were too bothersome.

Maybe the boys joined the party when they finally got home? If that were the case, then she would have woken up naked instead of in her panties and nightshirt. But if she had been too far in the trashcan, then maybe Tanner got mad? It wasn't like him to get mad about that... unless she said something she shouldn't have while drunk. *Ugh, that would suck!* But she should have some kind of memory, right?

The harder she thought, the harder she stomped on the gas pedal of the runaway steamroller flattening her brain. The clock read 2:14 p.m. Her monomaniacal desire for a shower didn't care about time.

Heavenly warm water washed away enough of her headache to make life manageable. It even reduced the nausea whirlpool to slowly rolling eddies. Of course, it took over half an hour for the therapeutic effects to kick in.

Almost three hours past noon, and Cali felt like had she wasted the whole day. She couldn't help wondering if she and Tanner had got into a slurred, embarrassing fight. Did he take the car in a fit of post-breakup rage? For the life of her, she couldn't pull clear images of him returning from last night's errand.

Cali passed by Dakota's room. The bed was made. Had it even been slept in? The irrational fears of World War 3 returned. Had it happened? Was she living in an apocalyptic wasteland? Then she walked by Linda's room. Still gorgeous even while sprawled on the bed and twisted in sheets. No Hook.

Padding down the carpeted stairs, Cali expected to be greeted by four sets of angry eyes. There were none. Just one snoring Dakota on the couch, her left breast again finding freedom from the confines of her bikini top, and no dick-n-balls drawn on her face. Cali felt a sense of pride from not succumbing to her own immaturity, but it was quickly washed away by that gnawing river of concern, flowing fast and furious. *Where are the guys?*

Cali braved the outside with the sun's rays doing their best to stab through her eyes. No men in the gazebo, on the beach, or in the water. The boat was tied to the dock and her car was gone. Still?

Too many questions for her hangover. Cali ran back inside and shook Dakota. "Hey, wake up."

Dakota jolted upright, her hair sticking up in ways that would make 80s heavy metal bands jealous. Rubbing her eyes with one hand, she used the other to pull her bikini top over her breast as if it was a part of her regular morning routine. "Wassup?" she asked through a few gummy smacks of her lips.

"Did the guys come back last night?"

Dakota ran both hands over her face to the point of smooshing her cheeks. She looked to the ceiling in contemplation. "Lemme think. Tequila, tequila, pot, beer, pot, tequila, beer, tequila, spinning world, fuzzy world, blackout. No. I don't remember the guys at all."

"Me either."

"Did they call or text?"

"I don't know. I think-slash-hope my phone's around here someplace. You gonna be okay?"

"I might puke my tits off, but after that I'll look for my phone too."

Cali rubbed a few quick circles along Dakota's back and then went back upstairs. Her guts stewed, this time from worry rather than hangover, although she couldn't deny the omnipresent nausea. Her phone was under her pillow—she said a short prayer as she flipped it open. No calls. One text from Tanner read, **sorry gonna be late**

"Fuck," she whispered as she dialed his number. Voicemail. "Hey, it's me. Where are you? I'm a little worried."

As she hurried to Linda's room she texted, **everything ok? where r u?**

Unmoved, Linda remained in bed, her black hair like a sheet over her face. The last time Cali startled Linda, she almost lost her head., so she sat on the bed slowly, delicately, as if there were landmines under the fitted sheet. She stroked Linda's arm gentler than she would a Faberge egg. "Linda? Sweety? You awake?"

"Yeah, but I didn't think you swung that way."

"The guys didn't come back last night. I got one text and no calls."

"What?" Linda turned, winced, and brought her hand to her head. "Ow. Fuck."

"Yeah, Dakota and I got a case of that, too."

Linda untangled herself from the sheets, but moved deliberately as if they had potential to cause pain. She oozed across the bed toward her phone on the nightstand. "Shit. No calls or texts."

"Hey, lesbians," Dakota said as she entered the room, holding her phone as if neither Cali nor Linda had seen one before. Her eyes more open, but her hair no smaller. "No calls from Jordon and some lame-ass text about being late. I tried calling and got his voice mail. What the fuck?"

"Okay," Linda said, her hangover voice somehow as soothing as her regular voice. "Let's not jump to conclusions yet, or panic."

"I agree," Cali said. "You two take showers. I'll make coffee and keep calling Tanner."

"All right. That'll give us a chance to wake up and think more clearly."

Dakota stared at her phone as if it wasn't doing what she wanted it to do. "Yeah. Yeah, okay."

Cali caught the look in Linda's eye. Concern. Cali didn't want to press her for her thoughts; the timing wasn't right. Hell, it could be her imagination running wild due to semi-blurred vision and a pounding head. She didn't voice any observations or accusations, content to make coffee and phone calls.

The benefit of making coffee while everyone else showered? Enjoying the first cup, hot enough to scald the cotton coating her tongue and bitter enough to strip away the stale taste of pot and tequila. If only it made phone calls.

Ten tries, ten voicemails. Cali was deep into her second mug when Linda and Dakota joined her at the butcher block counter in the kitchen. Linda wore an oversized tee-shirt. Dakota shuffled along in a thin robe. They both reached for the coffee like brain-starved zombies. Dakota chugged, and then looked to the heavens. "God's water! Sooooo gooooood!"

Linda smiled. "So, what next? Call friends and family? Call… the nearest hospital?"

Dakota's orgasmic bliss got cut short. "The hospital? Do you think something that bad happened? They're capable of taking care of themselves. Jordon and Tanner are really fucking huge."

"I don't think anything happened to them, but it's a place to start. Once the hospital tells us the guys aren't there, then we'll know they're okay. Just lost or something."

Cali put her GPS on the countertop. "We don't need to do that yet. Dakota knows my dad is whackadoo about survivalist stuff." Dakota nodded. Linda raised her brows. "With that comes a level of safeguarding, which includes installing a tracking system on my car. It can be seen by my GPS."

"Whoa," Linda said. "That's hardcore."

"And creepy as fuck," Dakota added. "Is he spying on us?"

"What? Ew, no! He's not spying. He's not creepy. He's not hardcore. He's a little overprotective, and in this case, his non-creepy, non-hardcore over-protectiveness has come in handy. The car isn't that far away."

Dakota looked at the screen, but Linda drilled into Cali with an intense stare. There was more to Linda than she was letting on, and Cali suspected that Linda's thoughts were reciprocal. Maybe there was, but Cali didn't think so. Sure, her dad was a little eccentric, but what rich dad wasn't?

"Are we the blue triangle or the red circle?" Dakota asked.

"The triangle," Cali explained as she used her fingers on the screen to zoom out from the current view, until a few tan lines cut through the blotches of green. "This is the main road we turned off to get here, to Maxwell's dad's house. It curves away from the lake, but here's a tiny offshoot road. A little farther from the end of that is my car. We jump in Jordon's car and go to my car. It's about a five-mile drive, so it won't take long. I say we go there, then decide what to do next, depending on what we find."

Linda nodded along. "Let's do that. Might lead to more questions, but we'll at least get an idea about what's happening."

Cali had never played poker with Dakota, but she figured it would be too easy, Dakota's face a billboard for her thoughts and emotions. Advertising slack-faced sorrow, she mumbled, "We can't. Jordon has the keys."

Cursing their luck would do no good, and might make Dakota think it was her fault. She already looked like a kid in an empty candy store. Cali kept her tone upbeat, ready to tell Dakota there were other candy stores. "Don't worry. It's shorter if we walk through the woods."

"Really? I thought you said it's five miles."

"The way the road loops around, it's five miles. Cutting through the woods is a more direct route. About a mile and a half or so. Not a quick walk, but we can do it."

"Just a hike through the woods." Dakota almost had a spring in her step as she left the kitchen. "Let's get dressed and head out."

An expression of dire uncertainty swept across Linda's face—it looked alien on a woman who had been so chill. "Do you think it has something to do with fuses?"

"Not in the slightest. Do you think it has anything to do with the tattoo cream you and I snooped through our boyfriends' bags for?"

Linda's posture went rigid. Jaw muscles worked as if she were chewing on an idea. Linda whispered, "Maybe," then left the kitchen.

Cali started to wonder if Dakota was the only one without an ulterior motive for this vacation.

July 15th, 2000. 9:48 AM

Ptolemy strolled through the auto body shop like he owned the place, ignoring the posturing and the glares from the half dozen mechanics. He went straight to the back, to the goon sitting on a stool in front of a closed door. He brushed dust from his five-figure suit and gripped his over-sized duffle bag tightly. "I have an appointment with her."

The man's veined and tattooed neck was wider than his veined and tattooed head. He thumbed the buttons of his cellphone, his massive hand making it look like a postage stamp, and said, "No. You don't."

It had been six months since he'd been here, so Ptolemy was tempted to ask what happened to the last guy who sat on this stool, but he wanted things to go as smoothly as possible. "I do. It's last minute, but don't worry. I know about her security system."

The mountain of a man looked up from his phone. "Oh yeah?"

"I've been here plenty of times."

The goon stood from his stool. "I've seen men die in a lot of different ways, but there's none more fucked up than what's behind that door. Last dude who wasn't ready... well, I needed to see my therapist four times in two weeks."

"Don't worry. I'm ready." Ptolemy gave a curt nod, then opened the door.

Two lions greeted him.

The room itself was a glorified hallway. The white floor, white ceiling, white fluted columns formed a walkway leading to a white door. White vases rested alongside the columns, the only things between Ptolemy and the lions, hardly enough to keep the great cats from tearing him to shreds should they deem it necessary. Floor-to-ceiling mirrors covered the walls, creating the illusion of a thousand predators stalking him in an infinite room.

Ptolemy headed toward the door, completely unafraid. The lions walked nonchalantly on either side of him, watching him while he focused on the white door ahead.

These two escorting him had been handled by the Empress from birth, and given a regiment of exercise and grooming. They were monsters, beyond the beasts natured had intended. The tops of their shoulders reached Ptolemy's chest. Thick muscle rolled along their entire body, and their shimmering manes rippled with every step. An arrogance was there, the knowledge shared between the animals that they could crush, kill, and eat any living thing on Earth. There was also a protective love of their mistress, The Empress. That, of course, was why she had them greet all guests.

The Empress had a manageable client list. Client lists changed in this business, constantly shrinking, facilitating the need for new clients, and therefore a need to trust strangers. The lions screened who belonged and who didn't. These animals sensed fear, and they were trained to react to duplicity and protect their mistress from harm. Ptolemy shuddered thinking about how the Empress trained the lions to sniff out lies.

Ptolemy made it to the throne room's door without so much as a warning growl from his escorts. The lions skulked through their own entrances, the simple white flaps waving behind them. Ptolemy used the white painted steel door meant for guests.

The throne room, as The Empress referred to it, was a stark contrast to the hallway. Dark, its main light source was the spotlight above her throne, shining on the only person who mattered—the Empress. Tiny red, blue, green, yellow lights pulsed and streaked in the distance behind her, a goddess sitting before a universe of stars. The lions padded their way to her, each resting their perfectly groomed heads on their front paws, never taking their eyes off Ptolemy.

Empress sat erect in her golden throne, her arms on the rests. Here was where she loved to show off her newest gadgets. For this meeting she wore a gray mask that resembled a woman's face, yet without the eyes, nose, and mouth. Long, thick dreadlocks sprouted from the back, some interwoven with gold strands. She always had a stylish flair.

"Good morning, Empress," Ptolemy said with a slight bow.

She leaned forward, the mask's hair falling over her shoulders. "Shoot me in the face." Her modulated voice sounded clear through the mask, not a single crackle or buzz.

Ptolemy raised his brow. "I'm not going to do that."

"You're a guest in my house and you're going to deny my request?"

"I apologize for being discourteous, but your request goes against my personal code of ethics."

"Oh, I know your code, Ptolemy. No women, no children, no innocents. I'm an adult who is far from innocent and I give you consent to shoot me in the face."

"You're still a woman."

"And you're sexist."

"Yes, I am. Women are far more intelligent, cunning, and interesting than men, which is why I kill only men."

Empress laughed as she removed the mask. Her skin was the color of mocha and her eyes were a light shade of brown that glowed like gold coins on a sunny day. Much to Ptolemy's surprise, the long hair was hers. "You always say the right things to me."

When she stood from her throne, the lions raised their heads. With a simple wave from their mistress, they relaxed and watched her saunter toward Ptolemy.

"Impressive, no?" Empress asked, offering Ptolemy the mask.

He gave a slight nod, marveling at its lightweight. "Very. What's it made from?"

"Trade secret, but after a battery of tests, it can withstand a direct hit from a low caliber gun."

"It can absorb enough shock to keep the wearer from feeling it?"

"Oh, fuck no. It hurts like hell."

Ptolemy laughed, then handed the mask back to her. "I like what you did with your hair."

Pursing her lips and batting her eyelashes, she flipped her hair over her right shoulder, a call back to her modeling days. She held the pose for a few seconds before laughing at herself. "Thank you. My stylist did a great job with the extensions. He's the best."

"He's a he?"

"Why wouldn't he be?"

"A woman knows a woman's hair better than a man does."

"I want complete control of my life. Men are stupid, simple creatures who are easy to control, even the educated ones. Women take far more effort to control, even the uneducated ones."

"So, I'm a stupid, simple creature?"

Empress pressed herself against Ptolemy's chest and slid her hand over his crotch, her breath warm on his neck. "Don't even try to act indignant. I've controlled you more than once."

As was probably true with every man, Ptolemy had thought he was her pursuer, the one getting his needs met during their first dalliance. With a quick dismissal from her after their mutual satisfaction, he had learned how wrong he was. "I wish I could argue against that, but alas."

She traced his jawline with her index finger. "You set up this appointment. Do you have something for me to see?"

Ptolemy was disappointed that the conversation had turned to business so quickly. He raised his bag. "I was wondering if you could tell me more about what's inside here."

"Bring it to my bench. Lights!"

The lights snapped on and Ptolemy winced. The lions did as well, grunting, but ultimately kept their position.

The lights revealed this wasn't a throne room—it was a workshop. Benches lined the two walls, each thirty feet long. Dozens of monitors in sleep mode hung from the ceiling over the benches with a uniform distance between them. Different projects, mostly weapons in various stages of assembly, each hooked to a dedicated laptop. The far wall had two garage doors to the outside world, ready to open for any of the six vehicles—Porsche, Lamborghini, two Ferraris, and two Yamaha motorcycles, all designed for style and speed.

With the care of a mother handling an infant, Empress moved what looked like a Gatling gun for grenades aside, clearing space on one of the benches. Ptolemy set down his duffle bag and opened it.

She peered inside. "Nice looking quadcopters."

"Quadcopters?"

She removed both from the duffle bag, then set one on the workbench. She examined the other, turning it over and back. "You're a smart enough man, you should be able to figure out why they're called that. This has been a popular style of drone."

"I know what drones are. The military is experimenting with them, right? Someone stole these from the military?"

"Not necessarily. They're gaining commercial popularity."

"Commercial? You mean any idiot can buy one?"

"Yep. As simple as a few mouse clicks. Companies are trying to make them smaller to get them on store shelves."

"I'm going to have nightmares of these things clouding the skies. What a stupid idea."

"That's because men run the world. I'm not overly impressed with the drones themselves. It's what they're equipped with that's impressive."

Empress set the drone on her workbench and turned it to a precise angle. She flipped its rocker switch, and it released a continual spray of water, forming a misty nebula. Propping the other drone on her shoulder, she flipped its switch. A light shined from it and projected an image on the mist. A deer leaping away. "Hologram and wireless technologies."

The deer—it was a hologram. The men from yesterday tripped his motion detectors and then used the drones to fool him. Ptolemy felt stupid. It was an elaborate trick, but he had known something wasn't right about the deer. He should've acted on his gut feeling. "So, these drones were controlled wirelessly to create a hologram. Jesus Christ."

"Welcome to the twenty-first century."

"It's only seven months old and I've already had nine people try to kill me."

Empress ignored his statement, attempted murder being dismissive small talk in this line of work. She flipped one of the drones over and removed half of the casing that created the junction point of the four propeller arms. "Impressive technology. The good news is I have some impressive technology, too." She went to a separate workbench, and then returned with a handheld device. After plugging it in her nearest laptop, a solid red beam emanated from the device. She glided it over the drone's interior components. A few minutes of silence and a few keystrokes later, she said, "Forward Technologies."

"Excuse me?"

"That's who made these drones. Half the parts are manufactured by them and the other half are from suppliers they're known to use."

"So, whoever tried to kill me yesterday bought these drones from them?"

"No way. These are prototype machines. There is *no way* they'd leave the R & D labs without permission."

"Then someone *from* Forward Technologies is trying to kill me?"

Empress grabbed a small box full of thumb drives. She picked one out and handed it to Ptolemy. Sympathy softened her features as she took his hand in both of hers. "I gave you all the answers I can. This is one of my special drives, programmed to copy the entirety of the first computer they're plugged into. My advice—go there, find one that looks important and plug this in, preferably a server. Then bring it back."

"Thanks. I'll be back in a few hours."

"No worries. Now get out of here. Empress wants to play with her new toys."

Drones. Wireless technology. Holograms. Ptolemy felt old. The world was moving fast. Did he have a few more assignments in him? His latest assignment hurt more than usual. He had more questions than answers after his visit with Empress. Maybe it was time to retire sooner than later?

July 15th, 2000. 4:11 PM

Cali hadn't been sure what the week would entail, so she tried to think of everything while packing, including a hike through the nearby woods. Khaki cargo shorts, black tank top, and hiking boots. When she pulled a six-inch lock-blade from one of her suitcases, her father's nagging voice cut through her hangover, telling her to expect the unexpected. Into one of her pockets it went. The battery life of her cellphone was lower than she would have liked, but there was no time to charge it. She put it in another pocket, grabbed the GPS, and headed downstairs.

Dakota was ready and waiting outside. Of course, she wore a pair of Daisy Duke's and a pink crop top that offered a glimpse of under-boob, the word "bebe" written in glitter across her ample chest. At least she was wearing sneakers. White Gucci wedge-heeled high tops, also sparkling with silver. She was staring into the forest. "What do you think they're doing?"

"We'll find out in about an hour," Cali answered.

"Do you know what's there?"

"No. The GPS shows road names and other things like bodies of water. The big green patch is the forest. But it won't show buildings." Cali held out the device, but Dakota didn't even glance at it. She looked over Cali's shoulder at Linda who was carrying metal water bottles, one in each hand.

Linda wore an off-white peasant shirt with three-quarter sleeves. The shirt touched the top of her shorts, not long enough to cover her camouflage fanny-pack. Her handmade cutoffs looked almost as chic as the four pairs Cali had in her closet at home, each pair a hundred dollars or more.

"Nice fanny pack," Dakota giggled.

"Nice ass cheeks," Linda replied.

Dakota frowned, her baby doll features making her look like a toddler ready to throw a tantrum. "I packed for swimming, sunning, and partying, *not* hiking."

"What about the clothes you wore when you and Jordon arrived?"

Dakota's frown deepened and she turned on her heel, heading down the trail. "Don't wanna talk about it."

When Dakota was far enough away, Cali whispered to Linda, "That means she puked on them."

Linda smirked. "Ah, yes. Makes sense. Shall we join her before she gets lost?"

"We so should. My dad has a house deep in the woods. She and I went there one time to do a little communing with nature. She thought a vine was a snake, thought a snake was a hose, and then twisted her ankle trying to run away from a deer thinking it was a moose. I know you should absolutely run from a moose, but she ran because she thinks moose eat people."

"Wow."

Cali and Linda caught up with Dakota as she wobbled into the woods. After a few steps, her balance improved.

The first half hour was spent in tense silence while they considered their situation. Cali glimpsed at Linda every so often, hoping to catch a tell, a sign, a betrayal of any hidden knowledge. Linda's face remained as placid as the lake they wanted to be sunning by. Finally, Dakota asked, "Where do you think they are?"

Cali moved her index finger over the GPS screen, adjusting the landscape with every swipe. "The car doesn't look like its deep into the forest, but it's definitely off the main road."

"It could be parked at a house, right? A house with a super long driveway? Like where we're staying? Maybe they got lost or had issues and needed to stay the night?"

"If that were the case, they would have called," said Cali.

"Not if the house didn't have a working phone." Linda held out her cellphone. "I have no signal, so it's possible they didn't either."

Cali pulled out her phone to check. "I've got one bar."

Linda regarded her with a wide-eyed glare. "How?"

"My phone has an upgraded plan," she said. A white lie. Her phone was special ordered from a secret country only her father had ever heard of, and it offered a stronger signal. But after the way these two reacted to her GPS-wired car, Cali didn't feel comfortable sharing that info.

"See?" Dakota continued, "There's shitty reception out here."

"Okay, I get your point, but why spend the night in some strange place?"

"Maybe something happened to the car? Maybe they got a flat?"

"There's a spare in the trunk and those three know how to change a tire," Cali said.

"Maybe two flats or three flats? Or the engine blew, or whatever."

Cali and Linda exchanged glances again, the secret language of two people realizing they needed to watch what they said to the third. Dakota wasn't bright, but plenty sensitive, and making her feel stupid would probably lead to an argument or a fight. They had to stick together right now. "Let's say that happened. They could've easily walked back to the house."

"Maybe they got confused or turned around or forgot where they were?"

"There's only one main road from the house into town with a few gas stations along the way. And as backward as this area is, I bet those gas stations still have pay phones."

"Maybe they made it into town and hit a bar. Like, they went to the hardware store and had to wait to get the fuse, so they killed time at the bar and had too much fun. I know Tanner is quick to grab a beer and Jordon will follow right along and Hook, he... he..." Dakota glanced at Linda, silently seeking permission to continue blabbering.

"Hook likes to party," Linda said with a nod, her tone knowing.

"Yeah," Dakota continued, speaking faster now that she was on a roll. "Hook likes to party. All three of them like to party. Hell, *we* three like to party! We can't get mad at them for doing the same thing we did, right? So, maybe they got shit-faced *and* confused *and* lost *and* got a flat *and* needed to sleep it off... and... and I don't know!" Dakota's last words had a warble to them as she choked back tears.

...and they wrecked the car and are lying injured in a ditch somewhere, Cali thought, the words Dakota might have used to finish the sentence. Linda

144

must've heard the same thing. She put her arm around Dakota's shoulders, and Dakota leaned her head into Linda. Whoever Linda was or whatever she was hiding, she remained the nicest person Cali had ever met, a saint for accepting someone else's grief.

"Sorry about making fun of your fanny pack," Dakota said with a sniffle.

As gracious as always, Linda gave Dakota a supportive squeeze and smiled. "No worries. They'll make a comeback, and you'll be amazed at how far ahead of the trend I am."

Dakota giggled and Cali smiled. Linda was easy. Easy going, easy to love. The world seemed to be easy for her. After a soft, "Thank you," from Dakota, they began walking with purpose again, until Cali saw something ahead through the trees. Her shoulders tensed, and she felt as if the world would never be easy again.

July 15th, 2000. 12:49 PM

Ptolemy watched the freight bay through his Nikon. He stood on the fire escape of the abandoned building behind Forward Technologies, adjusting the camera's lens as he focused on a fair-haired man standing at a loading bay. Ptolemy was no shutterfly, but he was good enough with a camera to capture the man's face. He mentally reviewed his scheme—this man was the perfect tool.

People were static, to a degree. Ptolemy was known as The Mathematician because of his ability to predict the likelihood of a person making choice A or choice B within given variables. Life was a maze and people had no choice but to walk its path and make the best decisions available. Ptolemy counted on people trying to cheat the maze.

This high-tech company would have the finest grade security. But he wasn't a hacker—he only wanted the information the Empress desired. He could possibly break into the building at night, but with unknown security systems guarding a company that designed hologram producing drones, his chance of success was low. Instead, he decided to hack the human element.

The man he now watched was definitely a rat in search of some cheddar. This guy was meeting someone. His downturned gazes, the way he crossed paths away from the camera that was perched over the doorway. Yes, something less than legitimate was about to happen. And there it was— another man entered the picture. An exchange of envelopes, careful side-to-side glances, and then each turning to walk away. What bit of information had changed hands was unknown, but Ptolemy's target was probably the seller. Ptolemy released the Nikon's shutter again, having captured the exchange. He ejected and pocketed the camera's SD card. A man like that, cautious and twitchy like a rat, could be used.

When his mark left the loading dock, Ptolemy kept watch, having an idea as to where he was headed before abandoning the camera—he'd come back for it later. He patted his pocket containing the SD card, and the thumb drive from the Empress.

Ptolemy started down the fire escape stairs. He stretched as he went. Too much stationary time. He knew better and should have moved once or twice to keep his muscles limber. Ptolemy cut down the side alley to emerge behind the man. Shadowing him was easy because the thief seemed convinced he'd pulled off his scam.

Ah yes, as suspected, the man was heading down the street toward the park. It was a few blocks away and had comfortable benches. This rat was smug, so he'd want to sit and enjoy his moment. A tiresome, predictable cliché.

The man made a brief stop for coffee, and then on toward the park where he slid onto a bench. Ptolemy smirked. He gave the rat a moment to enjoy a sip or two, allowing him to think he'd pulled off the swindle. The rat jumped when Ptolemy slipped onto the bench beside him, his freckled face suddenly flushed.

Ptolemy held up the thumb drive. The man's eyes went from the drive to Ptolemy. Despite his youth, the man remained calm. He looked around the park as if assessing the situation. "What ya got there?" the man asked, then brought his cup to his mouth.

Ptolemy walked the drive back and forth between his fingers, and replied, "What if you had a program designed to copy the entirety of a computer simply by plugging this in? A hunter/seeker virus that does all the work for you? That would be worth something, right?"

The man took a long sip from his coffee, his grip tightening on the cup. His gaze had gone distant, like he was considering the possibilities. Yes, Ptolemy had offered the right cheese. The rat just had to step into the maze for things to begin. The man reached for the drive. Ptolemy flicked it from his grasp. "Not so fast. Here's the deal—you plug this into a company server. Feel free to copy the program. You're smart. You can figure out how to modify it to search for whatever you like. After that, I don't care. Sell it to whomever, use it to steal company secrets, doesn't matter to me, but I get the original drive back." Ptolemy opened his palm, once again offering the drive.

The rat frowned. "You're telling me I can fit a server's worth of data onto this?" His tone was haughty.

"Smaller, faster, better, right?"

The man glanced at Ptolemy. "When do you need it?"

"Yesterday."

"Should only take a few minutes. I have clearances, but I need to be sneaky about going to the server room. How long does the program take to run?"

Ptolemy thought about that. The Empress hadn't told him. It couldn't be long, or she would have mentioned it. "Fifteen minutes or so," he said, hoping he was right. "When you have it, call me. Bring it here. Right here. Anything different and…" Ptolemy held up his SD card. "I got pictures on here of you—a real clear image—from the loading bay. You got an envelope in your pocket. I don't know what's in that envelope, but I know who to give this card to. Right now, we're partners in this particular venture." Ptolemy then offered a throw-away flip phone from his pocket. "It's got my number. All you do is press send."

After wiping away the sudden sweat percolating from his brow, the younger man slugged his coffee, grabbed the thumb drive and the phone, and sauntered away without a backward glance.

Ptolemy lingered to enjoy the nice day while he waited for the man to do what he needed. The rat was in the maze. All it took was patience. Twenty minutes later, his pocket began to vibrate.

"Yes," he answered.

"I got it," said his rat.

Ptolemy breathed a sigh of relief. "Park bench."

"Sure. I'll see you—" was the response, then came a clatter, as if the phone had been dropped. A shuffling noise, then faded voices. Ptolemy ground the phone into his ear, desperately trying to hear. He barely made out the conversation.

"Need to talk to you." Voice deep and gruff.

"Who the hell are you?" Ptolemy's rat asked.

"I'm the one with the gun, that's who. Tell me about the guy you were talking to on the park bench."

"I don't know him. Never saw him before."

"They all say that. How about we take this conversation elsewhere?"

His rat, the Forward Technologies employee, protested as his voice trailed away.

Fuming, Ptolemy quickly headed toward Forward Technologies. Caution made him pause as he approached the rear of the building. A white paneled van was parked in the alley down from the loading dock. No one behind the wheel. A stylized cockroach emblem overlaid by a red circle and a slash on the side of the van, along with the extermination company name, website, and phone number. The vehicle looked like the real deal, but the hairs on Ptolemy's neck prickled. *What are the odds*, he wondered? Fairly good that this van was waiting for a load. Fairly good that either his mark or Ptolemy was that load. Another attempt on his life? The "exterminator" irony was not lost on him.

He'd have to go inside, the one thing he decidedly did not want to do, to go where his assumed assassin had already entered. No time to plan. Nothing to do but improvise. He hated to improvise. He stole another glance around the corner at the building to confirm there was no one else in the alley.

First thing—check out the van. The van's rear door was closed, but unlocked. Ptolemy confirmed that no one was inside. Living, at least. An older guy lay on the floor, shirtless, his head facing an unnatural direction. His skin was ashen; he'd been dead for a while. The hit-man probably saw this van around town and devised a plan to assume the exterminator's identity.

Ptolemy slipped on a pair of latex gloves and examined the van's tools and bags and shelves. He rummaged through a large gym bag—spare polo shirts and ball caps with the company name and logo. He slipped out of his jacket and shirt and threw on the polo. He stuffed his clothing inside the shirt and tucked the company polo into his pants to create a paunch belly. Then he grabbed one of the clipboards hanging on the wall and donned the ball cap. Ptolemy strode out of the alley and headed for Forward Technologies' front door.

In the lobby, with a smile spread across his face, Ptolemy nodded companionably at the man behind the receptionist's desk. The employee, whose name tag read "Randall," returned his smile. "Hey, Randall, how's it going? One of my guys just came in. He's new and I'm supposed to observe him for training. He's a little gung-ho and didn't wait for me. What's the easiest way to find him?"

The smiling receptionist tapped away at his keyboard. "Shouldn't be a problem. Let me check my computer." Through furrowed brows, he smiled and said, "Well, it doesn't look like we have an appointment with you guys, and I don't think he signed in."

"He didn't sign in?" Ptolemy asked. "This is so embarrassing. First, he gets the wrong building, and then he somehow gets in without signing in and... Did *you* see him?"

Randall's smile faded.

"Let me do you a solid," Ptolemy said. "I'll go find him and get the heck outta your hair."

Randall finger-tapped his desk. His smile returned, but it appeared forced. "Wellllllll, unfortunately we have a protocol for vendors such as yourself. It would be reallllllllly unorthodox to let you wander the hallways without knowing where he is."

"This is a high-tech building, right? Lots of important stuff here. You're the gatekeeper, right? So, how'd he get past you without an appointment?" Ptolemy slumped his shoulders as he took on a sympathetic stance. "O

Don't worry, Randall... I get it, I do. It's not your fault. I don't know about you, but my man's going to get fired for this. I wasn't paying attention, because I was doing my paperwork, checking my boxes like I was supposed to, and I waved him on not realizing he was going into the wrong building."

With every word out of Ptolemy's mouth, the receptionist's face became a shade pinker, until his cheeks moved past red into purple territory. The receptionist handed him a pen and pointed to the sign-in sheet. "No worries. I completely understand. No one should get fired over a simple mistake. No harm, no foul, right? Find him, grab him, and have a nice day."

Ptolemy took the temporary badge from Randall and clipped it to his shirt. He offered a slight bow before leaving the reception area. "God bless, brother. You, my friend, saved a life today."

The receptionist gave an awkward wave and turned away as soon as etiquette dictated it acceptable. Once through, Ptolemy strode purposefully for the elevator. The security office would be on the first three floors, so he rode the elevator and searched the halls one floor at a time.

At the third floor, he came upon a door labeled, "Authorized Personnel Only."

Ptolemy knocked, positioning himself at the best vantage point. A sleepy-eyed security guard in a gray uniform greeted him. "Dude, you can't be here. Randall called up and said you were looking for your buddy. Find him and get the fuck outta here."

The guard's name badge read, "Esteban" and he gestured for Ptolemy to leave. Esteban played into Ptolemy's plan perfectly—he opened the door wide enough for Ptolemy to see one other security guard in the room. Ptolemy popped Esteban in the cheek, then slipped inside the room and put a sleeper hold on the other security guard—"Chuck" per his name badge— before Chuck got out of his chair. He moved the unconscious Chuck gently to the floor, then shut the door.

Despite the high number of security cameras in the building, Ptolemy found what he was looking for. This was not his first time in a similar seat, and the software was easy enough to use. Point and click. Not only did he find the conference room where the hit-man kept his rat, but he also disabled the cameras on the third and fourth floors, and erased the past thirty minutes worth of data for the first four floors. They now had no recorded evidence of him being here, nor would there be any evidence of him after he left.

Ptolemy worked the remaining problem in his mind. From what he remembered seeing in the alleyway, a series of gas and electrical lines ran down the side of the building. Alongside of the lines was a half window on each floor. His first thought was to pull the fire alarm, but that would cause an immediate evacuation. He wanted lingering confusion. Off to the conference room with his rat.

Ptolemy appreciated the serendipity of the nearby men's room. From what he saw in the security office, the hit-man hadn't yet harmed the rat, probably thinking he and Ptolemy had a relationship extending beyond a single meeting. From here, all he needed was a little luck. Actually, the more he thought about it, he needed a lot of luck. *Time to make some,* he thought while slipping into the restroom.

Ptolemy checked under the stalls. He was alone—so far, so good. Inside the bathroom closet was a wheeled mop bucket. Perfect. The stack of cleaning rags was a bonus.

He flipped over the bucket and put it against the wall, then stepped up to the half window. He wound the rags around his hand, turned his face away, and punched the glass outward onto the street below. He cleared the jagged parts from the frame, then looked out. The alleyway was empty, and he saw the wires he'd hope to find. They ran up the wall to the transformers attached to the top of the building. Carefully aiming his gun, he shot right where the wires connected to the transformer.

Fat hissing sparks then sudden darkness. Dim emergency lights kicked on. Success. He hurried to the door, opening it enough to see out. Hoping people would assume the gunshot was the transformers blowing, he watched the conference room door while employees gathered in the hallway. One minute. Two minutes. More people, more talking, voices getting louder. Three minutes. Four. Finally, the conference room door opened, and the hit-man stepped out. He looked around.

Everyone in the hallway engaged in theories and scuttlebutt, asking questions, and adding to the growing tower of conjecture. The hit-man's scowl didn't deter the dozen or so employees from pulling him into their discussions. Finally, someone—probably a middle manager seizing the opportunity to show off his leadership—suggested that even though no alarms had sounded, they should move to street level, just in case. The hit-man protested and tried to get back into the conference room, but as he drew unwanted attention, he acquiesced, joining the others moving toward the east stairwell. He'd be back.

The hallway was clear, and Ptolemy slipped from the men's room to the conference room, his rat jumping out of his skin when he opened the door. The rat yelled with syllables running together as if one continuous word, "There's a guy dressed like a pest exterminator who's been keeping me here and he's looking for someone named The Mathematician!" His rat caught took a deep breath. "Is that you? You know what? Don't tell me. I don't want to know."

Glancing up and down the hallway, Ptolemy replied, "You get what I asked for?"

The wide-eyed rat skittered closer, and handed the thumb-drive to Ptolemy. "Yeah. Here you go."

Ptolemy pocketed the drive . "Did you get what you needed?"

"Yeah. Thanks for that. I'm gonna have a lot of fun with it."

Ptolemy walked down the hallway with the rat in tow, but slowed his pace.

"Why are we slowing down?" the rat asked. "Shouldn't we be getting the fuck out of here?"

Ptolemy put a finger to his lips, signaling for silence. Footsteps echoed from the stairwell. It would be the exterminator. Ptolemy slid his gun out from under his shirt and counted down. *Five... four... three...*

The stairwell door flew open. Ptolemy put a bullet between the exterminator's eyes before he took three steps.

"Fuck!" the rat yelled. "Holy fuck! Oh shit, man, you are a bad-ass assassin mercenary hit-man! God damn! A real assassin! Holy shit!"

"Yep," Ptolemy said, walking toward the dead body.

"Oh, shit, man! Cameras! There are cameras everywhere."

"Don't worry. I took care of those."

"Yeah! Yeah, of course you did. You're a professional, man, and you thought of everything to get us out of here."

The exterminator's gun was in a holster under his jacket, easy enough to find. A .22 LR suppressed semi-automatic handgun. Compact, lightweight, and nearly silent. Ptolemy slipped it in the exterminator's hand and pointed it at the rat. Ptolemy hated to do it, but he put a bullet between the rat's eyes.

Ptolemy didn't like using people and hated killing unnecessarily, but after interacting with the rat for only a few minutes, he knew the dead man was not an innocent person.

"Sorry, buddy, but you should have made better life choices," Ptolemy said. He used his shirt to wipe down his own gun. He slipped it into the rat's hand, then pulled the trigger once to make it look like he had shot twice, hitting the exterminator and the wall behind him. The scene was complete—a corporate espionage exchange gone wrong.

Ptolemy had what he needed. He took a moment to review all that had happened, replaying the events in his mind for analysis. Save for the unconscious guards and the easily embarrassed Randall, he'd had no other direct interactions within the building. Well, direct interactions with anyone living.

Off to Empress to see what was on the thumb drive.

The women stood at the edge of the forest, frozen by the fact that Cali's car was parked in front of a dilapidated barn, next to a mysterious black Range Rover. Cali wasn't sure why, but she felt like she was about to enter a different world. She instinctively examined her surroundings before taking another step. Linda and Dakota followed her to her car.

"What the fuck?" Dakota whispered, the words falling from her mouth. "That's your car, right?"

"Yeah," Cali answered.

"Then whose SUV is that?"

"No fucking clue."

A few scratches ran the length of her car's doors, undoubtedly from a haphazard drive along the only road here. The doors were unlocked and... The keys were still in the ignition? *What the literal fuck?*

An empty ice cream cup in the backseat. Beef jerky wrapper on the center console. Crumpled paper bag on the passenger seat floor. No other clues as to what happened or to the guys' whereabouts. Cali took the keys, and the women went to the barn entrance.

A black substance coated the entrance floor. Soot? Oil? Ooze? What was it? A little farther inside were metal tables, a few overturned, a couple bent. Shattered glass was everywhere. Random piles of white powder. Cali couldn't believe what she was seeing. "Is this... Is this a drug lab?"

"It can't be." Dakota spat the words out as if the idea offended her. "It can't be. There's no way the guys would come to a *drug lab*. No way!"

Linda and Cali shared a look, agreeing with the assessment no matter how vehemently Dakota decried it.

"It's not one anymore," Linda said. "I mean, look at this place. It's destroyed."

155

Linda wasn't wrong about that. A third of the loft had collapsed, planks and sheets of wood blocking the back doorway. Cali was surprised that the barn was still standing, seemingly held together by moss, mold, and graffiti. The lab could have been abandoned years ago, but the acrid chemical smell made Cali think otherwise. So did the dust patterns on the floor. Footprints and drag marks. Blotches of dark red, the color of old brick, on the ground. Her skin went cold. She ran through the different possibilities in her mind, but only one made sense—blood. There had been a fight, an upheaval violent enough to cause mass destruction. Dakota was already beyond agitated, and since Linda—judging by the look on her face—had come to the same conclusion, Cali kept her mouth shut.

"This is so fucking creepy," Dakota said, her voice warbling on the verge of tears.

"Just to be clear," Cali started, "We're not going to walk into this barn, right?"

"Hell no!" Linda and Dakota said in unison.

"Okay, good. I just wanted to make sure that we're confused, not stupid."

"But we still need to find the guys," Linda said, resting her right hand on her fanny pack.

"Yeah. All right, we need to look around. We're going to stay together and we're not going inside this creep castle."

Linda led the way, walking around the side of the barn. Dakota was in a trance, mild tremors playing with her hands. Cali guided her as they followed Linda. The dank smell of rot accompanied them while they made their way to the field behind the barn.

Rust colored streaks led from the back of the barn into the field, and a path cut through the tall grasses. The streaks dissipated, but it was evident that something, or someone, had been dragged from the barn. Dakota stopped in her tracks, yanking Cali's arm. "Is that blood? Oh, God," Dakota said, her hands trembling harder. "Oh God oh God oh God ohGodohGodoh-God!"

156

It was Linda's turn to calm Dakota. Putting a reassuring hand on her shoulder, she said, "Hey, Dakota? We don't know what's going on yet. This blood looks old, really old..." It wasn't old. Slight shimmers of freshness clung to the larger globules drying on a few of the weeds. "... and it's by a barn. Maybe a hunter bagged a deer and cleaned it here? Maybe the barn held cows and it was time for the farmer to do what he needed to do? The point is we can't jump to conclusions without getting as much information as possible. Does that make sense, Dakota? Are you with me?"

Dakota's eyes remained wide, her head bouncing up and down somewhere between a nod and spasm. Linda gently cupped Dakota's cheeks and turned her head away from the blood. "Dakota? Hey, hi, it's me, Linda. I know you're scared, and I know what this looks like, but listen, are you listening? You saw the car, right? There's no damage to the car, so the guys weren't in an accident. Jordon and Tanner are big dudes, so no one is going to fuck with them. You're not alone, Dakota. Cali and I are right here. We don't know what's going on, but we're smart, capable women, so we're going to figure this out together."

Linda was so convincing that Cali almost believed her. Her words, her strength, seemed to have a calming effect on Dakota and that was all that mattered. Linda inhaled and exhaled in a deep rhythmic way, and she encouraged Dakota to do the same. When Dakota's eyes no longer resembled pie plates, Linda let go of her face. "I'm okay," Dakota said, turning back to the field. "I'm okay."

Cali mouthed, "Thank you," and Linda replied with a wink.

"We have to follow the path, don't we?" Dakota asked.

"We do," Cali answered. "But we'll do it together."

Linda continued to lead the way, her hand returning to her fanny pack. The weeds were tall, shoulder height or higher. Saplings sprouted up in random places and a few oak trees had moved beyond that stage. Sprawling, leafy branches obscured their view as to what might lie ahead. The trampled weeds forming the path suggested they were recently flattened. A few repeated indentations in the soft dirt confused Cali, until she recognized the shape as a footprint. She stood in one; it could have held four of her feet.

The trio walked faster until the green field faded to the brown of the forest floor, the tree's thick canopy muting the sunlight. The women stopped when they saw the structure. "A house," Dakota whispered. "A house!" Her voice grew in volume and excitement. "I see a house. The guys must be there."

A small, two story house. Just like the barn, the parts of the brown wood siding not covered by graffiti had green streaks of mold. Dakota stated the obvious. "This place looks abandoned."

"I agree," Cali said, her tone encouraging, so Dakota wouldn't feel belittled.

"Is that an outhouse?" Dakota asked while walking toward it.

"Dakota," Cali whispered angrily. "What are you doing?"

Ten feet from the outhouse, Dakota stopped and pointed to it. "Don't you get it? There's no way Jordon would use an outhouse. That proves the guys didn't stay here last night."

If the situation weren't so serious, Cali would have laughed at such logic and Dakota's complete lack of understanding about the concept of desperation.

"Unfortunately, sweety, that might not be true," Linda said. Her ability to stay calm and to keep others from freaking the fuck out was uncanny. Maybe she had some form of crisis management training? Maybe she took classes before heading off to third-world countries? Whatever magic it was, it worked. Dakota nodded and looked back at the house. "Should we go in?"

The back door looked like it could fall off its hinges from even a slight breeze, but it was closed. "Let's go around to the front first," Cali suggested.

Obviously, this place was a dumping ground for the locals, adding evidence that the house was deserted. But the amount of garbage was fascinating. She had attended art shows comprised of sculptures made from junk, yet this was far more compelling. The piles formed two rows, and the women walked down their center aisle. "This is crazy," Dakota whispered as she gazed up at each peak.

At the end of the piles was an old car. Judging from the high percentage of primer gray and rust, whoever deigned to revitalize it had given up.

Probably a stupid teenager who decided to come to this vacant house and party with all his stupid friends, and the car wouldn't start when it was time to leave. Dakota sneered. "Looks like someone had a sledgehammer party on this thing."

Cali agreed. The dents unnerved her. Each one was craterous, the impact point way too deep to have been made by a human being, even a muscled dude-bro driven by machismo like Tanner. When the women rounded the corner to the front of the house, worry for Tanner suddenly hit Cali in the gut.

The front entrance had no door and none of the windows had glass. A small ground-level porch with half-rotted boards. The planks were so compromised that there was a hole right in front of the doorway. On either side of the porch was more trash, mostly plastic bags, broken bottles, and discarded cigarette packs intermingling with decomposing leaves. A massive sheet of metal leaned against the wall on the left side of the porch. Jagged strips were peeling away from it. At first, it appeared that a layer of rust covered it. Cali was no metallurgist, but she knew that rust didn't glisten in the late afternoon sunlight.

Fear grew so quickly within Cali's chest that it threatened to crack her ribs. No scenario kept her from concluding that this was blood. Tanner's blood? Or Hook's. Or Jordon's.

"Oh, God," Dakota cried as she pointed at the house. "His shoe."

Inside on the wood-planked floor was a boat shoe, once white, now streaked with dark red. Sobbing, Dakota started to walk toward it. She got to the porch before Cali stopped her. Standing between her friend and the doorway, Cali said, "Dakota, wait. We don't know what's in there. We all have a lot of questions, but before we go rushing into a strange house... we need... a... reason..."

A bear. Across the dirt road, at the edge of the forest was a bear. Cali had never seen a live bear before, but something didn't seem right. It was running on its hind legs. By the time it was halfway across the road, she recognized that it had human arms and legs. It was a man in overalls wearing a bear's head. Sprinting toward them.

July 15th, 2000. 5:05 PM

Zebadiah gently scattered dead leaves over the trip line, careful not to set off the trap he'd finished making. This part of the woods was perfect for a trap, right at the bottom of a slight hill where two rows of brush would guide prey right to it.

He backed away to admire his handiwork. Everything blended nicely with the surroundings. Papa always said Mama had a special liking for these woods. Told him the woods themselves was special. She'd spend entire days and nights out here, doing God knows what, maybe doing the devil himself. Zebadiah felt the wood's distinctive mood. Papa gave Zebadiah the barn and the house, but Mama gave him the woods. She was still here in these woods; he felt her, too. He had to protect them the same way he had to protect his barn and his house.

He used his pant legs to wipe the forest grime from his hands, not that these dirty overalls helped much, it just added to his sense of accomplishment. This was the third trap that he had set, and that was after he cleaned up last night's mess. He was done setting traps for today. Tomorrow he'd set more, but he needed to explore the trash piles to see what resources he had to work with. He needed more ropes and wires.

Treading back to his house, he made note of which trees had sturdy, dangling vines. Maybe after some food and rest, he'd come back and get them. Or maybe go to the lake and explore the area? He hadn't been to the lake yet since he came home. There were houses down there and campsites. Girls liked campsites, especially ones close to the lake. They wore little bathing suits that barely covered their devil's horns. Zebadiah liked devil's horns. The way they looked. The way they bounced when a girl ran. The way they bounced when he played wedding games with them. Yes, it was time for Zebadiah to think about the needs of his fuckstick.

Papa always called it that. In prison, he had heard many, many names for it. None of those names made sense and he didn't like them. Besides, he was no longer in prison. And now he was different. Better. He was a bear. Maybe he was even *more* than that? More than a man or a bear, more like… a god.

Gods didn't die. Neither did he, even though he should have. Only the weak worshipped gods, as his Papa said. Zebadiah knew men could be strong, but women couldn't. The police woman who arrested him had hurt him, but she needed men strong enough to contain him. Women needed men. Women were weak and gods were strong, even stronger than men. Zebadiah was stronger than men. Zebadiah was a god with a god's fuckstick. No… a godstick. It was time to find some women to worship his godstick.

Almost home. Papa always said a lot about home. Home sweet home. A man's castle. And someone was trying to invade it.

Through the trees, he saw movement by his house. Where he stood, the branches were low, and the bushes were thick with lots of leaves blocking his view, but he knew what he saw. Someone was trying to get in his home *again*!

Just like a man or a bear, a god had a right to defend his home by any means necessary.

He intended to charge from the woods and slaughter the trespassers, but as he shifted through the branches and bushes, he decided to alter his plan when he saw the women. Women were trespassing. Pretty ones, too!

This forest must be magic like his Mama had said! Because he was just thinking about wedding games and his godstick and now the woods provided him with three worshipers. Two blondes and a brunette with glasses. The blonde worshipers had large devil's horns, especially the one with the super bright shiny hair. Why was she crying? No matter. Girls always cried, especially during wedding games.

The women stood in front of his house. Perfect! With them so close together, he should be able to get them all at once. Zebadiah sprinted from the woods.

July 15th, 2000. 5:28 PM

"*Run!*" Cali yelled.

Dakota shrieked as all three women ran into the house and crashed into each other. Caught up in a jumble of feet and arms, Cali stumbled and veered to the right, momentum sending her toward the stairs. She didn't want to go up, but she was running too fast to stop herself. She slammed into the landing's wall and made a ninety-degree turn up a few more steps into a room.

The second floor was like a set of train cars, this room led to the next, and that room led to the far room. No doors on any of them, nothing to obstruct Cali's view of the window over the front door.

"Come on, let's go through that window," she said, but realized her friends hadn't followed her up the stairs. She heard Dakota scream from the first floor. *Fuck! No!*

She stopped herself from running back downstairs because whatever happened to Dakota would happen to her. Did that bear-head wearing ogre kill her? And what about Linda? *Oh God, were they dead?* Was the hapless little blonde girl she met in kindergarten gone forever? What about brave, strong, unearthly Linda? *What do I do?*

Cali ran through the second room and into the third, to the window. The drop seemed much farther now than when she had first thought of the plan. *Why do I have to be the one who has to go out the window?*

The rooms had trash in the corners and along the walls, remnants from years of being a not-so-secret party house. This room and the one before it was a bedroom, the mattresses still there. She grabbed the one in this room, brown and slimy, and dragged it to the window and propped it up. Hopefully Bear Head would believe she was hiding behind it.

Footsteps. Footsteps from the first floor clomping closer to the stairs. *Hurry!*

In the second room the mattress was propped at an angle against the far wall. Perfect. Cali crouched and shimmied behind it, praying that whenever that nightmare of a man reached the second floor, he'd notice the mattress in the far room and not this one.

She pulled her phone and knife from her pockets. She tried 911. "Your call cannot be completed as dialed" played. *Are you fucking kidding me?* She had service, but this backwoods area failed her. She thought about calling again, but even with the volume all the way down, it seemed as if the voice was speaking through a megaphone.

Footsteps shook the whole house. Or maybe it was her heartbeat shaking the house. Sweat poured out in waves, her back wet, hair sticking to her neck. The footsteps, those fucking heavy footsteps, were on the stairs.

Cali trembled as she put away her phone and opened her lock blade, holding it outward, ready to stab the first thing that came around the corner. Inhaling big gulps of mildew stench made it difficult to concentrate. *Calm down.* She needed to calm down. *What would Linda do? I don't fucking know! She could be fucking dead.* Linda wouldn't entertain such negative thoughts. But Cali couldn't stop picturing Linda and Dakota dead on the floor, necks broken, blood flowing from their mouths. They were dead. They were dead and it was her fault for running away. *No! Stop thinking like that.* Control. Control breathing. Control thinking. Control focus.

Remember your training. All forms of fighting started with a basic principle—do not panic. But she was taught how to handle face-to-face confrontation, frontal assault. Her hands-on experience was in a controlled environment. Yes, the men she trained with were bigger, but Jesus God in Heaven, this crazy fiend was huge. And he just stepped onto the second floor.

Thump. Thump.

Each footstep vibrated up Cali's spine, tailbone to skull.

Thump. Thump.

A couple more steps and he'd be in the second room.

Thump. Thump.

A pause. He entered the second room and paused. *Don't breathe. Don't move. Don't make a single fucking noise.*

Cali's heart measured time. It felt like a thousand beats per second, but she estimated it to be two. She counted ten beats. Twenty. Thirty. He hadn't taken another step since entering the room. Had he taken his boots off and became so light on his feet she couldn't hear him? Was he just standing there staring at the mattress waiting for her to make a mistake? Forty beats. Fifty. She couldn't hold her breath much longer, her lungs needing to explode into a rushing exhale that would give away her position and get her killed.

Thump.

Thump.

Did he move on? Or farther into the room? Then she heard it. His footsteps moving quickly away from her.

Control. Control your exhale, she told herself as she chanced a peek. He was no longer in the room.

She had to hurry.

She slid out from behind the mattress, careful not to knock it over, and scurried to the wall separating this room from the other room. She crept along the wall, making sure to stay on her toes and not scuff her feet. His feet shifted, and then another noise—the mattress getting tossed aside. There was no more wall to hide behind. She had to risk exposing her location.

Holding her breath again, she peered into the next room. Perfect! He was leaning out the window. She rushed into the room. Before he could turn around, she slammed her shoulder into his ass and drove him forward with her legs. Screaming to give herself an extra boost, she pushed.

He twisted, but he was at an awkward angle. And she wasn't about to let up. She screamed again and stabbed his leg, quick jabs over and over. "Fall, you fucker!"

Out the window he went.

Wasting no time, she locked her blade and pocketed it as she ran down the stairs. A mix of emotions hit her when she saw Linda lying on the ground. Happy to see her, but frightened that she might not be alive, Cali knelt beside her. For a second, she froze—just outside the front door Bear Head lay in a heap.

As silent as possible, she rolled Linda over. A small bruise radiated from a bleeding cut on her forehead like a purple halo, but Linda's cheeks and lips had color. She was breathing and had a pulse. One lens of her glasses was cracked, so Cali removed them and put them in her pocket. She shook Linda by the shoulders and patted her cheek. No reaction. She didn't want to do anything louder for fear of waking Bear Head, so she scanned the room for ideas. A hallway along the stairs led to the back door, past two more rooms. Cali's heart jumped when she saw a pair of legs sticking out from one of the doorways.

Cali ran to the room, and found Dakota sprawled out on the floor. She recoiled from a horrid stench. It permeated the area and came from who knows what or where. Thankfully, Dakota was breathing and had a pulse.

Cali's mind raced. She needed to do something and needed to do it fast, no telling how much time she had before Bear Head became a problem again. Outside. She'd drag them both out the back door and hope they'd wake soon.

Fingers intertwined under Dakota's breasts, Cali dragged her into the hallway toward the backdoor, but something from the second room caught her eye as she passed it. She decided to keep on task. She'd investigate when she went back in for Linda.

Outside, she laid Dakota against the house. She shook her and patted her cheek. No response. No time. Back inside, to the room where she'd thought she saw…

Dead faces stared at Cali. Organs and body parts and blood covered the floor. The sour smell of rot threatened to choke her. Her breath hitched in her throat—Tanner was suspended from a chain. His head was cleaved in half, tongue lolling out of his mouth. Dried blood caked his face, his clouded blue eyes staring blankly at her.

Cali couldn't move, the shock from the horrors inside the room refusing to let her run. Hook was suspended behind Tanner, his bottom half missing. Beside him was what might have been Jordon. But it couldn't be his body, because this mangled chunk of meat didn't look human, more like

165

someone took Jordon's head and put it on a slaughtered animal's body. Chunks of meat were suspended from the ceiling. Not cattle, but human.

Too much. This was too much.

Cali screamed.

She turned to run, but the last thing she saw was a bear's face.

Cali's ankles felt heavy, and her shoulders burned. Dear God, the pain in her wrists! The aches and throbs came in waves, each one pushing her toward consciousness. That, and the crying.

Cali knew that crying. She had heard it plenty of times over the years. Dakota. Dakota was crying!

Eyes opened; Cali twisted. Pain shredded her right side, like she had rolled in broken glass. Hanging. She was suspended by her wrists, chains wrapped around them. A length of chain circled her ankles, too.

"Nooooo!" Dakota shrieked. "No! No! No!"

"Stop!" Linda yelled. "Stop!"

All the "W" questions crashed through Cali's mind like bulls through Pamplona. The "where" was the barn she had seen earlier, metal tables to her left, the loft's half-fallen section to her right. She was hanging from a hook protruding from the front of the loft, the part that hadn't collapsed. The "what" and "why" were obvious as well.

Across the barn from Cali were Dakota and Linda, each naked and dangling from the ceiling in front of the stables, chains pinning their wrists above their heads. Linda had chains around her ankles, Dakota did not. Scattered on the floor were their clothes, shoes, and Linda's fanny pack.

"Let us go!" Dakota screamed. "Let us go, you piece of shit!"

The man wearing the bear's head stood in front of Dakota. He loosened the laces of his boots and then used his feet to kick them off. Thick fingers worked the buttons of his overalls, and they dropped to the ground. Pale white scars covered his skin. Cali swore that his skin held a shade of green. He left the bear's head on.

He stepped closer to Dakota.

"Nooooo!" she screeched again, this time flailing like a hooked fish pulled from the water.

"Get away from her!" Cali yelled. "Get the fuck away from her!"

"Over here!" Linda screamed. She kicked her legs toward Bear Head, but he was about five feet too far away. Even with chains around her ankles, she managed to extend her legs with control. "Start with me, you big piece of shit! Over here!"

The closer Bear Head got to Dakota, the more she thrashed. Kicking and twisting her body, she cried and screamed. Rivulets of blood ran down her arms. Gnarled fingers reached toward her breasts. Dakota kicked at his hands and chest. Catching her ankle with his hand, he tugged. It was hard enough to rattle the chains, and it was as if he pulled her soul from her body. Tears flowed from a blank stare, her leg moved in a pantomime run, the way a turtle's legs worked when flipped on its back. The motion did nothing to hinder Bear Head, gripping his dick with his hand and moving closer.

Cali and Linda screamed wordless shouts of anger and fought against their restraints. Bear Head moaned, then took a step back. For a split second, Cali thought their rage had worked, had somehow stopped him.

His dick went flaccid as an octopus tentacle and drooped over his hand. He moaned again, a muffled scream escalating in volume. Panicked gestures consumed his movements. Shaking and yelling as if trying to awaken himself from a nightmare, he backed away. Closer to Cali.

She tightened her shoulders and brought her knees to her chest, praying he'd keep backing toward her. What… what the hell was he doing? Bear Head started punching his own dick. He hit himself harder and harder with meaty smacks. Cali had no clue why he was doing that; she just tried her best to judge how close he needed to be before she sprung. She'd have only one chance at this.

His body was turned enough for Cali to see his erection growing. The bigger it got, the slower he moved toward her. Grabbing his dick with both hands, he stopped moving and looked up to Dakota.

Cali thrust her feet outward with all her might, snapping her body like a whip and extending as far as she could. Judging her attack well, she got the chain over his head and around his neck. The chain dug into her ankles and she tried to pull him to the ground, but he was too strong and resistant.

From this angle, she tilted her head back and got a better view of the hook protruding from the base of the loft. Small and holding only one link of chain.

Bear Head pulled, but not hard enough to take the fight out of her. He teetered off balance.

"Choke him, Cali!" Linda yelled. "Rip his fucking head off!"

Cali appreciated the encouragement but didn't think it was likely she'd be able to honor the request. She needed to pull this freak a foot closer. She took a deep breath and flexed every muscle she had, and a few she didn't know existed, in one quick burst. It was enough to make him step back, enough to allow her to bend her arms and loosen the chain's tension.

Tilting her head back again to see the hook, she snapped her arms, intending to pop her chain-link free. The chain danced, but the link didn't move. Pain radiated through her shoulders. She snapped again with the same result. Cali grunted, and a tidal wave of adrenaline swept through her body. She snapped her arms again and the chain jiggled enough for the link to come off the hook.

An explosion of pain radiated between her shoulders, where she landed. The fall happened too fast. Her back slammed against the barn floor, but at least she brought Bear Head down with her. She needed to refill her lungs. Getting the wind knocked out of her muffled everything, even Linda's screams seemed far away. "Cali! My fanny pack! There's a gun in my fanny pack!"

Darkness skirted along the edge of Cali's vision. Breathe! A primal switch flipped, and she took in a gulp of air. *Knife*, was her first thought. *Get my knife... wait, what is Linda screaming about?*

"To your left! Next to your head to your left, Cali! Gun in my fanny pack!"

Muscles around her ribs burned as if each bone went nuclear. Cali forced herself to roll, to obey Linda, to grab the stupid fanny pack. Though her wrists were still chained, she had enough movement to yank the zipper. Then her legs went taut.

Bear Head started to move.

Terror froze the fire burning through her body. This was life or death, no time for pain or wooziness. Her ankles weren't shackled, just wrapped once by the chain. She shook her legs to loosen the chain, and then pulled when Bear Head turned over. Metal pinching along the way, she slipped her ankles out as he stood.

Cali pulled the gun from Linda's fanny pack, a .32-caliber short-barrel SP101. Cali had plenty of experience, thanks to her father. A hint of reservation passed through her mind—she had blasted targets before, but never a person. No. *This* wasn't a person. *This* was a beast wearing a fucking bear's head. *This* was a monster, a rapist, and a killer.

POP! POP! Center mass, his chest.

His thick fingers curled; he reached down for Cali.

POP! POP! Another two in his left eye.

He reeled back and fell.

Cali swallowed hard. "Fuck," she said with a huff. She was never a fan of true-crime stories, especially ones about a deranged individual who found solace in brutality. The morbid curiosity, the titillation of exploring the darker side of humanity was never in her. Yet sitting on a barn floor as a prop in another person's play with her hands chained, she was determined not to be a victim, rather a survivor.

The chains around her wrists were done in the same fashion as her ankles, no cuffs, or shackles, just wrapped. The fire returned, burning in her hand as she twisted and pulled free, ripping her skin, creating cuts and multi-colored bruises.

Cali hopped to her feet, and ran to Linda. After hoisting her down, Cali helped remove her chains and then they hurried to Dakota. They lifted her with ease, but she had gone limp.

"Dakota? Sweety?" Cali started. "It's over now. It's all over. We need your help to get you down."

No response, her head wobbling while she stared at Bear Head's corpse.

"We can leave now, Dakota," Linda tried. "We can put on our clothes and get the fuck out of here and go back to the lake house."

"Clothes?" Dakota whispered.

"Yep. This isn't some 1970s science fiction where we have to run around naked. All our clothes are here. Let's get dressed and get the fuck out of here. What do you think of that?"

The tiniest of light flickered behind her eyes as if she remembered she could control her own movements. She looked up as Linda and Cali lifted her again, this time unhooking herself.

Cali and Linda dressed quickly but needed to help Dakota even though she only had three articles of clothing. Cali did her best to encourage. "You're doing great, Dakota. We're going to have to walk back to the house, but once we get there, we'll all get cleaned up and we'll call the authorities and get this all taken care of."

"What about your car?" Dakota sounded like a lost child, unsure if she could believe anything she heard.

"We'll check on the way out, but I think the battery will be dead."

Dakota agreed with slow nods, her gaze moving to the world outside the barn, tears rolling over her cheeks. "Okay. Let's get out of here."

Cali put an arm around Dakota's shoulders to guide her. Linda grabbed her gun and slid it into her short's pocket. Linda shrugged and said, "Can't forget the gun. There could be some guy wearing a wolf's head, or a snake man, or a cat woman out there. Who knows what's in those woods?"

Cali passed Dakota to Linda when they got to the car. She plopped into the front seat and turned the key. Nothing. "Guess we're walking." She got back out, faced Linda, and said, "Care to explain to the class why you have a gun?"

Another shrug. "Well, you know, a girl—"

"—Can never be too prepared? Yeah, I'm not buying that. I also can't help but notice that you no longer need your glasses. They're in my pocket, by the way, just in case you do need them. I think we've all been through enough together. We've earned the truth."

Linda's jaw muscles worked as if she were chewing on her words before spitting them out. She rolled her eyes and gestured with her head toward the direction of the lake house. "Let's walk and talk."

As the trio hobbled their way into the woods, Linda said, "I'm a DEA agent."

Dakota's eyes snapped into focus and she pushed away from Linda, perfectly capable of walking on her own now. "What?"

"So that's why you were with Hook," Cali said with a chuckle reserved for sick jokes.

"Yes, exactly. He was a small-time party pusher, so we never even noticed him until recently. Rumors said he got financial backing to ramp up his business. This seemed a bit coincidental since there were a couple assassinations recently, brothers who made drugs in this area. There's also a newer player in town named Maddox. We weren't sure how Hook was connected, so I went undercover to find out what I could find out. It's obvious that Tanner and Jordon are his backers."

"Jesus Christ, Tanner," Cali mumbled to herself. Why would he do that? How did she not see this? She did see it, though. She saw it the past few days and made little effort to investigate, to challenge inconsistencies, or to ask more questions. All she did was ransack his suitcase and dive right back into the deep end of her blissful ignorance when she didn't find anything more than an obnoxious quantity of condoms.

"There's no fucking way Jordon would be part of that," Dakota said.

"I'll need to find the guys and talk to them about that," Linda said.

Dakota teared up and wiped her nose with the back of her hand. She sobbed. "You don't have to worry about arresting them. They're dead!"

Linda's face went pale as she looked to Cali for answers. "What? How?"

Cali swept away tears of her own as soon as they formed, her gut tightening from the thought of what had happened. "That... that *thing*... in the barn. In his house, he had a whole room of... of bodies. The guys were in there..."

"Fuck," Linda whispered. "I'm sorry."

"Not your fault," Cali said. "You didn't turn them into drug dealers, just lied to us about hunting them down."

"I didn't lie about anything."

"Oh, God, don't start lawyering me about the morally ambiguous line between lying and withholding the truth."

"Fine. I lied by not telling you I was a DEA agent, but that's not something I can go around and tell everyone about, is it? I couldn't tell you that I was investigating a drug ring your boyfriend might have been involved in, could I?"

Cali's boyfriend had been murdered—no, slaughtered—and hung up like a piece of meat in an abattoir. Her best friend's boyfriend shared the same fate. She had been strung up, hanging by chains, almost a plaything for a deranged freak. Cali needed to grieve, to vent. She wanted to come together with the two other women who lived through the same horrific ordeal, but now one of them didn't have quite the same feelings about the situation, didn't face quite the same loss. "I meant lying about the person who I thought was amazing. I thought we made a connection."

"We did. All my stories are true. Every opinion, thought, and feeling I shared with you is real. There was nothing I did or said during our time together that was a lie."

"Get a fucking room," Dakota sniffled, still wiping away tears.

"It still feels like you're someone else now," Cali muttered.

"Yeah? Well, I feel like you're hiding something, too." Linda pulled out her cellphone. "Still no signal. How about you, Dakota?"

Dakota pulled out her phone and mumbled, "No. Nothing."

Cali didn't say a word, yet Linda looked at her as if she had. "Upgraded plan, my ass. You're hiding something."

"No, I'm really not."

"You know how to fight. You know how to shoot. You didn't lose your shit under pressure. And we found your car because of a GPS locator. There's more to you than just a pretty, blonde college girl with a rich boyfriend. Any particular reason why you haven't tried your cellphone yet?"

Lies and misdirection spun all kinds of fantastical stories around Cali's mind, a few even sounded believable. She was too tired to work through any of them, and she was done with lies for today. "My dad is a survivalist junky. Like, uber-crazy about it, especially for a guy with an office job. I don't know why, but he is. When I was old enough to walk, I was old enough to train. All kinds of martial arts and fighting styles. He taught me how to use weapons when I became a teenager. He's into gadgets, too, such as GPS tracking devices and hardcore cellphones with stronger than normal signal strength."

"Wait," Dakota snapped. "You mean your cellphone has a signal? Why the fuck haven't you called anyone like the police, or Linda's DEA buddies, or the fucking army?"

"I already tried 911, but either this area doesn't have the service, or it's down. Right now, my battery is almost dead, so let's get back to Maxwell's house and we'll have Linda call her DEA buddies."

"Whatever," Dakota mumbled. She walked faster.

The forest floor sloped gently downward. Thick patches of fern sprouted around the bases of trees that grew closely together. Bundles of leafy bushes grew in the sparse areas where sunlight could make its way through. The trio walked in the same direction, keeping far apart from each other. Cali had a lot to process; so did the other two women. Maybe the silence would do some good and they'd be ready to communicate and share their feelings when they got back to the lake house. Ready to hug and cry and get pissed at the universe for doing this to them. For now, Cali thought it might be best to keep her mouth shut and focus on the crunching noises of the forest floor detritus. The noises fell into the rhythm of their footsteps, almost relaxing, until they didn't seem right. There was a bit of an echo, noises that didn't quite fit with anyone's footsteps. Cali stopped and turned.

Movement. Too many trees and branches and bushes and leaves for a good look, but a knot formed in the center of Cali's stomach. Then she saw it. Through the mass of foliage—a bear's head.

"He's still alive! Run!"

Linda and Dakota took one glance behind them. Dakota screamed, then sprinted ahead. Cali ran behind her while Linda angled her course to close the distance between them.

The downward slope helped with their pace, Cali running faster than she thought possible. When the slope of the land started to flatten, where two patches of bushes angled toward each other, Dakota caught her foot and stumbled. Cali prepared to pick her up off the ground after she fell. But Dakota didn't fall.

She flew backward.

What the fuck?

A thick branch slammed into Dakota. No, it was a log. A log tied to a rope. That bastard had set traps!

Cali ran toward Dakota, but Linda intercepted her. Hand over her mouth, Linda pulled Cali into the thick brush. She struggled, and Linda whispered, "Make too much noise and we're all dead."

Linda was right. Bear Head would be here soon enough. They had two bullets left, but she had already put four in him, including two in his eye. How was he still moving?

Dakota lay in front of the bushes where Cali and Linda hid. Limp. Broken. She blinked and coughed—a splash of red painted the leaves in front of her. Cali's eyes welled with tears. Her best friend was in pain with a monster coming for her. Dakota coughed again. She glanced toward Cali and Linda. She wheezed, trying to breathe, trying to talk. With a yelp, Dakota turned to look at the other set of bushes, and reached out for them.

The ground vibrated as Bear Head stomped into the area. He looked down at Dakota, then to the bushes she was reaching for. Faster than what seemed possible for a man his size, he ran to the bushes and crashed through them. Looking around, he swiped at them, hunting for something that wasn't there. He growled—a disgusting gurgle that would forever haunt Cali—then gave up.

He dropped to his hands and knees. Sniffing like an animal, he crawled closer to Dakota. Her body shook as she cried. One final snort before he grabbed a fist full of Dakota's hair and dragged her away.

July 15th, 2000. 6:32 PM

Zebadiah shook his head and growled, frustrated. He'd had three worshipers, but now he only had one to take back to the barn. How did girls escape his chains? They were girls, after all!

After collecting them in his house, he brought them to his barn. He had found plenty of chain in the trash piles, more than enough to wrap around their wrists and ankles. Plenty to hold girls. But then... Then his god-stick didn't work.

He wanted to play wedding games with the shiny blonde girl and play with her devil horns. They were so round and big! First, he made the girls naked and strung them up, as they should be. He was ready, but his godstick wasn't.

Why? Why wasn't it working? It had always worked before! But that was *years* ago. He never used it in prison, even during lights out. Too many men around. He wasn't comfortable using it by himself around other men, and he *never* wanted to give them the wrong ideas. They used theirs on him again and again, and he never wanted them to think he liked it, because he *didn't*!

When was the last time it worked? The police woman. She had kicked it. Maybe he should have let the shiny blonde kick it? He was too panicked to think of that. The thought of never being able to use his godstick again frightened him—so he punched it. Again, and again, with meaner and meaner punches. It had worked! But that other blonde girl ruined it. The clever one who tricked him into falling out of his own window.

Somehow, she got her ankle chains around his neck. Yes, he remembered now. She caught him off balance and yanked, even got herself off the hook.

The fall had surprised him, because he didn't know a girl could be strong enough to knock him down, and by the time he got to his feet, she had

176

a gun. Two shots to his chest did nothing anymore. But two to the eye? His world went black. Only for a few minutes.

When he woke, the girls weren't in the barn, but he could hear them talking and walking into the woods. He wondered how he could see at all—the clever blonde shot him in his eye. Maybe his eye grew back? Yes, that had to be why he could still see.

Zebadiah had put on his overalls and boots and chased after the girls. Prison gave him unusual feelings about being naked. He liked to be naked for wedding games, but not any other time. He didn't like being naked in prison. That usually led to other prisoners playing wedding games with him.

He followed the girls through the forest as quietly as possible, trying not to make any noise. He doubted they'd hear him anyway as much as they talked. Girls talked so much. Then they argued. Then they stopped talking, and that was when the clever one heard him. He wasn't sure if he wanted to play wedding games with her anymore. He wanted to kill her.

She wasn't clever enough to notice a trap, though, until it caught her shiny blonde friend. His trap worked perfectly, but he wished it had caught the clever one, because the shiny blonde looked in bad sorts. Just lying there. A weird feeling wriggled through him that he couldn't figure out. He was proud of how good his trap was, certain Papa would have been proud of him too, but disappointed that it worked too good and might have killed her. Wait. She coughed! And she reached out to the set of bushes closest to her like she wanted them. The other two girls must be hidden in the bushes.

But they weren't there.

Frustrated, Zebadiah gave up his search and trudged out of the bushes. The shiny blonde looked dead; the bottom half of her face covered in blood. He dropped to his hands and knees to investigate. He'd still play wedding games with her, but he preferred her to be alive. Warm was better than cold. He inhaled deeply, breathing in her essence. The smell of her sweat. Her blood. Who she was. He breathed her in, and he owned her now. He grabbed her by the hair and dragged her away.

When he reached the top of the hill, he paused to make sure she was still alive. Eyes half shut; her blinks were slow. Every time she coughed her whole body shook. He needed to get her to the barn faster, so he slung her over his shoulder and picked up his pace. But the faster he walked, the louder she moaned and the more she coughed. He had worked too hard and waited too long for wedding games. He needed this, but she might not be warm if he rushed to his barn. He could drop her on the ground and play wedding games with on the dirt and dead leaves, like the bear he was. No. He was a god, and gods got what they wanted. He wanted wedding games in *his* barn, like the way he played those games before prison. He'd just have to walk slower.

This gave him time to look around for more places to set traps. He needed to think of something other than wedding games. It'd be too uncomfortable to walk around with a hard godstick. He saw another alleyway of trees a few hundred feet to the west, a natural way a person would run if…

A noise.

Zebadiah whipped around, causing the shiny blonde to moan and cough up more blood. Something was behind him. He squinted, and scrutinized every inch of the forest, every tree, rock, bush. Nothing. Closing his eyes, he inhaled, but only smelled the shiny blonde. He knew what he had heard, though.

The shiny blonde moaned again. Zebadiah didn't have time for paranoia. He continued toward his barn, slower than he would have liked while looking over his shoulder every few steps. Papa always said girls were trouble.

July 15th, 2000. 4:15 PM

Ptolemy sat at a desk in The Empress's workshop. He had two laptops in front of him. One displayed Forward Technologies' financial statements and the other had employee personnel files.

"This makes no sense," Ptolemy mumbled. He had spent two hours looking at years of Forward Technologies' employment data searching for a known name. The first pass yielded nothing, so he used other resources to dig deeper on most of the employees. He wanted to see if they were using their birth names. Dozens of women changing to married names or back to their maiden names, an immigrant who wanted a more American sounding name, and one person with the last name "Dick" who must have gotten tired of the jokes and changed his name to "Smith." No one sounded familiar. The lone suspicious person in the entire directory was the President and CEO, Roger Templeton, and that was because he had the same last name as the drug brothers. Ptolemy had searched for any connection, but couldn't find any. Other than that, Roger was clean. The more Ptolemy researched Roger Templeton, the less he found. He didn't seem to be particularly good at his job, though, with Forward Technologies perpetually teetering on the brink of collapse. "This company barely makes any money."

"I'm not surprised," Empress said. She also sat in front of two opened laptops of her own. "Their security software and consultation packages are nothing exciting, barely above industry standard."

"And their contracts are small, private companies. One publicly traded company; no government contracts."

"The toys they're working on are so advanced that they have no practical applications other than military. Hologram technologies. Advanced robotics. I mean, look at this one. They're working on a single user ultra-all-terrain vehicle. This thing is designed to climb mountains and maneuver through forests. Sure, millions of wheelchair bound people would love one of these things, but it's nowhere near cost effective enough to think of commercial possibilities and every model seems to be designed to house weaponry."

"Investing this kind of time and money into these types of things usually indicates military contracts."

"It's almost like this Roger Templeton guy is making all this shit for the fuck of it. Of course, if I had tens of millions in legal, disposable dollars, I'd have fun experimenting with the crazy ideas bouncing around in my head."

Ptolemy laughed. "Earlier today you asked me to shoot you in the face to test your newest toy."

"Exactly. If I had tens of millions in legal, disposable dollars I would have put that newest toy on an *assistant's* head and asked you to shoot him or her in the face. Since my dollars are illegal and not disposable, I have to risk my own face."

"The trials and tribulations of being a small business owner."

"So, if they're not selling these toys, then how are they staying afloat?"

"I'm glad you asked, Empress. It appears there is another company, Albathia Pharmaceuticals, also owned by Roger Templeton. This company is putting the tens of millions into the bank accounts of Forward Technologies."

"Yeah? What the hell is Forward Technologies selling to Albathia Pharmaceuticals?"

"Nothing. Since they're both owned by Templeton, the money is coming in as inter-company transfers."

Empress and Ptolemy faced each other. She sniffed the air between them and said, "Smell that? I smell shenanigans."

Ptolemy laughed again. "Not only that, but there is also literally nothing else about Albathia Pharmaceuticals. No website, no information anywhere. Just an address and phone number listed on legal documents. Their financials are in here as well and they're even more cryptic than Forward Technologies'. Income from names I can't find via the internet and only one expense... Legal fees."

"Oh, damn. I think we left the realm of shenanigans and found ourselves some tomfoolery."

"I couldn't agree more."

"So, what's your next move?"

Ptolemy stood and stretched away aches earned from two hours' worth of sitting in the same position. "I'm going to pay Albathia Pharmaceuticals a visit."

"Now?"

"Believe it or not, it's downtown. I have a dinner tonight, so I was going to head home and get ready. Paying them a visit won't take me too far out of my way."

"Sounds like you've got a plan. Do you need any help?"

"I should be... Actually, do you happen to have any disguises?"

*

Ptolemy had hoped his recent visit to Forward Technologies would have been the last of his improv for today, but alas, he needed to learn about a company that funded a company that gave proprietary and secret technology to a trio of assassins who had tried to kill him. He needed more information, and he needed it now. There were few ways to make himself invisible while walking into an office building. "Deliveryman" was not one of Ptolemy's favorites. It was inelegant. However, it was practical, and it worked. No one glanced at him in a hat and windbreaker adorned with the logo of a major delivery company. The sunglasses were his, but the fake mustache was another gift from the Empress.

The small, four story building was in a section of town that gentrification might turn to next if it had nowhere better to go within the next decade. The offices in the building were like training wheels. If a company thought it was stable enough to move out of the owner's garage and hire a few more employees, then this was the building for them. Four suites per floor, each suite was large enough for an open area, a couple of offices, and a conference room. Except for the third floor, where Albathia Pharmaceuticals called home.

Only two suites on this floor, one on either side of the hallway and no name on either door. Ptolemy entered the one with light spilling out from underneath its closed door.

Ptolemy plopped the empty box on the front desk and said, "Delivery for Roger Templeton."

The receptionist jerked up from the magazine he was reading and scowled at Ptolemy. "Receptionist" wasn't quite the word Ptolemy would use for this beast. Even seated it was easy to tell that the guy was over six feet tall. Head shaped like a bullet; the crooked nose let Ptolemy know that other people's fists had sculpted his face. He wore a black turtleneck with sleeves covering rounded muscles like a coat of paint. This was going to be easier than he originally imagined.

The receptionist leaned forward and said, "You got the wrong place, so why don't you head on out of here."

"This is Albathia Pharmaceuticals? This is the right place. This package is for Roger Templeton."

"No one here by that name."

This man was a hired goon, probably instructed to let incoming calls go directly to voicemail. The good news—Ptolemy now knew what protocol to use on this guy. "Sure, there is. I know he's in the back, so go get him. He personally needs to sign for this."

"I said there is no one here by that name."

"Dude, you don't have to be a fucking dick about this."

The receptionist's knuckles cracked as his fingers curled into fists. Through gritted teeth, he said, "Look, I get that you're just trying to do your job, but trust me, you're not doing it right."

"Interesting. That's the *exact* same thing I said to your mom last night after I slipped her a five for a blowie."

That was all it took. Ptolemy jumped back, barely escaping the man's reach. Out the door and down the hall. The receptionist followed, spewing red-faced profanities while Ptolemy ran at half speed to make sure the guy was the perfect distance behind him. Ptolemy burst through the stairwell door.

He ran down one flight of stairs and opened the door to the second floor. Instead of going through, he continued down the stairs to the next landing. He readied himself, listening. Ha! His bait and switch ploy worked. The receptionist ran through the door to the second floor. Once Ptolemy heard him stomp down the hall, he hurried back up to the third floor.

Let's see what we have going on in here, Ptolemy thought as he entered the offices of Albathia Pharmaceuticals.

Nothing.

The door behind the receptionist opened into empty space. No people. Nothing in the offices or conference room. No file cabinets or desks. Not even a scrap of paper or trashcan to put it in. Nothing.

Clearly this was a fake company, possibly for money laundering purposes. How did it connect with the trio of assassins from yesterday? Did it have *anything* to do with Roger Templeton, whoever he was? And what about the other assassins? Did this have anything to do with his hit on Maddox at the barn?

Ptolemy rarely lost his temper, but he found himself in the middle of a perpetually vexing puzzle. He was getting angry. Angry enough to drop the receptionist with a single punch when he came running around the corner.

"Sorry about that," he mumbled to the unconscious man. But it had helped alleviate his rile., now more composed as he exited the offices of Albathia Pharmaceuticals. He had to go home to get ready for dinner tonight, and he looked forward to removing the mustache, because the glue had started to itch something fierce.

July 15ᵗʰ, 2000. 7:08 PM

Cali remained hidden in the bushes with her knees to her chest. A tremor started in her right hand. The shaking wouldn't stop, and her left hand joined in. She let go of her shins and shook her hands. She curled her fingers and squeezed. And then pounded on the ground.

Cali hated this idea, but Linda had told her to stay hidden while she followed Bear Head to make sure they knew where he was going. She wanted to join Linda, wanted to plan her revenge, wanted to run away, wanted to burn the whole forest down. Anything other than sit alone with her thoughts.

Cali pounded the ground again as memories of Dakota flowed through her mind, a raging river of ups and downs, smiles, and frowns. Laughter. Crying. Struggles with school, trouble with men. Vacations and adventures. The bathroom of Dakota's parents' house on her eighteenth birthday. Her father was an agent for her actress mother, and she had to film on location. Dakota had an opportunity to join her parents, but the location was a small town somewhere in a Southwestern state, one that brought forth an eye roll from Dakota anytime the name was mentioned, a town Cali couldn't conjure. After drinking too much, as she did *every* time she drank, Dakota needed someone to keep her hair from falling into the toilet bowl. Cali had held Dakota's ponytail more than any hair tie. After the standard process of puking and then professing how amazing Cali was for being such a great friend, Dakota went off script. Usually she rinsed with mouthwash, fixed her hair, and then rejoined the party. Instead, she took a moment to thank Cali, let her know that she was her only true friend and wanted to express that by…

"Let's become blood sisters," Dakota slurred.

"What?" Cali asked.

"Blood sisters. You know. I cut my hand, you cut yours, and then we shake hands. Our bloods mingles and we're connected for lifes. By bloods."

"Sweety, that's the kinda shit boys did in frats back in the 1950s."

"But it will keep us together forever. It will—" She hiccupped. "It will innerwine our future destnees to our futures together."

"I'm pretty sure our futures are tied together without needing to do this, Sweety."

Eyes blinking unevenly, Dakota looked at Cali. Streams of tears rolled over her baby doll cheeks. Her rose petal lips quivered as she said, "Please. I don't want to be alone in the futures. Everyone leaves, and there's no one, Cali. There's Melody, but she's more your friend than mine. My parents don't... They don't want me, and girls only want me to get the attention of boys and boys just want my tits and twat. You, only you, Cali, want me as me, not for boys or tits or twat. Please. If you'll never leave me, then do this for me."

It took way more effort than expected or necessary, considering they substituted a safety pin found in a drawer for the traditional macho knife. Cali pricked her finger and then gave the pin to Dakota who winced every time she touched the pin to her fingertip. Frustrated and scared, she gave the pin to Cali and asked her to do it. The original hole in Cali's finger had stopped bleeding, so she made a new one, then used her armpit to secure Dakota's arm. Despite the effort, Dakota squealed and squirmed, and twisted away every time the pin pierced her flesh. Cali accidentally pierced her own finger for a third time. As soon as Dakota's newly made wound bled, they touched fingers, Cali's flowing streams to Dakota's gnat-sized droplet, and then hugged.

"Please don't leave me," Dakota sobbed.

"I won't."

But she had. She let Dakota be dragged away by a monster. She left her blood sister to die.

Cali brought her shaking fists, scuffed, and bloodied, to her face and ground them against her tearing eyes to rub away the images of her lost friend. This couldn't be happening. This wasn't real. There was no such thing as a man wearing a bear's head. She'd open her eyes and return to reality.

Only reality didn't change. Dakota's blood still stained the leaves.

Linda told Cali to stay while she grabbed the gun and followed Bear Head. She said it was safer that way. How could anyone be safe with that creature around? How was that creature still alive? Cali had shot him. She had shot him, hadn't she? Maybe she only *thought* she shot him in the eye. It was an extreme situation. Perception was distorted. Time. Sensory. All of it *seemed* like she shot him in the eye, but more like the bullets grazed his skull, enough to drop him for a few minutes.

No.

Cali shook her head. That wasn't what had happened. She had shot him twice in the chest and twice in the eye. Sensory distortion caused by panic be damned. She knew what she did.

That man—that thing—wasn't human. He had them strung up in a barn. And tried to rape them. And survived getting shot. And chased them. And took Dakota… And… And…

And the tone of a cellphone ringing. It was her phone against her ear. Without thinking, without even knowing, she had dialed a number. Who did she call?

"Hi, precious. What's up?"

Cali's breath hitched. Her voice sounded tiny in her own ear, impossibly young. "Daddy?"

"Cali? Are you crying? What did Tanner do? Did he make you cry?"

"He's dead."

"What did you say?"

"He's dead. Tanner's dead. So are Jordon and Hook and they were slaughtered by this… This… *Thing*… This thing… This psycho has their bodies in a room in a house and he took us to a drug lab barn and strung us up and tried to rape us and… Oh, God!"

Silence.

Cali thought her battery had finally died until her father asked, "What did this psycho look like?"

"He's huge. He's really fucking huge. And… You're not going to believe me, but… I swear to you, he's wearing a bear's head."

"Impossible. I killed him and burned the barn down. I know I did."

Cali suddenly became aware of the early evening chill, a cool wind blowing over her, through her, icing her soul. "Wha… What did you say?"

"Cali, listen to me. I know where you are. I'll be there in less than an hour. Find a safe place to hide and do not move. I'm coming, precious. I love you. I'll get—"

"Dad? Daddy? What do you mean you know where I am? Daddy?"

The face of her phone was blank. The battery died.

What.

The.

Fuck?

Cali sat like another stone formation in the forest with her dead phone in her hand. White noise consumed her mind, framing her father's words, "I know where you are." She hadn't noticed that Linda had returned until she knelt in front of Cali.

"Cali? Are you okay?" Linda asked as she grabbed her by the shoulders and shook. The phone fell out of Cali's hand, and Linda snatched it from the ground. "You used the phone? Who did you call?"

"My dad," Cali whispered.

"Okay, I'll call my—"

"Phone's dead."

"Fuck. Okay, we have to go back to our original plan—get back to the lake house so I can call this in."

The plan. The original plan. It wasn't the original plan because an integral piece was missing. Cali snapped out of her stupor. "What about Dakota? We have to get Dakota."

Linda rubbed her hand over the lower half of her face as she looked away. Tears formed in her eyes. "She's dead."

"What? No. She can't be. She *can't* be." Cali had enough of death today. Everyone was dying except for the one thing that should have. Cali wanted to scream, to run, to hit, to collapse and curl into a ball, to cry, to sink deep into the earth and let darkness consume her. She jumped to her feet and looked in the direction of the barn. "We have to get her."

Linda stood. "Cali, I know you're upset, but I can't let you do that."

Cali knew Linda's words came from a place of logic, so she tried to keep from spewing her anger on her like a lava flow, but she couldn't hide her emotions. "You can't *let me*?" she snapped.

Waving her hands as if to erase her last words, Linda said, "Okay, that came out wrong, but going back into the barn would be suicide. We have to go back to the lake house. I'll call this in, and my people will take care of that son of a bitch. I promise, but we have to go back to the lake house."

Cali scowled and looked up the hill, toward the direction of the barn. "We can't leave this area. He's on his way."

"Who?"

"My father."

"What's he going to do?"

Cali clenched her fists. "I don't know! I don't fucking know!"

"What did he say?"

"He said… He said that… Jesus, this can't be right… He said *he killed* Bear Head and burned the barn down."

"Whoa."

"I can't… I can't wrap my head around that. I don't know what that means or why he said that. He told me he knows where I am, and I need to find a place to hide until he arrives."

It was Linda's turn to run her hands through her hair and look around. "Fuck. Did he say how long it'd take him?"

"Less than an hour. Then the phone died. I didn't get a chance to tell him where the lake house was or any details. I need to be close when he arrives. You can go back to the lake house."

Linda took Cali's hands and squeezed. "I am not leaving you here by yourself. We just need to lay low for an hour."

"No." Cali looked behind Linda at the log suspended by ropes. "I have a plan."

July 15th, 2000. 6:20 PM

Ptolemy was the second to arrive at the restaurant. He could have been earlier, but he needed a few moments to contact Broker and send the files he had on Forward Technologies and Albathia Pharmaceuticals. He needed a second set of eyes.

Kamu Dangan was the first to arrive; he was always the first. A few years ago, Ptolemy showed up to the predetermined restaurant a full hour early, but Kamu was already there, sitting by himself at a table for four while enjoying a Sake and reading a book. Ptolemy had since given up trying to beat Kamu to dinner, only ten minutes early tonight. Same Sake, different book.

After ordering a Beaujolais from the maître d', Ptolemy took a seat. "Good evening, Kamu."

"Ptolemy." Kamu closed his book—a retrospective of early twentieth-century American architecture—and set it aside to give his full attention to Ptolemy. At least it appeared that he had Kamu's full attention, but Ptolemy knew better. Sixteen patrons in the restaurant occupied six tables, and Kamu knew the specifics on all of them. Ptolemy could make educated guesses about which tables hosted business meetings and which tables served as setting for dates. One of the business meetings and two of the dates were illicit, this much was apparent to Ptolemy. He relied on his ability to make logical deductions given the limited information—hand gestures, facial expressions, body language. Kamu's abilities far surpassed Ptolemy's. When Kamu looked at someone it was as if he knew what they were made of, right down to the molecules. Which made him a perfect assassin.

As a member of the Shinigami's Helper clan from Japan, Kamu was the best of the best. Ptolemy's targets altered the fates of a handful of people. Shinigami's Helper altered the fates of entire countries. And Kamu was their

189

best. Had there been a fly in the vicinity, he could have removed both wings and all six legs, midflight.

Ptolemy took a sip from his wine. "I can't tell if the year between these dinners is getting shorter or longer."

"Time is funny like that," Kamu said, voice smooth and even, a voice most people found uniquely pleasant. "It bends, yet remains rigid. The bend is our perception of how fast it moves. The rigidity is that we each grew a year older, no matter how we perceived it."

Ptolemy held his glass in salute and said, "You are absolutely correct. My mind can't tell if it's been a year or not, but my joints sure can."

Kamu chuckled. "You've been active enough to work your joints?"

"Yes. That, and someone is trying to kill me."

A grumbling voice from behind Ptolemy said, "Considering what you do for a living, I always assumed that was a daily chore you had to deal with."

Mako. Behind him his twin sister, Meg. They were the world's largest siblings, in Ptolemy's mind. Mako was six foot nine, 310 pounds with a body fat percentage under five. Mako shared this information often, never once being asked to give it. Meg was six-five, two-thirty or so, as she would put it. This information was never high on her priority list. Mako's bald pate gleamed from the lights above; Meg's shoulder-length blonde hair shimmered. Again, the pride in personal choice of hairstyle meant more to him than her. "I don't want anything distracting from my pretty face," Mako once said. Their faces had enough similarities for a reasonable person to assume they were twins. Both had hard features, and her nose was smaller only because Mako's had been broken so many times.

Everyone in the group exchanged handshakes and smiles. While perusing the menu, Meg asked, "Is someone really trying to kill you?"

"Nine someones so far. The ones that stand out, though, were a trio of professionals who came after me in my house yesterday. Of course, they were new style kids who were all flash, so they had no guns."

"Your house?" Mako asked, incensed. "That's pretty fucking personal. Do you think your broker turned on you?"

Ptolemy waited to answer until after they gave their orders to the waiter. "No. There is absolutely no evidence of that. I haven't failed a mission, so it can't be a disgruntled client. I'm assuming it's someone tied to a past target. Whoever it is keeps hiring these new, inexperienced kids."

"Maybe an old rival trying to whittle down the competition by using the competition?" Kamu suggested. "It'd be a win-win for them. If you succeed, then there are fewer players on the field. If you fail, then your rival has removed their biggest threat."

"Interesting. I don't think that's the case, but I'll certainly do some digging later."

Kamu nodded.

"You said the three that attacked you yesterday had no guns?" Meg asked.

Ptolemy hmphed. "They thought their hand-to-hand skills were greater than they were. Although they had a couple of drones. Small, four-bladed remote-control helicopters."

"Drones. That's impressive. Mako and I have played with a few. We strapped some guns to them, and they became a lot of fun."

"No guns on these, but the trio used them to create a hologram."

"Whoa," the siblings said in unison.

"Nothing out of a sci-fi movie, just a crude image of a deer to distract me."

"That's still a hell of a gadget," Meg said.

"They were made by a company called Forward Technologies. You two ever hear of them?"

"Heard of them? Yes. Know anything about them? No. They've never contacted us, and we've never tried to contact them. Rumor has it the owner is an eccentric recluse."

"Eccentric recluse," Ptolemy repeated, trying to fit that piece of information into the puzzle with no image.

"Man, you know who would have been all over that?" Mako asked, then answered his own question. "Hawke. He loved gadgets and toys."

"So do you and Meg," Kamu laughed. "When we talked yesterday you were going on and on about the new gloves you two are testing."

Mako's face went from lined granite to mountainside crags when he frowned. "Don't say it like that. I don't want Ptolemy thinking Meg and I are the ones trying to kill him."

Ptolemy wouldn't believe the twins were trying to kill him. He trusted them. They no longer killed for money, not directly at least. "Consulting" was what they called it. They occasionally trained new recruits for international security firms—a euphemism for mercenary organizations pretending to be legit companies by paying taxes on their kill contracts. Sometimes they were contracted to test a company's security system, maybe even lead a team of bodyguards to protect high-ranking company executives and government officials. They loved the bodyguard jobs because there were never any issues. "People think they are more important than they really are," Mako would say. "Ego is the biggest line-item expense on a company's income statement," was Meg's explanation. She took care of the books for their business. The twins enjoyed what they did, but the jobs they loved most were product testing.

"I don't think it's you two who are trying to kill me." Ptolemy took another sip of his wine. "So, tell me about the gloves."

Mako had a face like burled wood on an old tree, until he got excited about the latest and greatest weapons technologies, then he became cherubic with glee. "They're amazing. Meg and I each got a pair. They're in the Hummer, with a lot of other cool shit. We can show them to you after dinner."

"Nice. What do these gloves do?"

"Gun gloves!" Mako lost containment of his exuberance and said it loud enough for a few patrons to glance over their shoulders.

Ptolemy wanted to laugh, but was afraid of how Mako would react, so he stifled it to a chuckle. "Gun gloves? I have to be honest, Mako, that sounds…"

"Really fucking stupid. I know!" Mako's smile grew with every word. "They're completely impractical and it's doubtful they'll ever move past the prototype, but they're so fucking fun."

"So… They're gloves that shoot bullets?"

"Yep! Three barrels over the knuckles of each hand and they hold a fifteen-round clip. Rigid tops so you can't bend your wrist upward past a certain point. They're ten pounds each, so if you run out of bullets you can *really* beat the holy fuck out of someone. Oh, I *love* hitting things with those gloves."

Now Ptolemy laughed. "Sounds like the absolute last things someone should have given you. Meg, do you have gun gloves in the Hummer as well?"

It was her turn to beam. Her smile softened her face but added a touch of crazy to her blazing eyes. "Better! I have electro-gloves."

Ptolemy couldn't believe what he was hearing. The usually stoic Kamu looked just as shocked. "You… You *can't* be serious."

"As serious as a defibrillator hooked to a nuclear power plant. Which is kinda what my gloves are like."

Ptolemy had a million questions and was terrified to voice any of them. Luckily, dinner arrived.

As was their tradition, they ate in silence, out of respect for the reason there were there—to remember the two team members who couldn't join them. The anniversary of their last assignment as a team. The anniversary of Ptolemy becoming a widower. God, he missed Athena.

Insurgency was a common concept in the Middle East, the powerless trying to stand against the powerful while the powerful wanted to gain more power. The United States had always been in the middle of it, yet somehow simultaneously on the edge of it. The governors of a few provinces in Afghanistan talked in secret about peaceful unity, and those whispers made it to the right ears of the American government. The Afghani governor who opened the peace idea sent his son to talk to the neighboring provinces. One liked what the ambassador of peace had to say, then a second and a third. The fourth—an old school warlord—did not agree with what the son suggested. The warlord's vision of the future was a mirror of the past. The son went from emissary to hunted within a few words. His father contacted the United States. After a few choruses of the "Our hands are tied," song and dance, they designated a pickup point outside the town where he was last seen, but bureaucracy wouldn't allow them across the border. The assignment came with a big fat check for Ptolemy and his crew—get the young man from a mosque that was sympathetic to his ideals outside of town to where American transportation awaited.

Athena and Hawke were the hands-on team. They walked to the mosque and collected the governor's son. The young man wore a perahan tunban, simple white linens adorned with a gray vest, and a lungee turban, the loose end sweeping to the front over his shoulder to obscure his face. Hawke's perahan tunban was almost identical, but he wore a kufi on his head to keep his vision from being obscured. Athena wore a white Burqa-chadri—a full-body covering with a face piece. A casual glance and they looked like most of the people milling along the streets. Athena and Hawke set the pace, a leisurely stroll on a sunny day. Blend into the ordinary.

The rest of the crew acted like a boat guiding its passengers down a river. Mako was the bow, fifty yards in front, cutting through the current for a smooth ride, while Kamu was the stern, ready to rev the engine should they need it. Meg was starboard and Ptolemy was port, both moving along the rooftops with their HK M4 carbines. Not the ideal weapon for the circumstance, but moving quickly from building to building with any kind of sniper rifle would be too cumbersome. The rooftops were only two stories off the ground, so Meg and Ptolemy weren't sacrificing accuracy should they need to use their weapons. Or if they *could* use their weapons.

The operation went like silk… Until it turned into broken brick. Mako kept his eyes up and interacted with no one, whispering into everyone's comm units about what to expect. Kamu made sure nothing suspicious was happening behind the package, so Athena and Hawke could keep moving forward without the need to turn around. Moving from one roof to another was easy for both Ptolemy and Meg. The end was in sight, the American jeep with a driver and the engine running right where it should be.

Ptolemy recalled everything, a perfect snapshot in his emotional scrapbook. The smell of the stone he leaned against. The beads of sweat rolling from his hairline, down his forehead and riding the edge of his nose. The dryness of his lips as he licked them, suddenly thirsty for a swig of water. A voice rising above the crowd noise, the music, the barking dogs. "Bomb!"

Weapons up. All four points of the boat had their guns trained on the bomber.

A child no more than seven years old with an obscene amount of C4 strapped to a custom-sized vest.

Four barrels pointed at the bomber. No one squeezed their trigger.

Athena and Hawke grabbed the governor's son by the arms and ran into the closest building. The child, wailing, tears flowing down his face, followed. The building disappeared in a cough of fire and an exhale of billowing smoke. The American jeep sped away.

The four-boat points had no time to register what had happened. By drawing their guns, they made themselves easy targets for the bullets whizzing through the air. They escaped and regrouped; they were trained professionals. The men shooting at them were simple thugs who believed in the extremist ideals of their governor, née warlord. This particular insurgency toppled faster than a house of cards in a tornado.

Guilt was the impetus to disband. Ptolemy often wondered if he could have pulled the trigger knowing what he knew now. He assumed the others were thinking the same thing from the sullenness over the table.

The boy was destined to die, on the street or in the building. A simple trigger squeeze and the number of dead might have been single digits, and the building would have been a shelter instead of a grave. Thirty-one people dead. Kamu returned to Japan. Mako and Meg turned to consulting. Ptolemy turned into a single father. Still, they met every year.

Mako raised a glass after everyone finished their meals. The others followed. "To Athena and Hawke."

They declined dessert and finished their drinks in silence.

"There is one thing to consider when gathering the names of who might be after you," Mako said, setting his empty glass on the table.

"No," Ptolemy said, hoping to stop Mako's conspiracy theory before it began. No such luck.

"They never recovered his body."

"They never recovered anyone's body from that explosion. If the incendiary device didn't turn those thirty-one people into hamburger, then the falling building turned them to paste."

Mako shrugged. "If anyone could have gotten out of that, it'd be him."

"Hawke is not alive. Neither is—" Ptolemy couldn't say her name aloud, a superstitious fear that if her name ever left his mouth, it would take memories of her with it. "Why would he be trying to kill me? Why wait so long?"

"He's pissed that we left him there. And you know Hawke. He's a planner, a master of the long game."

"We had to leave because we were getting shot at. It'd be one hell of a long game."

"True. But think about it. Your broker contacts you. You know nothing about him, but he knows everything about you."

Ptolemy had never thought of that possibility. He always thought Broker was a woman. He trusted Broker with more than his life. Too much trust to a person he had never met. No—he believed he knew who Broker was and it wasn't Hawke. If Broker wanted him dead, he'd be dead. He was still sorting through his thoughts when his cellphone buzzed.

Normally he wouldn't answer his phone in the company of others, but this call was a surprise. Cali.

As he spoke with her, his heart sped up. She was crying. It was rare for her to cry. At first, he assumed that douchebag Tanner did something douchey. His heart almost seized when Cali said Tanner was murdered by a man wearing a bear's head.

Her line went dead.

The other three at the table stared at him with wide-eyed confusion. Even though Mako was pushing his buttons with bullshit theories, they were family. He didn't need to ask if they were willing to help. He threw cash on the table, stood, and said, "We have to go."

July 15th, 2000. 8:01 PM

In front of Cali was the last twenty feet of forest. After that, a hundred feet to the barn. She knew what she'd find, but she couldn't focus on that. She needed to concentrate on getting that thing out of there.

"Are you ready?" Linda asked.

Cali didn't know how to answer. Her rage and sense of vengeance were ready, but the logical and sensible side of her brain wasn't so sure. Linda was trained for this—not necessarily for a bear-head wearing beast, but for dangerous situations. Cali showed herself that she could handle dangerous situations, too. This plan was going to work, even if by sheer force of will. Before Linda had to ask again, Cali nodded her head.

Linda stepped in front of her. It was as if Cali awoke from a nightmare. Linda's eyes, soulful and eternal, the most comforting sight in the world. She grabbed Cali's trembling hands and said, "I am very sorry for lying to you this weekend, but what happened between us is real. I absolutely love you, and after this is all over, we'll mourn together and cry together and smoke pot and get drunk until we puke. I'm here for you, okay? Now and after this is over."

Cali's hands stopped shaking. There was a lot to unpack with Linda. Cali didn't know who she was or what was happening between them, but Linda said she'd be there when Cali was ready to figure that out. Linda gave Cali a hug and Cali squeezed with every ounce of emotion to absorb all the strength she could. After spending time in a drug-making barn and running through a forest, Linda no longer smelled like an angel, that perfect blend of vanilla and cinnamon. Fear and stale sweat now, but that didn't matter. "I got this."

"I know you do." Linda gave Cali's hands one last squeeze, then made her way through the forest to approach the barn from the back.

This was it. Cali took a deep breath through her nose, and tightened Linda's stupid fanny pack around her waist. She exited the forest and ran to the barn's entrance.

Bear Head's back was to her, his overalls a crumpled pile around his ankles. Dakota was hanging from the ceiling again; the chains rhythmically rattled. Death was a blessing. *Focus,* she told herself. *Don't look at anything else.* "Hey! Asshole!"

The chain rattling stopped. Bear Head looked over his shoulder, turning enough for Cali to see blonde hair.

Don't look! Don't fucking look or the plan goes to shit! Cali extended both middle fingers and backed away. "You still don't have me, you piece of shit, and you never will!"

He growled and reached down for his overalls.

Cali ran back the same way she came, a fast jog at first to make sure she didn't lose him. A quick glance over her shoulder. He was out of the barn and past the cars already. *Fuck, he's fast!* Cali broke into an all out sprint.

Trees blurred past. Cali focused on what was in front of her, ignoring the stings from stray twigs lashing her arms and legs and cheeks. Snapping branches and footfalls behind her were getting louder. Running faster wasn't possible. Serpentine was her only option, but she wanted to make sure she wasn't going to swerve into his path. A glance over her shoulder. Enough to lose her balance.

Just as she turned her head, the terrain sloped downward. The ground wasn't where she thought, and she lost her footing. Fighting her instinct to sprawl out, she drew her arms to her body and twisted, landing shoulder first. A half roll, half summersault, she got a better look behind her while sliding down the hill. And screamed.

Roaring, the monster lunged, throwing his body at her. She saw gnarled fingers and glistening teeth. His humid, fetid breath hit her face. Reflex wanted her to curl into a fetal position and kick at him, but she fought against it. *Get up!* She rolled a few more times to avoid his attack. He landed flat on his chest, but his fingers found her hair. Cali yanked away, leaving behind a handful of hair. Back to her feet. *Run!*

The creature's size belied his speed, and the footfalls were behind her again, shaking the ground. Every thump might have been her heart frantically encouraging her to run faster or warning her that she was almost out of time.

Focusing on the sounds behind her—the crunching leaves beneath his feet, his gruff breathing—she tried to time her next move. *Now!*

Planting her left foot, she leapt to the right just as he reached for her again. He lost his balance and stumbled. That was all she needed to get ahead of him and lead him to the two rows of bushes she had become familiar with. He quickly regained his balance and stride, right behind her again. She prayed that he was so focused on her that he didn't recognize where they were. She had moved the trip line a few feet closer than where it had been.

The small gap between the rows of bushes was getting closer. Faster. Tears stung her eyes as he swiped at her hair. She soared over the trip line and then dropped to the ground. Air whooshed over her body as the log passed above her. He hit the trip line.

Cali relished the feeling of satisfaction from the meaty slap accompanying the log crashing into his chest. Her plan worked! She waited for the log's backswing before she jumped to her feet and ran to her fallen pursuer.

On his back, he coughed and wheezed. No blood from his mouth, no empty-eyed stare like Dakota had. No *true* punishment for his crime, but Cali would have vengeance.

Standing over him, she stared into his eyes. The head was not a mask, the fur, the teeth too real. This sick fuck was wearing the head of a real bear. And his eyes — how the fuck did he still have a left eye? His eyes were human, though, brown, and bloodshot. Angry. No pain or fear like Dakota's eyes during her last moments. Maybe pointing a gun at his head would get the look Cali so desperately sought?

She unzipped the stupid fanny pack and pulled out the gun. "Kill the fucker," had been Linda's exact words. Cali planned to do just that, and wished those eyes would change.

She'd never get a chance to see his fear. He reached up and grabbed her thigh.

199

She dropped to her knee, trapping his massive hand between her hamstring and calf, and jammed the barrel of the gun into his left eye. The shot was muffled, but effective. Black slime erupted as his head twitched. His arm went limp.

There was no mistaking her aim this time, but to be extra certain, she pressed the barrel to his right eye and sent the final bullet into his brain. She spat on him as a bonus.

She jogged back to the barn, crying the entire way, hand still buzzing from the gun's recoil.

Linda was there kneeling beside Dakota, sobbing. Cali's newest friend: one who loved her enough to take care of her oldest friend, take her out of the chains, lay her on the floor as nicely as she could, put her clothes back on. "I'm so sorry."

Cali knelt on the other side of Dakota and ran a hand over her hair. If not for the blood staining the lower half of her face, her neck, her chest, she looked exactly like a doll, her skin now even more porcelain. This wasn't right, this wasn't how she should have gone. Cali never expected Dakota to have a perfect life and hypothesized it would include an early and empty marriage to Jordon, a few ignored children, working hard to be a full-time trophy, but she should have made it well into her eighties while knocking off two decades from her age thanks to Botox and surgeries. Her looks meant a lot to her, and Cali was going to do everything she could to honor those wishes.

Her car was currently useless, but in the trunk was a survivalist's wet dream, including a set of impotent jumper cables. Those were only useful with another working car. She didn't care about those now anyway. She grabbed the blanket, the roll of paper towel, and the six pack of bottled water.

Linda was a good new friend. She sat next to Cali and without saying a word, they cleaned away Dakota's blood as the sun quietly slid behind the horizon.

July 15ᵗʰ, 2000. 8:42 PM

"The barn should be coming up," Ptolemy said as he shifted in the passenger seat and pulled his mask over his face.

"Should be?" Meg asked from the back seat. "I thought you said you were here before?"

The Humvee bounced and jostled everything inside, despite the people and the weapons being securely strapped in. Mako fought to keep it on the dirt road while trying to avoid the craters threatening to break the axels. They passed a dilapidated two-story house with large trash piles next to it. "I parked just off the main road and cut through the forest. I wasn't on this road."

"Do you know if this road takes us straight to the barn?" Mako asked.

"I don't think it does. I remember a road leading to it. It was smaller and shittier than this one. I feel like it'll be a right and it should be coming up soon. We just need to— There! Right there."

Mako hit the turn hard, wheels flinging dirt and gravel. The professional side of Ptolemy fussed about leaving too much evidence. Tire tracks. Paint flecks from the branches scratching lines into the Humvee sides. Evidence be damned. He needed to rescue his daughter.

Ptolemy steadied himself to keep his head from bouncing against the rooftop or the window. Mercifully, this wasn't a long road. It opened to the dirt-packed area he remembered.

They approached the barn from the side. Maddox's SUV was still parked in front of the barn as well as Cali's car.

It took less than a minute for the four passengers to disembark and arm themselves: Meg and Mako with their newly acquisitioned gloves, Kamu with his sword—a traditional tsurugi—and Ptolemy with his AR-15. It was loud and sloppy, but he'd worry about the consequences after his daughter was safe.

Kamu disappeared into the darkness while Ptolemy and Mako flanked Meg as she led the way. They reached the vehicles. Mako broke off to circle behind the SUV and get a direct sightline to the front of the barn. Ptolemy and Meg approached the front from a shallow angle. The Humvee cast enough light across the front of the barn to produce shadows along the entrance. And the shadows moved.

Meg switched on her gloves, blue sparks skittering along her fists. Ptolemy whipped around the edge of the entrance, gun trained on the first thing he saw.

Cali and an unknown girl with black hair were kneeling on the ground, looking in his direction, wide-eyed with surprise. A blonde, Cali's friend Dakota, lay on the ground. Ptolemy lowered his weapon and tore off his mask. "Cali."

"Daddy?" she cried, a grogginess to her voice as if she were waking up, unable to distinguish between dream and reality. Whether she trusted her own eyes or not, she got to her feet and ran to him. "Daddy!"

Ptolemy threw his strapped rifle over his shoulder, and swore bones broke from her squeeze. She sobbed uncontrollably and mumbled into his chest. "Dakota's dead. Tanner's dead. Hook and Jordon are dead."

"Ptolemy!" Mako yelled as he charged closer, leading with his fists. "I don't have visual on the hostile!"

Cali clutched Ptolemy, pinching him in a desperate grip around his waist, and screamed. The brunette jumped to her feet.

"Whoa! Mako, lower your weapons. Meg, back up. Cali, these two are with me. We have a fourth, but he's doing recon."

"These people are with you?" Cali asked, shaking.

Mako and Meg lowered their hands. Kamu emerged from the shadows.

Ptolemy pulled her away and looked into her eyes. "Yes. When you called me, you said a man wearing a bear's head was after you. Where is he?"

The brunette approached, arms crossed. "Dead," she said. "Cali killed him."

Ptolemy asked Cali, "You killed him?"

"I did," she said, wiping away tears. "I put two bullets in that fucker's eyes."

"Nice," Mako said under his breath, garnering an elbow to his ribs from his sister.

Ptolemy's heart broke for his daughter. He'd seen what that monster was capable of. Cali had endured his violence, and the loss of people close to her. Memories of her as a little girl playing with her dolls, visions of her as a smiling teenager filled his mind. All he wanted for her was happiness, not monsters. He was angry that her life had been in jeopardy, but a sweeping wave of relief washed through his chest, reminding him that she had prevailed. Not only did she take care of herself in a dire situation, but she also had the skills to end it.

Ptolemy looked the brunette up and down. "Who are you?"

She cleared her throat. "Linda Salazar, DEA agent."

"DEA?" He glared at Cali. "What the hell are you doing with a DEA agent?"

Cali shrugged.

Ptolemy cursed himself for not pushing Cali harder for names of the people who'd be joining her this week, but this was not the time for Q & A. The possibility existed that she was just one of Cali's friends, one who happened to be in that line of work... Which seemed too coincidental since they were standing next to a drug lab. He regarded Linda, then nodded toward the barn. "I assume you were investigating Maddox and his operation."

Linda uncrossed her arms and cocked her head. "You obviously know a few details about this place. Anything you'd like to share?"

Ptolemy the professional cursed Ptolemy the father for the slip up. Ptolemy the father reminded Ptolemy the professional that this was yet another reason to retire. Both agreed that the best course of action was to change the topic. He said, "Thank you for keeping Cali safe. I assume you went through just as much?" Linda nodded, then looked down at her own cuts and scrapes. Her eyes then moved to Cali. Judging how her stern expression melted into reverence, Ptolemy detected some deeper feelings for his daughter. He sighed. "I can't thank you enough for what you did."

Linda's body language changed, softened. She was no longer a DEA agent, now a friend of his daughter, and a victim. She said, "I should be thanking you for raising her the way you did. She saved my life at least twice and singlehandedly took on and killed the hostile. She's... She's fucking amazing."

"Not amazing enough," Cali mumbled. Arms wrapped around her own waist in a solitary hug, she went back to stand next to Dakota's body.

Ptolemy pointed to the Humvee and said to Linda, "We have a sat-phone in the car if you need to phone in."

Linda pointedly looked at his gun and then to each member of his crew. "Naah. I'll call in after we get this situation taken care of."

With a softer tone, he asked, "Where are the guys?"

Almost whispering, Linda answered, "Behind the barn is a field. On the other side of that is a house. That's where they are."

Ptolemy nodded. "You said Cali killed the hostile? Where's his body?"

As Linda began to give details about what had happened, she became visibly uncomfortable, often glancing at Cali. "He's farther into the woods." She pointed. "That way. When Cali and Dakota and I first escaped, we thought we'd taken care of him, thought that Cali had taken care of him. She shot him four times, but I guess that wasn't enough. He chased us right into a trap and it, um, it was how Dakota... Cali and I reset the trap and then came back to the barn. I gave Cali my gun and she led him to the trap and... She did what she had to do."

"You confirmed the kill?" Ptolemy asked, his tone more professional than he had intended.

"I put two bullets in his eyes, Dad," Cali answered. "So, yeah, kill confirmed."

"Amazing" was the word that Linda had used to describe Cali. That was an understatement. A twenty-two-year-old girl with enough poise and awareness and strength to go face-to-face with a monster. A true monster in every sense of the word, one of nightmares that was strong enough to give

Ptolemy the fight of his life. She had put two bullets in his eyes. However, he had put two dozen into his neck.

Ptolemy unclipped a flashlight from his belt and handed it to Linda. "How about you show Kamu where this took place?"

Linda nodded and glanced to Cali before she led Kamu into the forest.

Ptolemy approached the twins. "Linda said the bodies of their boyfriends are in the house across the field. How about you two investigate?"

The twins nodded at the same time and turned to leave. Ptolemy snorted. "You're not taking the gloves off?"

They glared at him as if a second head had sprouted from his shoulders. Mako reminded him, "The mission isn't over."

Ptolemy rolled his eyes. "I doubt you'll find anything more hostile than a rogue deer along the way."

"Then we'll have venison for our freezers."

"Deer can be very hostile," Meg added.

"You two desperately want to use those gloves, don't you?"

The twins looked down at the brilliant blue arcs of electricity dancing between Meg's hands. She said, "I may use these on my brother if no hostile deer cross our path."

"You wish. Plus, we are absolutely going to use them," Mako said. The twins snapped their wrists, and light beamed from the tops of their hands. Mako concluded with, "We're not going to wander through a dark field filled with rogue deer without our flashlights."

Ptolemy stifled a laugh as the twins left. Once they had gone around the side of the barn, he moved next to Cali and put an arm around her shoulders. She leaned her head against his chest. She didn't take her eyes off Dakota.

"I'm proud of you," Ptolemy said as he rested his cheek against the top of her head.

"Thank you," she whispered.

He didn't know what else to say, if he should say anything at all. This was her first true exposure to death. Real death, not the manicured versions in staged funerals that she had attended, the ones for old relatives with for-gotten names. Death was different for everyone and he let her mourn. The minutes slipped away in silence, until… "Dad?"

"Yes, Cali."

"Why do you and your friends look like you're ready to take over a small country by force."

"Well… There's a lot to explain."

"I'm listening."

He sighed while he contemplated. How was he going to explain that he was a merchant of death? How would she react when she found out that death had paid for everything in her life?

"You know I was in the military. I played chess with the Grim Reaper many times. I've walked through a mine field; had an entire building collapse near me; had thousands of bullets shot at me, but only two hit me; been in strange countries; and been chased by a rabid dog, once. It should be fairly obvious by now that I do not have a desk job. I—"

"He's not there!" came from behind them. Linda. The flashlight beam streaked across the vehicles as Linda and Kamu ran from the forest. "He's gone."

"What?" Ptolemy and Cali yelled at the same time.

"There is no body," Kamu said as he and Linda joined Ptolemy and Cali.

"Are you sure you were in the right place?" Ptolemy asked.

"Yes," Kamu replied. "The trap was a simple trip wire that released a log tied to a rope. We found the trap, but no body."

"I shot him," Cali mumbled. "I shot him six fucking times. I shot him in his fucking *head*."

Ptolemy believed his daughter's words were true. He felt her confu-sion, knowing that he, too, had shot the man multiple times. What kind of drugs were Maddox and his crew making in the barn? This went beyond the adrenaline of invincibility associated with substances like angel dust. This person wearing a bear's head was still moving strong after fatal gunshot wounds.

"Where the hell could he be?" Ptolemy asked, taking the safety off his rifle.

"The house." Meg. She was stumbling toward them using the barn's wall as support. Her left arm hung from her shoulder, bouncing against her hip as she walked while keeping her weight on her right leg. Blood dripped from her nose and chin. Weary-eyed, she repeated, "He's in the house."

July 15ᵗʰ, 2000. 8:33 PM

Darkness again. Zebadiah had been shot. Again. He opened his eyes and sat up. The sun had just gone down, but he could see the rope tied log hanging from the trees. His trap. The clever blonde girl used *his own* trap against him! Then shot him in the eyes, *again*. No more!

Back to the barn. He got to his feet, and inhaled deeply through his nose, taking in the world around him. Something struck him as peculiar, though. Smells. He inhaled again. The smells! So many confused him at first. Tree bark, dead leaves, dirt, animals—both dead and alive, and… People? Yes, people. People by his barn.

The girls were there, but he smelled death. The shiny blonde was dead. No matter, there were still the other two. But… There were more people. He needed to be clever, cleverer than girls. Instead of walking directly to the barn, he trekked deeper into the forest, and then aimed for his barn. He'd come to the barn from the side, closer to the field behind it. Then he'd…

Zebadiah stopped. The smells moved. He closed his eye and inhaled, taking in the entirety of the world. Two people moved away from the front of the barn. Two other people moved away from the back of the barn, toward his house. *His* house. Those two took priority.

He smelled the two people walking through the bitter aroma of the tall grass, their footsteps releasing earthy smells of dirt. He crept from tree to tree, and eventually came to his outhouse. Hiding behind it, he waited for the two people to exit the field. They were not what he expected.

A bald man and a girl. The girl was big, bigger than any girl he had ever seen before. The man was big, too. He was as big as Zebadiah when he got out of prison. Zebadiah was bigger than that now, maybe a head taller than the bald man and a shoulder wider.

The bald man and the big girl shared the same expression, the corners of their upper lips ready to expose teeth like wild animals, their eyebrows

208

almost touching from deep frowns. Prisoners had faces like this after they spent time lifting weights. They both wore tight black clothing and boots. And they had metal hands, lights shining from them like flashlights. Maybe they were robots? Or people mixed with robot parts? It seemed reasonable to Zebadiah since, after all, he was both a bear and a god.

The two intruders whispered to each other as they approached the side of the house. Were they going to go to the back or the front, or split up? They paused, whispered to each other, and then slipped around back.

The back door was closed, but no longer had a lock, thanks to that piece of meat who knew his name. Zebadiah could sneak along the trash piles, but that didn't seem smart. He had a good vantage point, so patience might be smarter. He'd wait for the right moment. These new people could easily enter his house. Zebadiah judged how fast he had to run to cover the distance from the outhouse, a run he made many times as a child.

The pair opened the back door, and then jumped back. They coughed and shook their heads, burying their noses inside the crooks of their elbows. The aromas from the meat room reached Zebadiah from where he stood, beckoning him, making him more than a little hungry. Hunger was good when getting ready to fight.

The intruders talked to each other. Zebadiah couldn't hear their words, but they sounded angry, and their postures had changed. They held their fists like they were ready to punch, and then blue sparks danced all around the big girl's hands. The two entered the back door.

Zebadiah started his sprint.

They didn't see him until he stormed the house. They were still fast, though.

Ready to tear into the bald man, Zebadiah roared. The man turned around and bullets tore into Zebadiah's chest. Bullets didn't stop Zebadiah. The bald man was fast enough to drop to the ground as Zebadiah lunged for him. The bald man kicked, boot soles slamming against Zebadiah's chest.

Flipping ass over head, Zebadiah smashed into the wall beside his front door. He scurried to his feet, but more bullets ripped through him. The bald man's hands—bullets came from the metal hands! No matter. He'd rip the man's arms off. But the big girl got in the way. She rushed over and punched him repeatedly, each hit coming with a jolt of electricity blasting through his skull. He swiped at her, but missed. She jumped away as the bald man lurched forward. Each of the man's punches came with more bullets. They stung, but didn't stop him, barely slowed him. He punched back.

Zebadiah had learned how to fight in prison. Those who got their enemy to the ground turned out to be the winner. He and the man exchanged blows, hits to each other's bodies, each one a powerful thump. The house vibrated, dust raining from the ceiling. The bald man grunted each time Zebadiah hit him. Zebadiah was winning, he was punching the man to the ground! Then the girl attacked.

The bald man teetered backward. That was when the girl struck from behind, pressing her electric hands against Zebadiah's back, shoulders, arms, head. Again and again and again. When her lightning zapped him, he'd freeze. The bald man joined her, punching when she let go. He recognized their pattern. Punch twice, step back, zap. Punch twice, step back, zap. The half second between the bald man's punch and the girl's attack was all Zebadiah needed. He twisted just as the man swung. His metal fist crashed into the fireplace hard enough to scatter broken bricks across the floor.

Zebadiah pushed the bald man into the big girl and then jumped out the nearest window.

He needed a weapon. Scrambling to his feet, he grabbed the first thing he saw—the ax he used to kill the meat who knew his name. He ran toward the front of his house. Since no one followed him out of the window, he expected them to come out the front. He was right.

Zebadiah slashed, but the bald man dodged the attack and kicked the ax from his hand. The bald man then tackled Zebadiah, putting his whole weight into the effort, and slammed him against the car. He pushed himself off Zebadiah and yelled, "Now!"

The girl touched the car. Zebadiah's world went jagged as sparks flowed along the frame. She let go, and the bald man launched himself with his fist pulled back. Zebadiah threw himself to the side as the bald man punched, his metal fist denting the car with a loud clang. This man was strong, and Zebadiah was getting tired. He no longer saw a man when he looked at his opponent, rather, a god like him. A god who punched with metal hands that threw bullets.

Zebadiah's arms weren't moving as fast as he wanted them to; he swung, and a metal hand swatted his fist away. Then with a mighty roar the bald god wrapped his arms around Zebadiah and lifted. Arms pinned to his sides and feet off the ground, Zebadiah screamed as metal fists ground into his back. Squeezing his fists, he flexed to break free of the man's grip. He never got a chance because the girl joined in.

Behind him. She must have been behind him since he didn't see her but felt her hands on either side of his head. His world went jagged again. Streaks of white sparkled in front of his eyes, his personal lightning storm. If he were to die, it would be by the metal hands of an angry god, a god like him. *Not* a girl, no matter how large she was.

A buzzing fire spread through his body like a swarm of bees.

He didn't know how long he had been electrified, but it stopped. Maybe she got tired, maybe she ran out of lightning—who knows. His tongue flopped around in his mouth, bouncing from tooth to tooth. Through the pain, the confusion, the hurt and panic, awareness dawned on him. He had a tongue again! His mouth was longer, his teeth sharper, too. This was no longer the face he was born with, the face he had as child and prisoner. This was the face of a bear. These were the teeth of a bear. Zebadiah was going to use them as such.

Before the girl had the chance to zap him again, Zebadiah opened his jaws wide and sank his teeth into the bald man's shoulder. This man was no god. If he were a god, he wouldn't have stopped squeezing. If he were a god, he wouldn't have let go. If he were a god, he wouldn't have tasted like a human.

The bald man released Zebadiah. He pushed himself away, minus the chunk of his shoulder in Zebadiah's mouth. Zebadiah flexed his chest and threw out his arms, sending the girl backward. He spun and slammed the back of his fist against the big girl's arm, hard enough to throw her against the house.

The bald man punched Zebadiah in the jaw. If he had been able to use both hands, the bald man might have regained an advantage, but his injured arm didn't move too good, his flowing blood painting it red. Zebadiah was tired and hurt, too, but he was a god, and this was a man. A human. Meat.

Zebadiah took another punch to the face. This one he allowed so the bald man would be off balance enough for Zebadiah's attack. Snapping his jaws at the bald man's face, he charged. Grabbing the bald man's shoulders, he pushed as hard as he could, his legs churning. He drove the man into the same trash where he'd thrown the little man who talked fast, the same pile with lots of jagged, pointed metal sticking out everywhere.

The bald man screamed just like the little man from last night. However, this man didn't die even though a piece of rebar protruded from his shoulder. Howling like a trapped mountain lion, he planted his feet and leaned forward, the rebar disappearing into his shoulder. He took one step, then another, and freed himself.

Curling metal fingers into fists, he flexed his chest and roared. Zebadiah had seen prisoners do this when they were so angry that they lost the ability to think. This bald man would prove no different, and sure enough, the man charged. Zebadiah jumped out of the way and rounded him from behind. Blood slicked the man's back, flowing from the holes in his shirt, from his shoulders where he had been bitten and stabbed. His shoulders. The blood. The meat.

The smell changed Zebadiah, triggering a deep and powerful hunger, infusing his whole body with a desperate strength. Time slowed, each heartbeat an hour, calling to him and filling his ears with an earth quaking thump. He needed to feed, and that smell set his insides on fire.

Zebadiah was on the bald man before he could turn around, his fingers tearing at the man's right shoulder while sinking his teeth into the left. The man tried to spin away, but Zebadiah was faster and stayed behind him, digging deeper into the meat. Metal fists kept hitting Zebadiah's head. No more!

Having torn away most of the bald man's shoulders, Zebadiah dug his fingers into the raw gouges, grasping bones. Pressing a knee against the bald man's back, Zebadiah pulled.

"Mako!" the big girl shrieked. Girls always screamed.

The bald man wobbled and took a step toward the big girl. One arm looked like a crumpled sleeve, the other dangled from a bloom of muscle. The bald man took a second step, then collapsed.

The big girl cried and clenched her fist, tiny blue lightning bolts crackling. Her other arm dangled, the metal hand useless. Zebadiah waved the bald man's arm bones, ready to pound her with them. But she didn't attack. She ran.

Zebadiah thought about chasing her. She had a limp to her run, so she'd be easy to catch. But he was hungry. The bald man had a lot of meat on him. Eating took priority.

He'd catch the big girl soon enough.

July 15th, 2000. 8:58 PM

"He's in the house," Meg said as she stumbled around the corner of the barn.

Cali felt like she had fallen into a frozen lake, everything inside of her cold, desperate, and begging for air. How was this possible?

Twilight had dissolved into night, the wash of the Hummer's headlights illuminating everything in front of the barn. Her father and Kamu ran to Meg, her father offering support as she shuffled with a grimace. "Where's Mako?" he asked.

Meg shook her head. "We engaged the target, but he had the upper hand. At first, I thought we were doing some real damage, but we weren't. He is huge, fucking huge. Mako emptied his gloves, put every bullet he had into that... that thing. Jesus, Ptolemy, he's not human. He... it..." She'd started as cold as a tombstone, but as she spoke, her emotions bubbled to the surface, turning her into a sister who just lost her brother. Tears rolling over her cheeks, she continued, "That thing took a bite out of Mako's shoulders and ripped out the bones from his arms."

Cali's heartbeat felt sluggish. She was impressed that Meg had encountered Bear Head and lived to tell the tale with only blood on her face and an arm hanging limp. Granted, Meg was not a tiny individual, but she'd witnessed bones being ripped from her brother's body.

"Fucking hell," her father whispered.

Linda slid her hand into Cali's, fingers interlocking. Linda exhaled slowly through pursed lips. "Sorry. I skipped the classes on how to deal with unstoppable killing machines while going to DEA school."

Cali squeezed Linda's hand, appreciating her attempt to lighten the mood while coping with fear. Recent events propelled the situation beyond the levels of bravery she could muster. Linda was strong and smart, qualities

214

Cali considered herself to have as well and gave a soft smile of solidarity and reassurance.

"This man," Kamu started, "He… bit off Mako's shoulders…?"

Meg jutted her jaw as she looked away. "Yeah."

"How the hell could he do that through a bear's mask?" Cali's father asked.

Meg turned to him, her eyes bloodshot. "I'm not so sure he's wearing a mask. It's like the bear's head is his head. I don't know how or what the fuck happened, but the bear's mouth moved and bit and chewed."

"What you're saying is impossible," Kamu said.

"I believe it," Cali said.

"I do, too," her father said. "Which is why we need to leave."

"Fuck that!" Meg snapped as she pushed away from Cali's father. "I wanna grab what's in the back of the Hummer and nuke that fucker, the house, and this barn."

"Not a chance. It's dark out and we're in enemy territory against a hostile that we know nothing about, other than he's something more than human. I'm sorry, Meg, I came to get my daughter and get out. He's gotta be on his way to the barn as we speak, so we have to go and go now."

"Fine. Take her and go. Leave me the weapons."

"Meg, Kamu and I can't let you do this."

Meg stood straighter, putting weight on her injured leg. Faint blue snippets of electricity skittered along her glove. "The fuck you can't. Mako's my brother, not just another comrade."

Cali's father inhaled deeply, and then turned to Kamu. Kamu nodded. Her father exhaled. There was no time to argue. "Okay, Meg. Under different circumstances I'd stay, you know that, but I need to get Cali and Linda to safety."

The circumstances became quite different when a familiar shadow loomed over them. The monster had stepped in front of the Hummer's headlights. His silhouette consumed everything. No heat came from the headlights, but the shadow destroyed all warmth from the universe.

Cali's father whipped her behind him, one hand gripping hers, his other trained on his weapon. She felt the rearward thrust as he shot his gun, the recoil of each discharged bullet. The dark figure barely shook as the rounds tore through him. Night gave more dominion to him when a bullet shattered one of the headlights. The gun, now empty, had nothing to show for its efforts.

The creature raised his right hand. Cali didn't know how she missed it, but he held a sledgehammer. Bear Head stepped forward.

Meg clenched her fists. Kamu drew his sword. They flanked her father. The blue glow from the electricity bouncing around Meg's gloves transformed her face into a scowling angel of death. Other than the Hummer's lone headlight glinting off the sword, Kamu blended into the darkness. It was his home, his true weapon.

Linda started shaking again, her breathing louder and more ragged. Cali stepped away from her father and into the shadows, hoping the darkness hid her from the beast. Her father turned his head enough for his words to make it to her. "When we get him away from the vehicle, get to the Hummer and get the fuck out of here."

Running far and as fast as possible was all Cali wanted to do, but not at the sacrifice of her father. No, she would not sacrifice him. He and his friends had weapons and training. Hell, Meg went toe-to-toe with this thing. Cali didn't want to leave her father, but it was the practical thing to do. She set her jaw and said, "Okay."

The monster kept stepping forward, ignoring Kamu and Meg as they flanked him. He seemed determined to get to her father. No, not her father, Cali realized. Her. Bear Head wanted her and viewed no one else as an obstacle. However, Meg and Kamu were determined to be recognized.

Kamu struck first. Shorter than his target, he stayed low, rushing in to slash the monster's thigh. Two quick cuts and he retreated. Black ichor coated Kamu's blade, but his attack had no effect. Meg swept in and grabbed the monster by his neck. Arcs of lightning passed back and forth between the gloves. The beast froze and tensed. Cali got ready to run.

The creature quaked as he fought through the electricity induced spasms. With inhuman resolve, he brought his hand to Meg's face and pushed her away. He continued his trek forward as if lashed by a monomaniacal god's whip.

"Get ready," her father yelled. He withdrew two Glocks from his thigh-holsters. "Go!"

He squeezed the triggers. Bear Head stumbled and staggered, but he kept walking. Cali led Linda away, using the shadows as best she could. Her father shot Bear Head in the face with controlled bursts, continually backing away as the monster advanced. Cali realized his plan was to keep the thing distracted and blind so she and Linda could escape.

"We're not going to leave them, are we?" Linda asked when they reached the Hummer.

Cali went to the rear of the vehicle. "Fuck no."

"Good."

The Hummer's trunk was stocked like a weapons flea market. Assault rifles ran along both sides of the space. Handguns hung like decorations against the backseat. Precut foam lined the floor, nestled with loaded clips and grenades. Cali reached for the grenades, but Linda stopped her. "Even though I'd love to shove a few of these up his ass, they're not precision. If we're not accurate, we'd risk throwing them at your father and his friends. Here, let's start with these." She grabbed the gun closest to her reach. "An AK -103."

"Perfect. Give me one."

Linda handed it to Cali and grabbed one for herself. "Let's end this."

They stayed close to the Hummer, but out of the headlight. Cali guessed her father should be running out of ammo soon. Kamu and Meg continued their quick strikes, but they hadn't slowed the juggernaut. When everyone was out of the way, Cali and Linda brought the butts of the assault rifles to their shoulders, and put a few rounds into Bear Head's back. That got his attention. Cali couldn't see his eyes when he turned around, but she felt his wrath and the malevolence of his dark being seeping into her soul.

"No!" her father screamed. He pumped the remainder of his ammunition into the thing's back. No effect. He dropped his guns and jumped on the beast, wrapping his arm around Bear Head's neck. Meg rushed in and landed punch after punch while Kamu lunged forward to slide his blade into the beast's ribs.

Cali's finger hovered on the trigger. The potential to hit her father or one of his friends was too high. She could only watch as three trained killers struggled to slow the beast, their efforts yielding minimal results.

The beast swung his sledgehammer at Meg, but Cali's father yanked Bear Head's arm, pulling him off balance, causing him to miss. When the creature twisted and reached back, Cali's father released his grip and dropped to the ground. The moment his feet hit the dirt, he drove his shoulders into the back of the beast's knees. Seizing the opportunity, Meg threw herself against Bear Head, toppling the beast and forcing him to drop the sledgehammer. Kamu slid from the shadows, his blade raised over his head. The slightest flicker of light glinted off the sword as it sliced toward the monster's neck. Kamu wasn't fast enough. Bear Head shifted enough to take the cut to his arm instead of his neck.

On any other human, the sword would have cleaved away the arm. Against this beast? It stopped about halfway. Kamu wrestled his sword free, then readied it for a second strike, but had to leap away from Bear Head's fist.

Not relenting, Meg twisted and fought her way to a kneeling position, putting her full weight into her knee on his chest. Releasing a roar that would rival any forest predator, she dug her thumb into the bear's eye as electricity swirled around his face. His entire body spasmed, jerking and bouncing on the ground. Still, both his hands slowly reached for her.

Cali's father struggled with the sledgehammer, fighting to control the massive chunk of steel. Once he managed to raise it over his head, he teetered, then yelled, "Meg!"

She jumped off the monster as the sledgehammer plummeted toward the bear's head. It never made contact.

The beast caught the neck of the sledgehammer. Yanking, he got to his feet and tossed Cali's father toward Kamu as he tried to swing his blade.

Meg lunged at Bear Head, but he turned to block her efforts with his shoulder. She spun, whipping her heel around and connecting her foot perfectly with his jaw. He spun as well, but he swung the sledgehammer on the way around.

Meg was lurching forward for another attack. She avoided taking the full brunt of the hammer's head, but enough of the handle connected with her ribs. She cried out, face contorted in pain. Bear Head was moving faster as if impatient with the obstacles that kept him from his goal. He easily blocked every punch and kick from her father. He was even quick enough to grab Kamu when he led with his sword. Fist full of shirt, the beast slammed Kamu to the ground and threw him into Cali's father.

The beast turned toward Cali.

Cali had a clear shot. She didn't understand the physiology of fear or how adrenaline worked; she just saw everything in slow motion.

The dark spray from the back of his head as she put a bullet in his skull.

The slight twitch in his left arm as the bullet from Linda's gun passed through.

The second gout of sludge spewing from his head when she put another round in it.

The holes opening in his chest from Linda's next shots.

Jarringly, the world moved into full speed again. He was right in front of them, a hungry mythological beast needing to feed.

He dropped his sledgehammer and reached for Cali and Linda. Having a sudden awareness of her surroundings, Cali spun and dropped her shoulder, flinging herself over the hood of the Hummer. Linda screamed and threw her rifle at Bear Head, buying her the split second she needed to dive into the open passenger door. She scrambled through the vehicle, but when she reached the driver's seat, Bear Head grabbed her.

Linda flailed, kicking at the beast's hand while hitting the Hummer's gear selection lever. With one last surge and sprawled across the front seats, her hand reached for the gas pedal.

Cali watched in horror as he grabbed Linda's ankle. She ignored the aches and pains racing around her body—her knees, ribs, shoulder—and stood. The Hummer sped away in reverse. "Linda!"

It took a heartbeat for Cali to register that Linda had escaped. A few more to realize that there was nothing between her and Bear Head.

The dark forest was behind her, but this thing could outrun her, so fleeing was futile. The barn stood in front of her, but he blocked her path. Her father and his friends were to her left. One step at a time, she moved toward them. She locked onto the beast's eyes—slimy black marbles set in matted brown fur—and prayed that her father had a way of dealing death's card. An engine revved. Tires kicked up dirt. A rush of wind tossed Cali's hair as the Hummer sped past her and slammed into Bear Head. And didn't stop.

Spitting up gravel, the vehicle pushed the monster toward the barn. They barreled through the opening and plowed into the remains of the fallen loft. One of the barn's walls collapsed.

"Linda!" Cali called as she ran toward the barn.

A rough hand grabbed her around the waist, stopping her.

Her father.

"Dad? Let go! We have to get to Linda!"

"It's too dangerous. The tanks!"

The drug lab's propane tanks. Linda had probably driven right into them. If they were damaged, they could explode like rockets with no aim or direction.

Cali didn't care about the risk to herself, she needed to save Linda, who was trapped in the vehicle by the debris. She squirmed and twisted to get out of her father's grasp. She almost succeeded, until Meg helped contain her. Crying, she prayed for Linda to get out of the Hummer, get out of the barn before the tanks exploded. No god was listening.

The amber flower of ignited gas bloomed, fast and silent. The gas must have escaped a ruptured propane tank or two, enough to kindle parts of the collapsing barn. Then came the explosion of another tank. The fireball added to the burgeoning flames, hot enough to start a cascade of discharging ammunition. Deadly fireworks. Cali's father and Meg dove on top of her, taking her to the ground. Cali's breath was knocked from her, and her body felt like it was in an oven, claustrophobic and hot. Then a deafening explosion. The grenades in the Hummer had detonated.

All the air in the world disappeared, sucked into the burning void, leaving Cali nothing to breathe, suffocating her. Unsure how long she laid buried under her father's protective weight, she began to feel the absence of everything. Tanner was gone. Dakota was gone. Linda was gone. She coughed and hacked. A painful groan came from her father as he finally rolled off her.

After a time of no noise other than the fire consuming the barn—a pop here and there, the occasional sizzle of flame crawling over something wet—her father's voice pulled her out of her trance. "Cali? We have to go. Meg and Kamu sustained injuries. Do you remember how to get back to the lake house?"

Cali struggled to sit. Her father reached for her and helped her to her feet. She watched the barn, eyes burning from the dark smoke, not wanting to turn away from the danger that lurked within. "You know he's not dead, right?" she said to him. "Nothing can kill him. You know that, right?"

"If he isn't dead, then we need to get moving before he comes after us again."

Cali watched the flames a little longer, looking for movement, any signs of life. She waited for Linda to stroll out unharmed. Maybe the Hummer protected her? Maybe Linda had discovered a tunnel created by the debris to escape through? She'd pop out any second and flash that warm smile of hers while still wearing her adorable pink cat glasses and stupid fanny pack. With a shrug, she'd say, "What? All good. I've gotten out of burning barns all over the world." That was a silly fantasy. The stupid fanny pack was still around Cali's waist, the adorable pink cat glasses in her pocket.

The barn wall gave way and dropped what was left of the roof into the flaming wreckage.

Swallowing a ball of acid, Cali mumbled. "Let's go."

July 15th, 2000. 9:08 PM

His barn. Zebadiah was losing his barn. Papa was right. Girls were nothing but trouble.

After filling his belly with the wonderful meat provided by the bald man with the metal gloves, he came back to his barn to capture the brunette and kill everyone else, including the clever blonde. *Especially* the clever blonde.

Zebadiah had been right about the man in black. He had returned and brought friends—the big girl and another man with a sword. But they didn't stop him, didn't destroy his barn. It was the brunette! She slammed a Hummer into him! He tried to keep his footing, but the vehicle was too strong. It pushed him into the barn, and he couldn't stop it.

The wood of his favorite place on Earth broke in loud cracks as the Hummer smashed him through the barn. It stopped when it crashed into the fallen section of the loft. He lay on the hood, his legs pinned. The black-haired girl was pinned in, too, fallen wood pressed against the doors.

The windshield was cracked, so when Zebadiah punched it, his fist went right through. He tore out the windshield, surprised that glass acted more like paper. The girl screamed as she swatted at his hand. Then she stopped, distracted by something behind her. Zebadiah grabbed her arm, but she still looked out the back window. A few propane tanks had leaks, bouncing around the barn as the gas inside of them escaped.

The black-haired girl turned back to him, her hand gripping his wrist as if she trapped him. "I don't know what the fuck you are, but fire kills everything. Burn, bitch!" She reached her other hand under the steering column and pulled out wires. Zebadiah saw sparks. Then a ball of fire. Noises like shooting guns erupted from the back of the Hummer. Bullets tore through the girl and some had hit him, too. And then the whole back of the Hummer exploded.

Everything shifted as the barn fell. The back end of the Hummer had lifted, shifting enough to release Zebadiah. He fell to the ground and pulled the girl out through the window. He crawled as far as he could, but beams and boards fell all over the place—some on top of him— some blocking his exit.

He fought the urge to rest. Now wasn't time to rest. He heard cooking noises, the sizzle of meat. He smelled it, too. As smoke formed around his face, he realized it was him being cooked. Large blisters bubbled up along his arms, black sludge oozing out when they popped. Fire ran along his overalls, making them shriveled and black, searing them into his charring skin. Was he going to burn out of existence like the girl said? Was she right? The girl. He had the girl. He couldn't play wedding games with her, but she could still help him live. His new, sharp teeth tore into her arm first, snapping bones like pretzels.

The food helped. His bodied healed, but it still burned. The barn still burned. He continued to eat. His food was burned, too, so it didn't taste good, but that didn't matter. The fire burned away his flesh, but his food replenished it. Every time the wood shifted, he tried to move from under the beams, but they still pinned him down. So, he continued to eat. By the time the fire slowed in intensity, he had eaten all his food.

Zebadiah could wait no longer. It was now or never. A beam that once supported the loft lay across his hips. Planks from the loft itself pinned his legs while pieces of the roof piled on top of everything. Legs first. One foot was stuck, but he was able to kick at the wood with his other foot. He wasn't sure if he had boots anymore, either they had burned away, or they had melted to his feet. But the kicking didn't hurt, so he kicked harder and harder. The weight on his foot shifted just enough for him to pull it out. The beam over his waist proved to be more difficult to escape from.

Zebadiah first tried to push against the beam, but he had no leverage. He could spin, though. It was a struggle, but he got on his belly, hands on the ground by his shoulders. He pushed. Everything moved just enough for him to dig his feet into the ground and bend his knees. A little more and he brought his knees closer to his chest until he was on all fours, his back now supporting the weight of the beam and everything on top. Another push and he had one foot flat on the ground.

The weight of the barn's remains ran across his back from shoulder to shoulder. The barn. His barn. His sanctuary. Reduced to burning sticks of wood. Intruders came in and took it from him and when he tried to take it back, they blew it up. This made him angry. The more he thought about what the intruders took from him, the angrier he got. Angry enough to push harder. Harder! With one final push, he roared.

Freedom!

The night air tasted fresh and clean, unlike the dirty soot he had been breathing. He staggered out of the burning wreckage and walked to the front of the barn, where Bertha laid. This and the house were all that was left of Papa. Zebadiah wasn't about to let the intruders take that from him. It was his turn to take from them.

Closing his eyes, he tilted his head back and lifted his snout. A deep breath took in everything, all the smells of the world laid bare. Another inhale and he was able to pick them apart, sift and sort the aromas of the forest. One more breath in and he sniffed out what he was looking for. He felt strong, victorious. Vengeful.

He roared.

July 15th, 2000. 10:06 PM

The walk back to the lake house was quiet. They needed to focus on moving as quickly as possible, and Cali knew any energy expended on asking or answering questions would slow them down. Debating the question, "What the hell was that thing?" or getting the answer to "What the fuck do you do for a living, Dad?" would accomplish nothing at this point in time. They must get back to the house and regroup.

A roar from the direction of the barn drove their feet faster.

When they approached the back of the lake house, Cali inhaled deeply as if finally breaking through water right before drowning. Even though it was less than two miles from where she had almost died, the house represented civilization. There were no bear-head wearing psychos in civilization. Civilization was safety.

But the lights were off.

Cali fumbled with the keys to the backdoor.

"Why are there no lights?" her father asked.

"A fuse blew, and the generator must have run out of gas."

Her father clicked on his flashlight. "No matter." They entered the house. The flashlight was bright enough to light up the entire living room and kitchen area. It was sturdy enough to use as a bludgeon if necessary. "Any signal yet?"

Cali checked Dakota's cellphone. "It's got plenty of battery, but no signal."

"Okay. First thing we need to do is get Kamu to the couch and evaluate his condition." For the entirety of the trudge to the house, Kamu's head drooped and bobbled while he stumbled along, her father practically carrying him. More than once, if not for a random moan of pain, Cali had thought he was dead.

225

Her father guided Kamu to the couch. The smaller man's face twisted; the pain so great he started to shake. "Is there a first aid kit? Or an ace bandage? Half his ribs are probably broken. We need to stabilize him until we can get help."

Cali ran to the bathroom and rummaged through the cabinets and closet. She found both a first aid kit and a couple rolls of bandages. She hurried back to her father. Kamu's shirt was off, and bruising took up half his body. Splashes of blood coated his cheeks and chin.

"Whoa," slipped from Cali's mouth before she was aware she'd said anything.

"Yeah," her father said as he took the supplies from Cali. "This is temporary. Even if we assume the creature is coming for us, we still have a few minutes to rest. Long enough to catch our breath. I saw your car at the barn. Any other cars here?"

"Dakota's." It hurt to say her name. *Push it down, Cali. Deal with it tomorrow.* "But Jordon has the keys."

"That's okay. I'll hotwire it when it's time to go."

Cali took a step back. Her father said he could hotwire cars with a natural and dismissive tone. Like hotwiring a car was on the same level as changing a light bulb. Her father. The same man who refused to change the oil in any vehicle he owned was now talking about hot-wiring cars. The same man who wore suits and carried a briefcase to work was now dressed in black and wrapping bandages around another man's ribs, a man who wielded a sword after arriving on the scene in a weapons-filled Hummer. Her father spent more money on personal grooming than she did, now he smelled of the sweat and dirt that streaked his face and matted his hair. The same man who gave her life took life from others.

Cali hadn't realized that she was backing away from him until she bumped into the counter between the kitchen and living room. Startled, she jumped and whipped around with clenched fists.

"Good instincts," Meg said. Left arm wrapped around her waist, she was nursing an injury and self-medicating straight from a tequila bottle. "Your father taught you well."

226

"Thanks." Cali lowered her fists and placed her elbows on the countertop. Smooth and cool, another representation of civilization, unlike the scratchy, humid wilderness. "Considering I don't know who he is anymore."

Meg took another swig, keeping her eyes on Cali. Unblinking and dark, like a shark watching potential prey. She wiped her mouth with the back of her hand. "You know who he is. He's the man you've always known. So what if he has secrets. We all have secrets."

This wasn't a mere secret. A secret was her new, dead best friend being a DEA agent. A secret was her dead boyfriend's aspirations to be a drug lord. Her father's secret was life-altering. This was every moment of her life begging to be revisited and scrutinized for ulterior motives. Where was he going when he went to the office? Did he even have an office? Every time he was late to meet her, was it because he was narrowly escaping death? Or was he *killing* someone?

Cali didn't want to argue with a woman taller and more muscular than most men. Judging by the way Meg was looking at her, it was an argument she'd lose. Killer or not, it was clear that this woman was loyal, ready to defend her father, no matter if the attacker was his daughter or an unstoppable bear-headed man. Instead of responding to Meg's statement, she nodded to the gloves resting on the countertop. "Those are pretty cool. You make them?"

Meg's upper lip twitched. Cali assumed her stony face was attempting to smile. "I have no talent for making, only using. This is a prototype." With her free hand she turned one of those gloves over to show Cali the palm. "My brother and I test prototype weaponry. This was a field experience for the gloves. The insulation is very good. I didn't even feel a tingle." Meg flipped the glove over and pointed to the wires sticking out. "The casing is shit. Came off too easily, exposing the wires. This is the power source. If even one of these wires popped out, then whatever they'd touch would get fried. Considering they're too long and had to be tucked in means I got lucky."

"Sometimes it's better to be lucky than good." It was an attempt to bond, a way of sharing that they were both still alive after facing Bear Head, and they were both lucky. Meg stared with her blank expression and cold eyes. Internal tension started to twist around Cali's guts, the kind gotten from looking at a photo of someone's kid and guessing the wrong gender. Luckily, her father rescued her again.

"Could you grab some water for Kamu?" Cali's father asked Meg as he came over to the counter.

Meg grabbed a glass from the cabinet, filled it with tap water, and limped over to Kamu. Once she was by the couch, Cali mumbled, "God, she's intense."

"She has to be in this line of work," her father replied.

"Yeah? And what line of work is that, Dad?"

Her father sighed and gave a look that Cali had seen before. "I'm going to go start the car."

"Talk to me. Tell me the truth."

"I will. I promise, but first—"

"Dad. No. Now." To emphasize her desire, she grabbed his wrist. "Please."

Her father looked over to the couch, then to the sliding glass doors leading out front. "We don't have time—"

"You said we had a few minutes. That's all this will take."

"Cali—"

"What the literal *fuck*, Dad?" Cali squeezed his wrist. "Please. Please explain this to me. The Hummer. The guns. How you knew where I was. Your friends. Please."

"Okay. You're right, you deserve to know. I was in the army and had a penchant for judging the difference between right and wrong and then acting upon that judgment with extreme prejudice."

"Killing. You mean killing people."

"The bad ones, Cali. The ones that threaten, use, kill innocent people. After the army, I met your mother. She had similar skills."

Cali's throat tightened and twisted like it was on a pulled rope. Her father hardly mentioned her mother other than to vaguely extol her virtues with phrases like, "She was an amazing woman," or, "She fought her cancer with everything she had." Cali rarely heard her name, and whenever she asked about her mother's career, her father would say, "She had a boring job, like mine." Now, the first time her father shared more information than a rehearsed statement, it was *this*? "Mom was a killer, too?"

As if no further explanation was needed, her father continued. "We became mercenaries, a small crew who used our talents to help those who couldn't help themselves. Us. The three you met tonight, and another man named Hawke. A mission that turned out to be our final mission went sideways. We lost your mother and Hawke. I still had talents. I still wanted to remove those who deserved justice, but would never receive it. I… I eliminate problems for a fee."

"An assassin. An assassin. Jesus Christ, you just told me you're an assassin."

Still not pausing to address her comment, her father continued. "Last night, I had an assignment at the barn. A new player in the drug manufacturing world named Maddox was using the barn as a drug lab. I was there to take him out, but then that freak showed up. He killed Maddox and his crew. He attacked me and I thought I took him out by putting two dozen bullets in his neck."

Cali's shoulders hurt; her entire weight was being supported against the countertop as her knees melted into jelly. The anger in her chest was a diamond cut into shape by disbelief. She couldn't fathom how the man who attended her tea parties when she was four could be an assassin. That man kissed every boo-boo, lifted her spirits when she was down, praised her for her accomplishments, hugged her because he loved her. This man in front of her was pushing her father out of her life, erasing his existence. She was angry at him. She was furious with a woman she had never met, her mother, this irresponsible woman who had risked her life and died before her daughter's second birthday. Cali wanted to hit her father and scream at a dead woman. Unwilling to do the first, unable to do the second.

Cali ground the heels of her hands into her eyes until she saw starbursts of color. She wanted to reach into her brain and pull away everything about the last few days. She wanted to go back to the last moment of blissful ignorance. Before she learned her parents were killers. Before she learned her boyfriend was a drug dealer. Before she learned this trip was a farce. Back to the drive to this house. To the anticipation. Even though she and Tanner had been arguing, she was excited for a relaxing vacation. The drive hadn't been all that bad, until Tanner mentioned…

Cali shook her head as a defeated chuckle fell from her mouth. "Zebadiah Seeley."

Her father frowned. "What did you say?"

"I don't know why I remember stupid things at the stupidest times. On the ride here, Tanner mentioned Zebadiah Seeley."

"That name sounds familiar."

"He's the local boogieman. I guess he's real since it was probably him under that bear's head. Jesus! The boogieman is real, and my parents are killers, and my dead boyfriend and his three idiot friends are drug dealers."

"Three? You said it was just Jordon and some other guy named Hook?"

"Another of Tanner's friends was also supposed to be here this weekend. Maxwell. He couldn't make it, but I'm sure he's involved, too."

"Maxwell?"

"Yeah, Maxwell Templeton. This is his house. Well, it belongs to his father, Roger Templeton."

Her father went rigid, his eyes widened. "Okay. I know I hit you with a lot, but we need to get moving. We need to assume that Zebadiah, or whoever he is, didn't die in the barn fire and is on his way. Can you check Dakota's phone again?"

The faintest hint of a smile touched Cali's mouth as she held up the phone. "It's got a signal."

"Excellent," he said. He took it from her. "I'm going to get the car started."

Her father opened the sliding glass door and left her alone with two strangers. Strangers to *her*, not to her father or her mother. People that had been in her parents' lives. People they had trusted, depended on. People her father kept secret. He had lied to keep those secrets.

Lies. Her father crafted an entire life for Cali out of lies. The stupid notion of a girl looking for a man who was like her father flashed through her mind. After all, Tanner lied to her to hide his secrets. He had told her they were going out to buy fuses, instead they went to a barn drug lab. Had the fuse blown, or was that a lie, too?

A knot formed behind her chest and the only way to loosen it was to listen to her intuition and learn the truth. Grabbing the flashlight, she headed toward the basement stairs. And stopped.

"What the fuck am I doing?" she whispered to herself. The beam of light reached the basement floor with ease. The wooden steps were clean, and the wooden handrails looked sturdy. "There's a killer on the loose and the blonde girl is thinking of going into the dark basement."

She shook her head as if trying to awaken herself from a dream. Fuck it. She started down the stairs, scolding herself for being illogical. These steps were the only way into the basement, no other entrances, no exterior access. That knowledge didn't stop her from pausing when the fifth step creaked.

Moving the light from side to side, she scrutinized what she could see. No encumbrances from the bottom of the steps to the cinderblock back wall. *Idiot*, she thought as she continued. She needed to see for herself, needed to know. If there were no other fuses, then Tanner and the other two were trying to take advantage of the situation. If there were other fuses, then she had been played, this whole week a planned ruse. A sham, just like her relationship with Tanner. Just like her whole life up to this point.

The stairs separated the basement into two sides. The one side had shelving, half full of gas cans, paint cans, boxes of who knew what. The other side stored the bigger items such as kayaks, rafts, wooden chairs. Each side offered plenty of places for Zebadiah to hide. But the side with the shelves also had tools, so Cali rushed to them and picked up a hammer.

She looked it over. The strength and comfort that came from wielding a weapon was short lived. It was a ball peen hammer versus a seven-foot bear of a man that wouldn't die by bullets, sword, electricity, and probably fire. Cali set it back on the shelf. Right next to a box of fuses. "Son of a bitch."

The fuse box was on the nearby wall, and Cali screwed a fuse into the empty slot. Light from upstairs lit the stairwell. Satisfied that Zebadiah wasn't lurking behind the stacks of implements designed to make lake life even more enjoyable, Cali made her way back upstairs. She entered the living room as her father came flying through the door.

July 15th, 2000. 10:14 PM

Ptolemy knew the lake house was not the perfect place to regroup midway through a mission, especially with no electricity, but it would have to do. They all needed to catch their breath, and Kamu and Meg were injured. They couldn't call for evac or assistance, their sat comms destroyed, and no power in the house meant no landline.

The thing they had fought burned to a cinder in the barn after being slammed into by a Hummer. *No way* it should still be alive, yet the back of Ptolemy's neck tingled with a feeling that he was still being hunted. He prayed he could get the car started.

Cali looked mortified when he told her he'd hot wire Dakota's car. Damn it if she hadn't forced him to tell the truth about his real job, making her think his life as she knew it was a lie. He wanted to tell her more, give the details that explained why he did what he did, and let her know that every moment they shared was true and real and good.

This had to be difficult for her. Beyond difficult. Two days ago, she was a privileged college student living a life many dreamed about. Since then, she lost people she knew including her boyfriend and best friend, fought an unstoppable killing machine, and learned her father was a contract killer. Hell, even he was having a difficult time comprehending a creature that wouldn't die, yet Cali had gone toe-to-toe with it more than once. Ptolemy was proud of her.

But then she had said a name. Templeton. She said that Roger Templeton owned this house.

"... I'm going to get the car started."

Phone flipped open, Ptolemy was calling Broker before he reached the sliding glass doors. Out on the deck, he heard Broker's voice on the other line. "Ptolemy? I've been trying to get ahold of you. Is everything okay?"

Again, Broker displayed concern beyond the professional standard. If she was who he thought she was, then she was right to be worried. "Remember the barn hit on Maddox? Well, there was more to it than that. Cali and her friends accidentally got mixed up in it."

"Cali? Is she okay?"

"Yes. Her friends, no. I got my old crew to help out."

"Has the threat been neutralized?"

Ptolemy held his breath and scanned the darkened yard for movement. The moon's reflection skittered over the placid lake. "Undetermined."

"Do you need extraction?"

Ptolemy made his way to Dakota's car, parked close to the deck. He was still wary of potential threats, specifically an unkillable death machine. "I have a vehicle available. We'll be leaving the area soon, but we're at a house owned by Roger Templeton."

"Wait… What?"

"That seems like one hell of a coincidence, right?"

"Let's tack on my information and ask that question again. I recently discovered that Templeton is the mother's maiden name of an old associate of yours."

"Really? Who?"

"Dustin Roger Hawke."

It had been a long time since Ptolemy felt this level of fear, but twice in one night it visited him, its cold arms wrapping around him in an intimate embrace, its icy fingers reaching through his chest for his heart. "He's dead."

"Is he?"

Ptolemy leaned against the driver-side door, all but collapsing. "We really think a man who's been dead for two decades is trying to kill me?"

Broker paused. Ptolemy heard her breathing quicken, as if she debated telling him something. "Anything is possible."

"How about Albathia Pharmaceuticals?" Ptolemy pushed himself from the car, more stable now, his hand on the door handle. "Did you find out anything else about them?"

Broker's modulated voice went back to all business. "Remember the line item on the expenses for legal fees? I got access to their bank accounts and followed the money trail. I thought I'd find patents or trademarks or other corporate nonsense. The money wasn't used for any of that. The money wasn't used for lawyers at all. The whole amount was used for bribes to get one man out of prison."

"One man? Must have been someone important. What's his name?"

"Zebadiah Seeley."

Something moved on the other side of the car, a shadow of a shadow. Ptolemy jumped back as the sledgehammer crashed down on the roof, crumpling it like wadded paper.

A mass of darkness looped around the car. The house lights behind Ptolemy popped on, the brightness exposed the monster lurking in the shadows. Zebadiah tossed his head back, surprised by the sudden brightness. He dropped his hammer to cover his eyes and then blindly reached out. Skin was twisted into various knots of ground meat, twists of pink oozing through the cracks of charred black; his burned overalls had been fused to his body. The bear's head, though, looked unmarred. Teeth glistening with flowing saliva, he roared. This beast was evidence that God had forsaken the world. For the first time in his life, Ptolemy was petrified.

Zebadiah grabbed Ptolemy by his shirt and threw him toward the house.

Ptolemy flew through the open door and hit the floor shoulder first. Pain radiated across his chest, but it could have been worse. He could still move, and he rolled and stood.

The beast came smashing through the glass doors.

Cali screamed from the basement stairs. She turned and ran back down.

"No!" Ptolemy yelled. "Cali!"

The beast turned his eyes to Ptolemy. Meg was swift to react, jumping in front of the monster, grabbing his wrists. Zebadiah roared. Meg roared back, expressing her desire for vengeance.

Ptolemy went in low, launching himself shoulder first into a kneecap. The snap of the monster's leg bending the wrong way was sickly satisfying.

Zebadiah dropped to his good knee and Meg took advantage. She released his right hand and clamped down on his left wrist with both of her hands. She pushed up and back. Ptolemy joined her. Standing behind Zebadiah, Ptolemy grabbed his forearm and pulled. The monster fought back, but Meg and Ptolemy exerted their will, dislocating his arm at the shoulder to the sound of a sickening pop. It wasn't enough.

Zebadiah pushed upward on his good leg to stand and thrust his head back, connecting with Ptolemy hard enough to knock him away. He shook out his other leg as if his foot had simply gone to sleep, and without a grunt of discomfort, the monster popped his shoulder back into place.

Meg was standing too close to Zebadiah when he attacked. Grabbing her arms, he pinned them against her body. There was nothing she could do to stop him from clamping his jaws on her neck. A gush of blood, and her throat was a gaping hole. He dropped her body, now twitching with death spasms, and turned his attention to Ptolemy.

In one fluid motion, Ptolemy jumped back, sliding across the counter between the living room and kitchen, landing gracefully in front of the sink. He snatched the knife block from the counter behind him and launched the knives. Four in Zebadiah's chest, two in his neck. They didn't slow him. Zebadiah grabbed the countertop and tore it from the floor, cabinets and all. He tossed it aside and charged, leading with open jaws. Ptolemy shoved the empty knife block into Zebadiah's bear-mouth. Pain exploded from his lower back as Zebadiah slammed him into the sink.

Then Zebadiah arched and froze. There was a slopping sound of meat hitting the floor, followed by the sound of a punch. Another arch and then a grunt from Zebadiah.

Ptolemy didn't know it was possible, but the bear's face showed confusion when the process repeated. Again. Ptolemy could slide enough to the right to see what was happening behind Zebadiah.

Cali.

She hadn't run to the basement to hide; she went down there to garner a weapon. A posthole digger. With a grunt, she jammed it into his back and pulled out a glob of black sludge.

The creature turned to face Cali.

"Get to the boat!" Ptolemy screamed.

His daughter did as he instructed, dropping the tool and sprinting out the shattered doorway.

Zebadiah lunged for her.

Kamu suddenly jumped in the monster's way.

He had his sword drawn with his right hand, and in his left, he held... A roll of paper towel? Locks of his hair were plastered to his face, pale and dripping with sweat. He smiled, wide and bright, his glee a sign of madness.

Zebadiah staggered forward, his arms outstretched, hands reaching for Kamu. Despite his injuries, Kamu moved like water on a slide, flowing with ease. Zebadiah grabbed, but missed. Kamu avoided the beast's hands, ducking and dodging every attempt. He used his sword to block, not stab or slice, and with every movement, Kamu spun around the beast, wrapping Zebadiah in paper towel. Around his arms, chest, neck. When the roll was done, so was Kamu.

Zebadiah grabbed Kamu by the neck and lifted.

Head less than a foot from the ceiling, Kamu used his sword one last time. He drove the tip upward through Zebadiah's arm and into the overhead light. A spark, a pop, and the house went dark. A flame flickered from the sparks, hitting the paper towel. In a flash, fire engulfed the paper towel.

"Run!" Kamu issued with his final breath before being slammed to the floor with a back breaking snap.

His friend's sacrifice gave Ptolemy enough time to escape. He ran from the house, past Zebadiah as he swatted at the spreading flames.

Cali was untying the boat from the pier when Ptolemy hit the yard; she was onboard when he got to the dock. Ptolemy heard a bear's roar and the sounds of glass breaking.

"Push away!" Ptolemy yelled. "Push away!"

Cali pushed and the boat started to float into the lake. Ptolemy kicked off the edge of the dock and jumped, needing every inch of his long legs to leap the distance. His feet hit the deck, and he crumpled, pain swirling through his knees.

"Dad!" Cali cried as she knelt next to him.

"I'm okay," he said, struggling to his feet. "Oars. We need to find oars."

"Here. I found— Oh my God!"

Ptolemy looked over to the docks in time to see a bear in the shape of a man consumed by fire, launching himself toward the boat.

July 15ᵗʰ, 2000. 10:23 PM

It took a full heartbeat for Cali's brain to register what was happening. A fireball flew through the air at her. The fireball had a form. Had a face. A bear's face. In the next heartbeat she dove off the boat.

She heard cracks and snaps—sounds of Zebadiah destroying the boat—as she hit the water. Legs kicking, she torpedoed through the water until she needed a breath before breaking the surface. Cali assumed the worst, and she swam as fast as she could without wasting a moment to look back. She headed toward a thick patch of aquatic plants by the shore.

She hoped and prayed her father was behind her.

Cali made it to shallow water and walked in a crouch once her feet touched bottom. She slid into a patch of weeds, through thick blades of grass and dense tips of cattails. *Control your breathing*, she repeated as she peered through feathery tops of the bulrush.

Now was the time to assess her situation, to see where her father was, where Zebadiah was. Her father was a good swimmer. She was confident he could hold his own, and that was before she'd learned he was a super soldier assassin who could probably hold his breath for ten minutes while fighting a school of sharks.

But she didn't see him. No splashing, no swimming. Not a single ripple. The calm water reflected the silver moon like a freshly polished mirror. *What the fuck?*

Taking small, quiet breaths, Cali inched among the grasses, moving closer to shore, and got a better view of the moonlit dock. Empty, no one using it to claw their way out of the water. The only noise was the soft lapping of water against the pebbled beach. With each step, the water level moved from thigh deep to knee deep. Her vision rattled as her pulse thumped behind her eyes, but she saw well enough. She still saw nothing.

Another step closer to shore, the water at her shins. *Options? What are my options?* Racing back to the lake house was her only fathomable choice. She knew it better than the woods, and there were tools inside. Weapons. She had damaged Zebadiah with the posthole digger. If she could find other weapons for her and her father, they could come up with a plan to stop him. *Where is he?*

She scanned the water from the center of the lake to the pier. Still no father, no monster. She'd have to take a leap of faith and sprint from the shore to the house. She wished she could see at least something.

Water swirled around her left ankle.

Cali squealed, jumped back, and looked down. Just an agitated school of feeder fish, but damn if she hadn't given away her location.

Strong hands grabbed her shoulders and yanked her back.

Swing. Punch. Push. As fast as the lightning from Meg's gloves, Cali escaped from the hands holding her, and floundered on shore. "Cali."

Her father.

Rubbing his jaw, he stood between her and the patch of grasses where she'd been hiding. He whispered, "Nice punch."

"Dad? Where were you?"

"I can be stealthy when I need to be."

"Did you see what happened to Zebadiah?"

"Not after he smashed through the boat and disappeared into the lake."

The grasses rustled; the feathery tips of the bulrush danced ever so slightly. A rush of water. Her father's face unchanged.

Cali tried to scream, but she remained frozen in a nightmare world that somehow moved too fast and too slow. Within a fraction of a second, her father's torso split down the middle as the bear's face burst from his chest. Entrails and blood hung from the bear as he rushed toward Cali.

Run! She couldn't. He was too fast, too strong. She fell backward as Zebadiah jumped on her, his knees on either side of her hips, his hands in the grass on either side of her head. Teeth gnashed as her father's blood slopped onto her face.

Knives.

The knives her father had thrown at him were still lodged in his chest.

Cali ripped two knives from him and skewered his eyes. He howled and she pounded on the handles, driving them in deeper and deeper until he reeled back. At last, she was able to squirm out from under him. Cali yanked out one of the other knives from his chest, and then sprinted back to the lake house.

Through the living room.

Up the stairs.

She took off her shirt.

The second floor was a hallway with two doors on the left, two on the right, and a window at the end. There was no way he'd fall for the same trick again, so she jumped into the bathroom to grab a towel. The room she and Tanner had shared was on the far right. As she hurried down the hallway, she dragged her shirt along the wall. In her room, she dropped her old shirt on the bed and grabbed a clean one from a drawer. She wiped the back of her sweaty neck with the towel, and then quickly scrubbed each wet armpit. Done with it, she tossed the towel on the bed, donned the clean shirt, and ran to the bathroom. Door closed. She waited.

There had to be a way to kill this fucker, and she was going to find it. All she needed was time.

Smell. That was the only logical way he had followed her through the woods, all the way from the barn. Of course, when it came to a man with a bear's head who was nearly impossible to kill, logic didn't seem to be an ingredient in this recipe of terror. He might have sensed body heat. Maybe he had some form of extra sensory perception, but she was wagering her life that he had used smell. The bathroom held many fragrances, hopefully enough to mask her so he'd pass by this room in favor of her scent trailing into the bedroom.

Or maybe he simply felt her, because she felt his presence. He was here, and she felt him before she heard him on the carpeted steps.

Control your breathing, she repeated, over and over until she caught herself holding her breath. He was on the other side of the bathroom door. She heard his quick inhales, him sniffing the air. Cali gripped the knife, expecting the door to blow off its hinges. *Go for the eyes,* she kept telling herself. *The brain is behind the eyes.*

After a grunt, the floor creaked—he was moving farther down the hallway.

Her ear pressed against the door, she heard his breathing trail away, his feet scuffling down the carpet. She turned the knob and opened the door a crack. Tip facing outward, she led with the knife, then peeked, hoping part one of her plan had worked.

Zebadiah's silhouette lumbered into the bedroom, exactly where Cali wanted him. *Perfect.* She slipped from the bathroom and hurriedly tiptoed downstairs. Focus. She needed to focus. She couldn't let the emotions from seeing the bodies of Kamu and Meg slow her down. If she acknowledged them, then she'd have to acknowledge her father, and she couldn't do that yet. Tears and a soft heart were useless now. She grabbed Kamu's sword and scurried to Meg's gloves, and knelt by them.

Sawing with the knife as fast as she could, she cut through the sword's handle wrap. *Faster, faster!* A piece of cord split away, then another and another. She only needed to cut away enough to expose the metal underneath. Now, Meg's gloves.

She knew very little about electronics, but she remembered Meg's words. "… exposing the wires. This is the power source. If even one of these wires popped out, then whatever they'd touch would get fried. Considering they're too long…"

Cali tugged at the wires, pulling them toward the power source and yanking them from their connections. Dozens of wires stuck out from each glove like frazzled hair.

Hurry!

A noise—a slam from the second floor. Hurried footsteps stomping closer to the stairs.

Cali wrapped the wires around the sword hilt's exposed metal. *Faster!*

Zebadiah reached the bottom of the stairs.

Even though the gloves were large on her, Cali was able to curl her fingers around the sword. A web of wires reached from the back of each glove to the sword hilt's exposed metal. Meg had mentioned that the insulation was good, and Cali was about to put it to the test. Simple rocker switches were at the base of the thumbs. The gloves hummed and the sword crackled with electricity.

A fountain of sparks flowed the length of the blade and created a blue hued strobe in the darkened room. Part two of her plan was a success. Anger had pushed away fear. Time to enact part three. She gripped the sword tighter and moved to the center of the room.

With plenty of training to back her up, she felt competent, but she was no sword master. She'd surely lose if her opponent were armed. Luckily for her, her opponent only had fingers and teeth. However, she kept in mind that the same opponent had been shot, stabbed, electrocuted, and burned.

The beast stood before her. A slight bend in his knees, he crept farther into the room, attempting to circle her while sizing her up. Zebadiah was no mindless animal. Cali moved, the two of them revolving around an invisible point. She watched his eyes. The flickering bursts of untamed electricity lit them at different intervals and intensity with an occasional flirtation of darkness. But she could see his black and glossy windows to Hell. She intended to close them before the night was over.

Taking two quick steps forward, she lunged. She aimed to drive the tip of the sword through his waist, but he was too fast, sidestepping her strike. He didn't attack, so she stepped forward again, this time swinging at his waist. Missed again! He jumped back, then swiped for her. She followed through with her spin and he caught a fist full of her hair. Yelling, she sliced at his arm. The awkward angle gave her no power behind her swing, but the blade cut his forearm and delivered a jolt. Snarling, he released her hair.

Cali's scalp throbbed. Just another ache to add to the collection. Every muscle was sore. Every joint screamed. Her heart hurt. This creature had killed everyone she loved. "I don't know you, but this is for everyone you took from me. My father. My friends. I'm going to fucking kill you."

Zebadiah smiled. Cali didn't know bears could do that, but the back of his upper lip curled. He grumbled, his mouth opening wider. There it was. Her edge over him. A man was somewhere within that bear head. Ego was the weak point in the armor of all men.

"This is also for those girls you kidnapped and raped," Cali continued. "You *had* to kidnap them, didn't you? You couldn't *find* a girl on your own because you were too weak."

Zebadiah's body language changed. His fingers curled to fists. He walked his circular path faster.

"Oh, I know all about the *weak* Zebadiah Seeley. Too *weak* to get a girl. Too *stupid* not to get caught."

In between snarling grunts, he shook his head as if trying to dislodge a thought.

"I'm going to beat you, Zebadiah, beat you like the *bitch you are,* because I'm *stronger* than you. And smarter."

That was it, the pushed button that set off a nuclear explosion.

With a roar that shook the entire house, Zebadiah rushed Cali. She stepped aside like a matador, dragging the edge of her sword across his waist. She turned faster, sliding the tip between a pair of ribs. He froze from the electrical paralysis, but fought through it, demonstrating his determination to catch her. She wasn't going to let him.

She pulled out the sword and ducked as his muscles reengaged to continue his spin, fast and awkward. Cali drove the sword through the small of his back. His body rebelled, his roar broken and stuttered. She removed the sword, and was prepared for when he whipped back around.

Zebadiah roared again.

Cali closed his mouth, ramming the sword through his bottom jaw and up into his skull.

There it was. The look she wanted to see. In the sword's flickering blue glow, his eyes shifted. Confusion. Pain. Fear. Right when they started to dull, she pulled out the sword and stepped aside, clearing the way for him to fall to his knees. One kick to the back of the head was enough to drop him. But not enough to finish him.

He wasn't moving, but she had seen this before.

Cali secured her grip and raised the sword above her head. Screaming bloody vengeance, she brought it down on his neck.

The gash went to the bone. The valley of black flesh oozed as Cali withdrew the sword. Panting, she felt a twinge of satisfaction. Her plan had worked.

Zebadiah's hand twitched.

The wound started to heal, the two pieces of flesh mending themselves together.

"No." Cali raised the sword again and swung. She hit the same spot, recreating the same gouge. The black wound started to heal. "No!"

Cali swung again and again and again. Chunks of flesh and muscle flipped through the air. Gobs of his oily blood sprayed her with each hit, spurts splashing her face. She kept hacking at his neck, screaming her throat raw with every chop. Her mind slipped, the barriers holding back her thoughts crumbled away. Memories of her father broke containment. Thoughts of Dakota rushed from her mind to her heart. Unexplored feelings for Linda swept through her. Cali's emotions took control as she cried and yelled and swore while swinging harder and faster.

She stopped swinging when she couldn't lift her arms.

Zebadiah's head was no longer attached to his body.

Yet he opened his mouth.

"Fuck!" Cali yelled as she kicked it away from his body, sending it outside, over the deck.

Burning from within, Cali fought with her arms to raise the sword one more time. She waited for the body to move, waited for even the slightest twitch. Panting and crying, Cali watched Zebadiah's corpse for minutes. No movement. Had she really done it? Had she won?

Cali drove the sword into his back one last time. Sparks cascaded down the blade and flowed to Zebadiah's overalls. A small flame formed. Cali slipped her hands out of the gloves and said, "Maybe you'll burn this time, fucker."

The fire grew as she stumbled out of the house. On the grass in front of her lay the bear's head. Zebadiah's head.

Eyes blinking, mouth moving.

At first, she thought it was involuntary movement typical in the recently deceased, but the jaw opened and closed like a fish on land begging for water. "What the fuck *are* you?"

The answer had to wait, because another question formed the moment she saw headlights coming down the driveway. A black Hummer, like the one that had brought her father to the barn. "Who the fuck are *you*?"

The brakes whispered to a stop, the driver door swung open, and a woman stepped out.

A woman who looked like Cali.

Other than the shape of her eyes and being about two decades older, Cali had seen this face in the mirror. Cali had already witnessed the impossible within these past couple days. She had no doubt who this woman was.

"Mom."

"Oh, God, Cali!" the woman cried as she hurried to her daughter.

Cali hugged her and burst into tears. She didn't care if she hadn't seen her for twenty years, didn't care why her father had claimed she was dead. She wrapped her arms around her mother and unloaded her emotions in body-wracking sobs. Her mother simply held Cali and cried along.

When Cali was able to breathe again, she took a step back. "What are…? How…? Where were…? Why…?" Her words floundered in the air, but her mother understood.

Hands on Cali's shoulders, she offered a sympathetic and calming smile. "I know you have a lot of questions, and I'll answer them. But we need to go. This area is secluded," She looked away, her eyes taking in the carnage. "But it's doubtful that a burning house will go unnoticed. I…" Her voice trailed off. She covered her mouth with her hand, stifling a sob. Cali knew what her mother was looking at. The bright moon spotlighted her father's desecrated body. She didn't need to look; she was still wearing his blood.

Cali's mother turned away after a few more painful seconds, but not toward Cali. Watching the house burn, she pulled out a cellphone. "I need body retrieval at my location. The Mathematician. Yes, you heard correctly. Leave the burning house for the authorities."

Cali's mother flipped the phone closed and stared at it. "I was talking with your father when the line went dead. I drove here as fast as I could."

"You were in communication with him?"

Cali's mother exhaled slowly through pursed lips. She looked up into her daughter's eyes. "Did he tell you that he and I were part of a small paramilitary group?"

"That you two were mercenary assassin killers? Yeah, he mentioned that."

"Our last mission didn't go well, especially for me and another member of our squad named Hawke. We were both presumed dead. Hell, I was almost dead, but a group of sympathetic locals found me. No one found Hawke so I, and everyone else, thought he was dead. It took me over a year to heal, and by the time I was able to get home, the team had separated, and your father moved on. He became a contract killer. I became his Broker."

"So, he knew you were alive. Why didn't he tell me?"

"He didn't know. I used a voice modulator. I'm sure he had his suspicions, but he thought I was dead. Everyone did."

"But... Why?"

"Why did I continue to let him think that? Because during our last mission, you were almost an orphan before you were out of diapers. Your father is... Part of his charm was *life*, even though he dealt in death. Being near him was invigorating, an addicting drug for my soul. I couldn't return and become what I needed to be for you while being around him. If I had come back into your lives, it would have been disruptive and dangerous. I couldn't stop going on missions. Part of being a mother is making this world safer for you. I would have been right there next to him in some dangerous environment with a gun in hand. You two had become acclimated to a life without me. Neither of our lifestyles were conducive to raising a child, so I kept my distance, staying in reserve for when he met his untimely end. As his broker, I tried to do everything possible to keep him from that."

Cali regarded this woman, a person she had never met before and didn't know. But did she really know her father? Resentment was a strong feeling, but she needed to tamp it down if she wanted to learn about her parents. "You said you were talking to him. Was he on an assignment?"

"His original assignment was to take out a drug lord named Maddox at the barn. Things got complicated. He came back to rescue you from Zebadiah Seeley. I was in contact with him because I discovered that Zebadiah was part of a plan to kill your father."

Cali cringed. "You mean to tell me that thing was hired to kill my dad?"

"More like a weapon that someone used."

"Who?"

"Remember our friend, Hawke? Well, it turns out he's as dead as I am."

It was hard to breathe again. Too much information. Too much *insane* information. Cali's mother put her arm around Cali's shoulders. Gazing at the burning house, she said, "You've been through a lot, Cali. There's much more I'm sure you want to ask. I called people to collect your father's remains, and we'll handle them properly, later. Let's get you home."

Cali nodded. "Yeah. Yeah, I'd like that, please. But first…"

Cali walked up to Zebadiah's head. She lifted it by the fur between its ears. His eyes locked onto hers. Upper lip rippling, his jaws opened and closed, still trying to bite, to eat.

"Throw that in the fire," her mother said.

Cali smirked. "No. I've got different plans for this thing."

June 14ᵗʰ, 2001, 1:48PM

Cali took a cleansing breath. The faint hint of wood polish tickled her nose as she inhaled. The desk was nice and deserved to be polished as often as possible. A solid reddish-brown cherry wood. Hand crafted with decorative carvings along the front and sides. Comfortable to rest one's feet upon while leaning back in the accompanying soft leather chair, as Cali discovered. She assumed the owner, Roger Templeton, would take exception to her doing this.

"He's on his way," Mother said. "You're going to be great, Cali. You've handled all the others with ease."

"Thanks, Mom, but he's a little different."

"I understand. I still think you'll be great."

"Okay. Game time. Once I wrap up here, I could go for some Thai for dinner."

"Sounds great. Signing off now."

Cali removed the earpiece and slid it into the pocket of her shorts. It was weird having her mother speak into her ear. Hell, even after a year it was weird having a mother. The first few months were the most difficult, working through loss and trying to understand why her mother had abandoned her. Cali had lost many people, so she decided to embrace finding one, having a mother in her life to help console her. Through the shared grieving process, she learned a tremendous deal about her father. Her life with him had been half a book and her mother supplied the missing pages. Then her mother started to supply even more. Cali learned a lot from her, such as how to break into an office.

The one she was in now belonged to a megalomaniac, a spacious corner office with two walls of glass. Gaudy artwork adorned the other walls in between shelves of books that had never been read. There was even a statue of Zeus, naked and muscled to the idealized body of masculinity. So tacky!

249

The door opened and in walked the owner of the garish office. A man in his early fifties, his age hidden well by his healthy shape and full head of brown hair. His expensive suit exaggerated his muscled chest which tapered to a thin waist. A deep scowl formed angry lines over his face. Cali assumed he must have learned that another one of his accountants had recently died. "Good evening, Roger."

"Who the fuck are you?" he barked.

Cali swung her legs off the desk and picked up the gym bag next to it. She walked to the center of the office and set the bag back down. "Come on, Roger, don't I look the slightest bit familiar?"

The older man squinted, then sneered. He nodded. "Calista Lindquist. You look just like your mother."

"I know. She's gorgeous, right? Now that you're standing in front of me, I can see where Maxwell gets his blocky, rectangular Frankenstein head."

Roger removed his jacket and tossed it on a nearby chair. "What do you want?"

"First, I wanted to let you know that I figured you out. Well, I had help, but I know it was you who killed my father. I don't have all the details as to why, yet. More specifically, why now? I'm assuming it has something to do with Dirk and Derrick?"

Roger chuckled and shook his head as he removed his tie and unbuttoned his shirt sleeve cuffs. "We're gonna do this? Okay, sure, why not. Those two were my nephews. Kinda dumb, and way too flashy, but hey, they're blood. They wanted to get into the business, and I gotta tell you, they were pretty good. Made sure their street guys paid on time and in full, and they didn't skim from me."

"So, they were middle management drug dealers. Got it."

"They were good kids. When your father took out Derrick, it was time for him to retire."

"Time for him to retire? So, you knew he was an assassin?"

Roger undid the top three buttons of his shirt, rolled his neck, and then laughed. "Knew? Hell, I used his services. A lot."

"You never thought to let him know that you were alive?"

"I'm assuming you know about the shit show in Afghanistan. My first thought was revenge against those assholes for leaving me there, starting with your father since he was the decision maker. When I got back to the states, I learned that Athena had died. I figured there wasn't much more I could do to make him hurt, other than kill you, of course."

"Of course," Cali replied. Roger seemed ready for what was to come next, so she adjusted the stupid fanny pack, bent her knees, and raised her fists.

Roger raised his brow and shook his head again, incredulous. "I ain't a baby killer, so I decided to say fuck it. The best part of being dead was being a ghost. People can't see ghosts, but ghosts can see people. I changed my name and watched the people from my past for a while until I figured out my next move."

Cali jumped forward, then back, avoiding his punches. He was much faster than she had judged from his looks. Cali, however, had unique experience with fighting men who were faster than they looked. She jabbed a few times but missed as he retreated. He was quick to attack again. This time, she lunged forward and planted her elbow in his nose. She stepped back. "Drugs. Your big career move was drugs."

Roger dragged his forearm under his nose and glanced at the blood. A goodly amount, by Cali's estimate. Enough for Roger's cocky smirk to disappear. "It was the eighties. Weird fucking time to be alive, believe me. Drugs were a hot commodity. Legal, illegal, didn't matter. My military mind for planning and organization and ruthlessness came in very handy. I focused on quality. I focused on management and distribution. As I got bigger, the competition started to take notice. I then discovered your old man decided to become an assassin. I figured, why the fuck not use his services? I called myself The Philanthropist to appeal to his weird sense of right and wrong. He thought I was spending money to clean up the filth when I was really taking out my competition."

"Until he accepted a job that interfered with your business."

"Until he killed my nephews. Ptolemy had taken out a few of my higher-ranking officers here and there from other jobs, but nothing that hurt.

Whenever that would happen, I simply used your father to do far more damage once I figured out who had hired him."

"Like Maddox?"

Roger attacked, showing his experience this time. His punches seemed slow and sloppy, telegraphing each swing before he released it. Too full of adrenaline not to follow the natural course of the fight, Cali didn't catch on that he was playing her until she took his fist to her cheek. His feint had worked, and she saw stars. He wrapped his arms around her, but she responded with a knee to his crotch. She hated to use a cheap shot, but she couldn't risk letting him get ahold of her like that. A man his size could slam her all over the office.

Cali stepped back as Roger crouched down like a baseball catcher. He shook his head again, this time implying disappointment. "Yeah, like Maddox. That fucker was aggressive and smart. And fast. A dangerous combination. While I was researching him and who he was and how he operated, he was taking big chunks out of my local market share. His big balls move was offing my nephews. Once your old man took out Derrick, I hired as many guys as I could find to take him out before he got to Dirk. Problem was, no one with experience wanted the job, so it was nothing but new guys. Fucking Ptolemy wiped out whoever I sent. He offed Dirk. That's when it became personal."

"That's when you gave up his home address."

"Yeah. And learned that Maxwell and his idiot friends, including your boyfriend, wanted to get in the game. They contacted Maddox of all fucking people. Well, I couldn't let that happen. Maddox was really good at hiding his labs, but I found one."

"The one in the barn."

Roger stood up and rolled his neck again. "A quick search told me who owned the place. A crazy fucker in prison."

Cali cracked her knuckles. "You spent a shit ton of money on bribes to get Zebadiah out of prison to kill Maddox."

"I hired your old man to kill Maddox. I got Zebadiah released to kill your old man. 'The Mathematician' liked to make sure his equations balanced. Zebadiah was one hell of an unbalanced variable. That was also why I told Maxwell to stay home that weekend. I was certain that his idiot friends would be at the wrong place at the wrong time. They were and they dragged you into it, too, but it's not my fault that you have such shitty taste in men."

It was Cali's turn to attack, but she was smart this time. Roger's words were designed to push buttons. He was expecting her to be sloppy. She, however, was smooth, fast, efficient. None of his punches came close. All of hers hit. Now it was he who let his emotions control his actions.

Wheezing and bloodied, he had a murderous look in his eyes. He let his arms dangle, trying to conserve energy. Cali sneered. "Well, before my dad died, he discovered your little secret about Albathia Pharmaceuticals funding Forward Technologies."

Roger spat a glob of mucus and blood on the floor. His shitty smile returned. "My laundromat? A few years ago, I decided to go global. A decent sized drug ring that spans a few states is easy to hide. One that spans the world? Many, many more prying eyes, so I needed to wash my money. Forward Technologies has always been a pet project of mine. I used Albathia to take the money from my clients and dealers, and transfer it to Forward Technologies to keep it funded. When I went global, I needed protection for my assets, and that protection needed cutting edge technology. I pay my taxes, and no one asks too many questions."

"Yeah, the downside to no one asking too many questions made it soooooo easy to clean out the cash accounts of Albathia Pharmaceuticals."

"What?"

"Oh, you heard me. Now, cleaning up the books for Forward Technologies was a bitch. I'm sure you noticed a few of your lawyers and accountants have been dying mysteriously as of late. Totally me. I had to remove those dirt bags so I could be left alone to work on making the finances look legitimate for the transfer. Oh shit, maybe I forgot to tell you—I totally forged all kinds of documents stating that Albathia Pharmaceuticals has been dissolved and that you're handing Forward Technologies over to your employees as of tomorrow."

Roger snarled and rushed Cali. She had heard nastier growls. Roger's was thoroughly unimpressive. She let him wrap his hands around her throat. "You bitch! You think you're going to steal from me and then pick up where your father left off? Well, you failed on your first mission!"

Time for the stupid fanny pack, the perfect place to hide a syringe full of nastiness that would paralyze a person while keeping them conscious. One second to inject it into Roger's arm, four seconds until he released her, three seconds to stagger around looking surprised, and a half a second to fall to the floor.

Cali sauntered over to her gym bag and unzipped it. There were only two things in the gym bag, one being a roll of black plastic. With the smile and body language of a high-end car showroom model, she unfurled the plastic, demonstrating to Roger that it was a body bag.

To make her life easier, Cali took a moment to arrange Roger's limbs, legs together, arms at his sides. Starting with his feet, she worked him into the bag. "Typical man. Always thinking he's the 'first' and not listening to a woman when she speaks. I already told you I killed a bunch of your dirty employees. You also assumed I wanted to follow in my father's footsteps. Not quite. See, he was stupid rich. Add to that the tens of millions I moved from Albathia into my bank account—thank you for that, by the way—I do not need to kill for money. However, now that I have such extraordinary means, I can focus on anything I want, such as a crusade. And I do have a crusade."

Roger was in the bag and Cali zipped it up halfway. He stared at her with hatred in his eyes, as if he'd escape this situation soon enough and dish out revenge. Cali loved that look.

Clapping her hands together as if patting away dust, she retrieved the second item in her bag. A bear's head. With open eyes, twitching ears, and moving jaw.

Oh, did Roger's expression change then, from anger to pure fear when Cali held the animated bear's head in front of his face. "Have you met Zebadiah yet, Roger? Well, here he is. Thanks to you, I have discovered there are monsters in this world, Roger. *Real* monsters, not just evil shitheads like you. You ruin lives, lives that *could* be put back together. Not these things.

They *destroy* lives. I'll never unsee what this thing did, Roger. I'll never unfeel what this thing put me through. Have you figured out my crusade, Roger? Have you figured out that I'm going to dedicate my life to making this world a better place by ridding it of these things? You have no idea what these things can do. So, I'm going to show you."

Cali dropped the bear's head into the bag and zipped it shut.

The chewing noises of flesh being torn from bone filled the office. Cali had heard them plenty of times before. The creature would use its tongue and teeth to macerate its way through Roger. After an hour or so, Roger would be unrecognizable pulp, muscle, fat, and bone. She'd remove Zebadiah, and then drag the bag to the nearest dumpster. After that, she'd keep an eye on Maxwell to make sure he didn't follow in his father's footsteps. Now that she got rid of the person who opened her eyes to the nightmares of this world, she could dedicate her time to hunting these nightmares.

A beautifully framed mirror hung on one of the walls. Cali took a moment to see if any bruises had started. A hint of purple on her cheek. That was it. She straightened her ponytail and then took a long look at herself. Tattoos. A bad ass monster hunter like herself needed some ink. She tugged the collar of her shirt to expose the field of unblemished skin below her left shoulder. She knew what her first tattoo would be. A stylized and intricate version of the word "Linda."

Epilogue

Papa always said Mama was a witch. Mama tells me that Papa was a blasted fool who felt nothin' good and knew even less. But about this one thing he was right. Mama's a witch. She tells me as much.

Mama whispers to me. She fills my head with her voice when I'm lonely or sings me songs of fire and blood when I get too scared. Or tells me secrets when I get confused.

"Why can't I move, Mama?"

"'Cause you ain't got no body, boy!"

"How ain't I dead then?"

"'Cause you're *my* boy."

"Can I get my body back?"

"You need to get back to where you come from."

"Papa's house? My barn?"

"Yes, boy."

"Mama? Why is my head that of a bear? I wore the bear's head, now it's my head."

Mama cackles, loud. "You are what you eat, boy! Ain't no one told you that? That's what the land did for you. The more you ate, the bigger and stronger you got."

"The land?"

"The land. The land your blasted fool Papa thought was his. It was the land that gave you life, healed you when you ate. Made you better."

"Why the land, Mama?"

"'Cause I blessed it. I blessed it in the name of a higher power. And you was conceived on it."

"Conceived?"

"Your Papa put his seed in me to grow you. And I had that blessed by a higher power, too."

"I belong to a higher power?"

"You do, boy, and when the time is right, you'll meet that higher power. Just like when the time is right, you'll return to our land and get your body back."

"Oh, Mama, I need my body! How? How do I get back to our land?"

"Don't worry, boy. Your children will take you there."

Children? I have children? Oh, Mama always knows the right things to say to me.

Viktor Bloodstone

is

Brian Koscienski

Chris Pisano

Jeff Young

www.novelguys.com